THE PILOT AND THE PUCK-UP

PIPPA GRANT

COPYRIGHT

Copyright © 2018

All rights reserved. This book or any portion thereof may not be reproduced or used in any manner whatsoever without the express written permission of the publisher except for the use of brief quotations in a book review.

This is a work of fiction. Names, characters, businesses, places, events and incidents are either the products of the author's imagination or used in a fictitious manner. Any resemblance to actual persons, living or dead, or actual events is purely coincidental.

Cover Design by Qamber Designs
Edited by Jessica Snyder

1

Zeus Berger (aka the biggest, baddest, most spider-fearing mother pucker to ever play in the NHL)

Coconuts are itchy. I should've gone for the watermelons.

But it was a bitch and a half getting that last-minute private fitting at Madame Cosette's anyway, and the woman probably would've had to stitch three bras together and then nail the damn contraption to my shoulders to get it to hold without losing a melon, so coconuts it is.

Besides, it's the heels that are gonna be the bigger problem. Damn good thing I have ankles of fucking steel.

And my minidress is stretched to max capacity over the coconuts anyway. It's also in danger of showing my other coconuts, if you catch my drift. And there's definitely a drift—or is that a draft?—on my other coconuts.

A wolf whistle echoes through the swanky private

clubhouse where I'm strolling in with my twin brother on my left and my brother from another mother on my right. A passing server drops a tray of champagne. Conversation stops. And a bunch of stuffy golf pricks gape at us like we're a mutant alien circus freak show crashing their million-dollar wedding reception.

We're three dudes who have more money than God, more muscles than all the Kardashians' bodyguards combined, and more fun than cotton candy and roller coasters.

And this is no wedding reception. It's a chance for pretentious rich asses to brag to each other about who gave more money to the foundation benefitting from this celebrity golf tournament tomorrow.

Ares is scowling, squinting around the room like he's looking for the dumbass prince who was stupid enough to bet me ten grand I wouldn't show up tonight dressed like a chick. Chase is on his phone, snickering like he's not half a foot shorter and a hundred pounds lighter than me.

I swipe his phone from him and shove it between my coconuts. "Quit sexting my sister in public."

"I was posting that picture of you getting dressed to Facebook," he replies. "Ares, fetch the phone."

Ares grunts. "Shut your face," he tells Chase.

I slap my brother on the shoulder. "Lighten up. I make this shit look good."

"Hate to break it to you," Chase says, "but your sister actually makes a better woman."

"You saying you wouldn't tap this?"

"Saying she gives a better blow job."

He easily ducks my fist, because the fucker's known

me too long. Plus, my heart isn't in taking him out. Chase is good for my sister, and he's a damn good friend to boot. Not that I'll ever tell him that to his face. Again.

Ares quits scowling enough to snicker too. "Girls don't hit," he tells me.

"You gonna let him talk about Ambrosia like that?"

"I know where he sleeps."

People think Ares is dumb because he doesn't talk in big words. But he's one of the smartest fuckers I know, in his own way.

Only dude in the world as big as me too, but in these heels—special ordered Mablanoks something or others—I've got him by four inches. Air's thin up here at over seven feet tall, but that ain't gonna stop me from having a hell of a fun time tonight.

"Gentlemen." A half-British, half-ice king voice intrudes on our private party before we reach the food table. The prince extends a hand to Chase and Ares before settling his grin on me. "And... I'm sorry, madam, it seems I've missed your name."

Never met the dude in person before—all our shit-talking happened over the phone—but I've seen his picture, read his hockey stats, and I know his stepsister. Like Chase, he's tall and beefy enough for a regular human—comes from some friggin' cold northern Atlantic nation with enough sheep for his own harem—but Ares and I are towering over him too.

"This is Ambrosia," Chase offers. "I have terrible taste in women."

"Lick my tits," I say to Chase before I grab the fucker and rub his face between my coconuts.

Ares grins.

Chase pinches my ass and I let him go. Two more servers do an about-face and scurry away with their trays of little bread bites that are smaller than my pinky and apparently pass as *food* at these things.

"You can call me The Goddess," I tell the prince.

Manning Frey's royal features split into a wider grin as he rocks back on his heels. Where I'm in a girdle, size 18 fuck-me shoes and a medieval torture device that's holding up my coconuts, he's in some tan suit and white shirt getup that was probably picked for him by a royal ninny. "Overselling ourselves, are we?"

I like the fucker already. Not because he owes me ten grand, but because I've got a feeling he'd be a good companion in his own coconut bra and minidress if we wanted to crash another snooty function tonight. "Not if a pansy-ass like you passes as a prince. I'm still taking home the hottest girl here tonight."

He juts his chin up. If he keeps grinning wider like that, his smile's gonna eat his whole face before long. "You're going to get a woman. While you're dressed like that."

Yeah, I know what it looks like. Me and Ares, we're the biggest mother puckers to ever strap on skates and wield sticks in the NHL. I'm sprouting a five o'clock shadow before I'm done shaving every morning. Each of my thighs is the size of one of those European sissy cars. Solid muscle too. My ma calls us big-boned. My sister calls us overgrown apes. I make one ugly-ass woman.

"Damn fucking right," I tell Prince Manning anyway. Because you don't get to be the biggest, hairiest, most feared badass on the ice by owning up to your shortcomings. No, I bear my teeth at those fuckers and take them *down*. Yeah, *bear* my teeth, because my teeth turn into fucking *bears* when I'm pissed. If you ain't got your balls, you ain't got nothing. "I'm gonna make her switch sides, then when we get back to my hotel room, I'm gonna make her switch back, and I'm gonna rock her fucking world."

"As completely wrong as that sounds, I've seen him do it before," Chase says.

Ares grunts an agreement, even though both of them know I'm full of shit and I know they're each looking forward to watching me fail. I share a look with my twin.

You're such a fucking dumbass, his says, because he knows it's biologically impossible for any woman in this stuffy, exclusive clubhouse to seriously be attracted to me like this. I flunked biology—the classroom part, I mean, because obviously I know what I'm doing with the biology in my briefs—and I still know it too.

Two words, my look replies. *Endorsement. Dollars.*

I don't give two shits if I score a chick tonight. I score plenty, on and off the ice.

Also?

Zeus Berger doesn't back down from a challenge. Even a challenge I can't win. And I smell a challenge coming on.

"Care to put some money on that?" Manning says, right on time.

"Double or nothing," I reply. Win or lose, no man will ever say I didn't put my heart in it. And I've got my winning personality on my side. I might be ugly, but I'm not out. Far from it.

Ares snickers again.

"Go on and pick the girl," I tell Manning. "Wouldn't want you to think I planned this."

He rubs a hand over his beard while he scans the room. "I'm beginning to see why Willow speaks so ambiguously of you."

"That means she only half-likes us," I translate for Ares. "Probably intimidated by our awesomeness."

"Or the fact that you threatened her fiancé with a ten-pound wheel of moldy cheddar," Chase muses.

"Fucker needs to put his foot down with his mother on all those wedding plans."

"On that, we're in complete agreement," Manning says crisply. He stops and nods toward the wall of windows overlooking the lake on the course's eighteenth hole with the Blue Ridge Mountains to the west. "Her."

I squint, because that half of the room is backlit by the light glaring in. "The chick who just shoved her finger into Levi Wilson's beer bottle?"

Ares perks up. "Boy band Levi?"

"Aw, shit, Bro's gonna be pissed she missed this," Chase mutters.

That's right—my sister is a boy band ho. Got a thing for Levi's old band, Bro Code—which she swears is a total coincidence, considering Chase has called *her* Bro since we were kids, a nickname she claimed to hate until she realized how much she liked Chase a couple months back.

"Not the beverage assaulter," Manning says. "The woman with her."

I shift my attention from the woman trying to shake a beer bottle off her finger while obviously stuttering apologies to the world's reigning pop rock god, and a familiar beat takes up residence in my pulse.

Long, dark hair. Tall. She's built—not heavy, but not turn-sideways-and-she'd-disappear skinny either. She's in pants that accentuate her curves and a no-nonsense blouse that can't hide her rack. Even in the backlight, there's a feline grace to her movements as she efficiently grabs her companion's arm, neatly twists the stuck bottle off her friend's finger, and hands it back to Levi Wilson.

I do love me some feline grace.

And even though she has the bearing of a woman much smarter than my usual type, there's some stirring over my southern coconuts that suggests I might be about to start a bigger scene.

These rich mofos would shit a brick if I popped a boner in this dress.

Heh.

But while I'm damn proud of my Neanderthal heritage —gets me a big paycheck on the ice every year, and sponsorships for everything from deodorant to car jacks off the ice, probably girdles before tonight's over too—even I know the quickest way into a lady's pants isn't always showing her the goods. So I tell Jupiter to cool it down there—what? You're damn right both me *and* my junk are named after kings of the gods—and nod to Manning. "You're on."

2

Joey Diamonte (aka Fireball)

THE LAST TIME I stood in for my business partner at a schmooze fest, I drank three overgrown frat boys under the table, won six grand sharking a day trading asshole in pool, and interrupted a congressman while his wife's yoga instructor was kissing a booboo on his dick.

Not my business, but when you have resting bitch face, one of the top ten badass jobs on the planet, and a special talent for ignoring social cues—like I was really going to marvel at the size of his dick? Come on. I have pencils bigger than that—well, let's just say people jump to the wrong conclusions.

And I don't take too kindly to being threatened.

So me being here tonight, surrounded by rich, famous snotbuckets? You know it wasn't by choice, and we didn't have any other options.

At least Peach—that's my business partner, and yes,

that's her real name—had the presence of mind to call my sister in to babysit this time. Not like *any* of us are happy about any part of this situation.

Except maybe Gracie.

Who's apparently in utter heaven. And unexpectedly klutzy.

One minute, my sister's about to faint over meeting Levi Wilson, and the next she's talking with her hands again and accidentally shoving a finger down the neck of his beer bottle.

"Gracie's been on four flights with me and never once tossed her cookies," I tell Levi as I pass his bottle back to him.

"You're the rock star here," Levi tells her. "Joey made me puke six times while we were shooting my video in her plane."

"Ohmydog, I love you," Gracie squeaks. Her hands go up again. Levi smoothly passes the beer bottle to a bodyguard impressively disguised as a snooty rich dude while Gracie once again does what she does best. "I used to kiss your poster every night before I went to bed. Joey always said I'd get herpes from it, but I was too young to know what herpes was. Now, she'd prefer I stay a virgin until I'm eighty. Not that I'm a virgin. Or that I don't have standards. If that's what you're thinking. I'm very picky."

That's Gracie.

I raised her well, if I do say so myself. Because Levi Wilson, who's basically been named the hottest, sexiest, studliest creature on earth by every magazine, blog, and woman under the age of forty pretty much every year for the last ten years, has put his bedroom eyes away and is now instead giving her the patient smile he probably uses with seven-year-olds.

He twists so he's at Gracie's side, slipping an arm around her shoulders, well above any danger zones, so I don't have to throat-punch him. "You want a selfie? Here, hand me your phone."

I pass him my phone, because Gracie—yes, verbal diarrhea Gracie, my pride and joy—has gone catatonic. He snaps a few photos and hands it back.

"Get any ideas and I will slice your dick off and feed it to street rats," I murmur to him as I line up to take some better shots.

He grins. "Already understood, Fireball."

"You are such a beaver blocker," Gracie hisses.

I give her the *yeah, what's your point?* cheek-and-lip curl.

She replies with a classic *you are NEVER going to be an aunt* humph.

"Levi Wilson," a male voice interrupts. Gracie goes from star-struck to mute with terror, and I don't have to turn around to know why.

I can feel two mountains standing at my back, and a quick glance in one of the gilded mirrors confirms—holy *shit*.

It's like a tan-skinned Hulk brought a pink-wigged, bearded Hulkette in hot pink Spandex that will probably be big enough and permanently stretched out enough to serve as a four-person tent whenever the giant's done with it.

I know exactly who these two are, and they'd better not be planning on trying anything with my sister, or I will end their hockey careers faster than a comet ended the dinosaurs, except with way more pain.

And more comets.

The two men with them are also taller than me, and because I'm here for work and my sister and business partner are both naïvely optimistic that I'm capable of talking rich people out of their money if I know who they are, I recognize both.

Chase Jett, the dark-haired, chin-dimpled, rags-to-riches billionaire is on one end. Manning Frey, the brownish-reddish-haired, bearded prince of Stölland on loan to Copper Valley's NHL hockey team is on the other.

There's so much testosterone radiating through the air we're all about to keel over from penis poisoning.

Especially from the twin dressed like an overgrown hooker troll.

"My girlfriend's your biggest fan," Chase Jett tells Levi.

"You wish I was your girlfriend," the Hulkette in heels says. He winks at me. "I'm flying solo tonight. You can call me Zeusette."

"You wish I was your boyfriend," Jett replies easily. "And I won't say in mixed company what I usually call you."

The manly twin—these two are so freaking huge that I actually feel a twinge of sympathy in my vagina for their mother, and my vagina typically weeps for no woman—grunts at both of them.

"Are those *coconuts*?" Gracie asks.

"Fuck, yeah," Zeusette says. "Good eye. Wanna feel?"

"I used to stuff my bra with cabbages. Much less rough on your skin," she says. "The baby cabbages we grew in our garden, I mean. Not the ones you get in a store that are like eight inches wide, because once you get over about four inches in diameter, you're overcompensating. Plus, it's hard to get past the cleavage police." She hooks a thumb at me. "Unless you're, well, built like a brick shithouse like you are."

I grip her by the arm and silently vow to kill my business partner for both backing out of this at the last minute and for sending Gracie along to *help and keep me in line*. Like it was her fault her grandmother had that accident. I know. *I know.*

I fucking hate these schmoozefests.

"Time for dinner," I tell Gracie. I point to a server across the room carrying a tray of what looks like mini wieners wrapped in bacon.

Gracie follows my finger and grimaces. "Before or after you threaten all of *them* with castration too?"

"If you're in the mood to cut someone's balls off, I volunteer the royal sheep-lover." Zeusette gives Prince Manning a slap on the shoulder. A normal man would've collapsed like an accordion, but the prince barely wobbles. "He's been making inappropriate moves on me."

"I merely acquiesced to your request that I fondle your bosom, madam. It's entirely not my fault you enjoyed it so much."

Gracie's smiling too big at Knuckleheads One, Two, and Three. And I only exclude Chase Jett because I know he has a serious girlfriend.

Case in point, he's ignoring his companions and talking to Levi about her. "My girlfriend really is a huge fan."

"Chase sleeps under a blanket with your face on it," Zeusette adds.

Ares grins while Levi laughs.

Jett gives Zeusette a *so what?* shrug. "You should see what your sister does under that blanket."

Both twins switch from snickers to scowls.

"Mr. Berger." The club manager—a slender man with glasses, a receding hairline, and the well-modulated tones of a dumbass who makes a living picking the shit off richer men's boots—steps into our weird-ass group.

Zeus elbows Ares—apparently a reminder of who the *Mr.* Berger is tonight—and Ares grunts out a "What?"

"*This* Mr. Berger," the manager says, pointing at Mr. Fake Boobs. "We have a dress code."

"What? I'm in a dress."

"Men are required to wear suits and ties."

Everyone looks at Ares, who's in jeans and a T-shirt sporting a cartoon of a platypus saying *Eat My Bannana*—yes, spelled exactly like that, and no, I don't get the platypus thing at all—then back to Zeus.

"You saying just because I feel like a woman today, I can't dress like one?" Zeus demands. I've seen highlights of him playing hockey a time or two, and I recognize the *I will rip your head off, stick my hand down your throat hole, and pull out your heart to mount as a trophy on my wall* glare that even the most hardened sportscasters discuss with undisguised reverence.

I might've tried to mimic the look a time or two on Gracie's boyfriends, because she has ridiculously horrible taste. She says I have unrealistic standards.

Zeus puffs his coconuts higher. "Or are you discriminating against ugly women?"

"Mr. Berger—"

"That's *Ms.* Berger to you tonight. Do your bosses know you're a twatapotamus?" He hops on one leg and pulls off a heel that would fit a Sasquatch, and I hope Gracie's not getting a view of Zeus down under, because while I'm fairly certain I could take him down, I'd prefer to not waste my energy fighting the brute. "Do I need to throw a shoe through your window to make my point about your discriminatory rules?"

"Put your loafer back on," Jett tells him.

"Friendly wager," the prince chimes in with his accent that's not quite British, but not quite *not*. I don't like the way Gracie's practically swooning every time he opens his pie hole. "All in the name of charity."

"Yeah, charity to not beat your ass," Zeus growls at the manager. "We need to arm wrestle this out?"

Ares rubs his beefy fist into his palm. The manager's going pale, and I can't help wondering if this is about Zeus getting his way, or if he's trying to make a statement about our society at large.

Coming up at ten, the Berger Twins, best known for throwing ice statues at each other amidst a friendly neighborhood snowball fight, take an unexpected stand in an unorthodox manner for the LGBTQ community at a fundraiser for underprivileged dyslexic kids.

Most likely, Zeus just wants some attention and his own way, and he's one of those lucky bastards whose shit always smells like roses.

"Afraid to wrestle a girl?" Zeus continues.

The manager blanches two shades whiter.

"That's right," Zeus growls. "Get outta my face before we call in the ACL-fucking-U."

While I might not appreciate the testosterone show, I do have serious admiration for the placement of that f-bomb. The manager slinks away—probably looking for security backup, good luck with that—and the twins share a fist bump.

"Gracie, you ever meet a prince?" Levi says.

"She's met Prince John, and that's as close to royalty as she's coming," I say.

Levi grins while the royal member of the Testosterone Squad bends over my sister's hand and plants a kiss on her knuckles, clearly unaware of just how much danger he's putting himself in by flirting with her. "Prince Manning of Stölland, my lady, at your service. Might I show you to the food table?"

Yep, I'm going to tear his nuts off and serve them to him on a bloody platter if he tries anything with Gracie, and no, I don't care that *his* royal bodyguard is almost as big as each of the Berger twins, because *no one* touches my sister.

She looks at me, some *Ohmygod, the coolest people are here* lighting her dark eyes. "Hit him in the crown jewels if he gets handsy. And remember that other trick I taught you."

She rolls her eyes. "He's not going to defile my honor on the cheese platter with all these witnesses."

The prince—poor man, still ignorantly unaware that I'll know every one of his dirty secrets before midnight tonight if he so much as looks at her wrong—gallantly gestures her ahead of him. "Right this way, lovely Gracie."

I move to go with her, but she shoots me another look. A Gracie special. *Chill out, I can't get pregnant by eating appetizers with the man, and you are NOT going ruin this for me too. Besides, I'll network better for you than you can yourself.*

She has a point.

A mountain of a man dressed as a woman steps into my view of my sister. "Stuffy crowd," Zeus Berger says to me. "No appreciation of the ladies. I missed your name. Can I borrow your lipstick?"

He's sporting a fucking *beard* and asking to borrow lipstick.

He grins.

I refuse to grin back. I've had enough blowhard dicks in my life—tonight especially, and we've only been here thirty minutes—to easily squelch the urge. "Call me Fireball. I don't wear lipstick."

"Damn, girl, could've fooled me. Think I need to know your secret."

"I eat my enemies for breakfast and wear their blood the rest of the day."

All of the men laugh. Except Zeus, whom I don't include as a man both because I'm not sure he wants to be counted among the men, and also because he's not laughing.

No, he's zeroing in on me as though he wants to know if I'm threatening to eat *him* for breakfast, and if I'm woman enough for the task.

"You arm wrestle?" he asks me.

"I'd hate to break one of your nails."

That's all it usually takes. One little *yeah, I can be just as big of an asshole as you can* tossed their way, and they decide a woman with a spine isn't worth the hassle.

Not Zeus Berger though. His grin goes wider, his eyes bluer, and if we were back in my hometown, he'd be pulling a *hold my beer and watch this shit* move.

And even though I know better, there's still a coil of interest stirring in my lady balls.

"Mud wrestle?" he asks.

"And ruin that pretty dress?"

"Could do it naked."

I eyeball the coconuts on his chest, which are impossible to look at without acknowledging that his shoulders are almost as wide as the wingspan of my plane, and yeah, there's some more loin-throbbing going on.

Rather unusual.

Show me a souped-up gunship ready for battle or a fighter jet breaking the sound barrier, and yeah, I'm gonna get hot and bothered. Strap me into a spaceship and give me a lift to the International Space Station, I'll probably orgasm on the spot. Sometimes a thick, juicy bacon cheeseburger makes me pop a lady boner.

What? I like food.

But in my experience—between working my ass off in high school to get a good scholarship, spending four years in engineering and ROTC classes, and then several more surrounded by blowhard pilots in the military—men tend to be all talk and no follow-through. If they bother to try to get in my pants in the first place.

My special lady cave?

It's like outer space. Few have tried to get there, none

have succeeded. And not for lack of willingness on my part.

It's only natural that my body would eventually quit reacting to men at all.

Until this giant of a man in a hot pink dress and matching troll doll wig.

Dog help me. Clearly I have issues.

"The proper order of female friendship levels is face masks, pajama pillow fights, and *then* naked mud wrestling," I tell Zeus, as if I'm an actual expert on such things.

"You can't skip the pillow fights," Jett agrees, nodding in mock seriousness.

"Shut up, glitter chin," Zeus says.

Levi's rocking back on his heels, clearly enjoying the show. "They don't know who *you* are, do they?" he asks me.

"Hard to stand out in this crowd," I reply.

Zeus's bright blue eyes are trained on me again. Not quite predatory, but not benign either.

More like I'm being weighed, measured, and evaluated as a worthy competitor.

Always did like the chase better. He wants to play a game, he's gonna find out I'm no cream puff.

He damn well better not be either.

"Who are you?" Jett asks me.

"Just a little ol' vomit comet pilot," I reply. Both because it's fucking fun to say, and also to see if the word *vomit* will make Zeus Berger blink.

It doesn't.

Excellent.

"Weightless?" Jett asks, and I have to give him credit for not only knowing about my company, but also for recognizing the code word for my plane and for not looking surprised when he asks the question.

So few people expect a woman to pilot the coolest airplane on the planet, much less own her own flight adventure company.

I incline my head.

He grins. "You got the plane here?"

Ah, a boy with too much money and a new toy. Exactly what I'm supposed to be here shopping for. I let my lips lift a fraction of an inch, because an investment from Chase Jett in Weightless would take my commercial zero-gravity flight company from a mom-and-pop operation—figuratively speaking, since I run it with my college best friend, whose name doesn't even appear on our website because everyone always underestimates a Peach—to a serious contender for NASA and SpaceX contracts, along with expanding commercial tourist operations.

If he proves he can agree to our terms, because we're not having *any* man tell us how to run our planes, which is the only reason we haven't secured private investors yet. Or even looked very hard.

That, and because I'm apparently notoriously hard to work with.

What's with all these people having trouble with standards?

"My crew's bringing it out tomorrow," I tell him.

"She'll make you toss your cookies," Levi says to Jett.

"Can always use a few more notches in my cockpit," I agree.

Chase nudges Ares. "Think you or Zeus would puke first in the vomit comet?"

"I don't puke," Ares says.

"I like comets." Zeus wiggles his brows at me.

"You don't *have* a comet, *Zeusette*," Jett reminds him.

"Shut up, jackass. Playing the part here." Zeus winks at me again. "Apologies for his crudeness, Fireball. He was raised by horny monkeys."

"Grew up with us," Ares says with an eyeball aimed at his brother that suggests he doesn't like being called a horny monkey.

"Some of us are more evolved now."

"Total feminist, hm? Planning on burning your bra?" I ask him.

"Fuck, no. I'm putting this shit up on eBay. I name these coconuts Athena and Aphrodite, sign 'em, wrap 'em in a bow, and some dumbass'll pay a few grand to put 'em on his trophy wall."

He's an egotistical ass, and yet it's impossible to not like him.

If I pulled the same shit, I'd be—

Huh.

Pretty much, I'd just be me. I'm pretty fucking badass. Just happened to be trapped in a body with tits, ovaries, and an ass, so nobody appreciates me the way they appreciate him.

Fuckers.

A server pauses next to us with a tray of canapés. "Cordon bleu bites?"

All of us stare at the tray. And if *I'm* thinking those would be more appropriately called Cordon Bleu Balls, I can only imagine what's about to come out of *Zeusette*'s mouth.

"It's food," Jett interrupts before the Berger twins speak.

"If you're a fucking bird," Zeus replies.

"Want meat," Ares says.

Levi, who's been eyeballing somebody across the room, waves in that direction then nudges me. "Don't let them fool you. They're harmless. Heard they go to knitting circle every Saturday night."

"Heard? You fucking made my gramma a doily when you were with us last weekend," Zeus counters.

Jett hands Levi a card. "Seriously, my girl plays your songs every Saturday night at a juice bar in New York. Name your charity, I'll fund it for a year if you crash one of her performances."

"I'll keep that in mind." Levi claps me on the shoulder. "Make 'em all toss their cookies. I want pictures. You bringing your sister to the tournament tomorrow?"

"She's allergic to golf."

"Tell her I'm keeping that beer bottle forever."

"Touch my sister and die."

He grins, leaves us, and I angle a glance around until I spot Gracie.

Ah, there she is. By the food with the prince. Surrounded by a group of guys who include a rock star, three normal-sized professional athletes, and a late night show host, hands waving wildly about as she tells a story. Or possibly gushes about how much she loves every one of them.

I'm glad she's enjoying herself, but I will personally rip

all their arms off, starting with their fingers and working my way up, if any one of them tries to get in her pants.

Is Gracie allowed to date?

She's a fucking adult and a successful bakery owner. Yeah, she can date.

But her life experience is limited to our dinky hometown on the border between Alabama and Tennessee. This reception is a cesspool of snooty, over-macho arrogance handed down from generation to generation, much like most of the wealth in this room, and I'm not having any of these fuckers think her innocent Southern charm makes her ripe for picking and throwing away.

"Lovely to meet you all," I lie to the Testosterone Squad, fully intent on excusing myself too, but Zeus is looking at me again—*through* me almost, which is about as disconcerting as having a wooly mammoth trying to peer into your soul.

If said wooly mammoth had piercing blue eyes that seem to suggest some intelligence hiding behind the hooded brow and some twisted kind of sex appeal.

"What's a vomit comet?" he asks.

I could go into specifics, all about the aircraft and the physics of parabolic flight, but that's rarely what anyone wants to hear about. After one last glance to make sure no one's getting handsy with Gracie, I look back at him. "It's a plane that can simulate zero gravitational pull," I tell him. "Basically, riding the vomit comet lets you feel like you're floating in space."

"It's so fucking cool," Chase says.

"Why's it called the vomit comet?" Zeus asks.

"Because people often puke on it."

"What do you do with it?"

"I fly it."

"Like you're the pilot?"

Again, I incline my head.

"That's badass."

"Thank you."

"Chase would puke his guts out first."

"You three are adorable."

"Damn fucking right. Wanna get out of here with me?"

A surprised laugh flies out of my mouth before I can stop it. "No."

"Don't worry. Just warming you up to the idea." He's an absolute goon, complete with a sparkle in his blue eyes that suggests he's playing me.

Like he *knows* I'm going to say no. And he's going to ask again, in even more outlandish ways, and he'll relish the hell out of being shot down over and over, all night long.

It's disconcerting, to say the least.

And intriguing. Can't help wondering how far he'll go.

I'm not unfamiliar with being hit on. I'm a woman in a man's world, I eat right, exercise, and take care of myself, and I can throw down at the bar. I'm not unfamiliar with arrogance—see again *woman in a man's world*—but Zeus Berger's style of arrogance doesn't fit in a normal box.

He's cocky, yes, but he either truly, delusionally believes that he can convince me to leave with him—while he's dressed like a woman, no less—or he gets his rocks off just by playing the game.

He gives his girls a tug, thrusts them out, and yanks his skirt down.

"Chase. Order six pizzas. Ares is hungry."

"Order your own damn pizzas," Chase says affably.

"You got to ogle my ass while I was getting into this girdle. You order the pizza. And a karaoke machine." He winks at me. "Later, Fireball. We got more chaos to cause. Don't leave without saying bye. A woman like me needs all the girlfriends she can get."

The three of them amble away. The pink Lycra does some fantastic things to Zeus Berger's ass. There's some surprisingly nice curve to it. He's so...well, *big*, that you wouldn't expect him to have *shape*. And I don't think the lack of jiggle has anything to do with being squished into the dress.

Not judging by the definition in his thighs.

That man is a powerful force to be reckoned with.

If Gracie weren't here, I'd consider his proposition.

Because that low pull in my belly isn't hunger, and it's not indigestion, and it's not excitement over a round of charity golf with billionaires, athletes, rock stars, and actors.

It's interest.

I shake my head.

Zeus Berger is an arrogant hockey player who's been trained in all the right things to say to compensate for his bone-headed ability to make the news for doing stupid shit like talking his teammates into doing a mooning flash-mob to the tune of "Jingle Bells" at the Mall of America.

And I don't know if I'm more mad that he got away with it, or that I never hang out with the kind of people who would invite me along for fun like that.

3

Zeus

I DON'T CHASE WOMEN. Never need to. During hockey season, they're always there, waiting. Off-season, if I want to pick up a chick, I hit a bar or a club.

When you're the size of a house and so loaded you could buy the whole fucking bar, with more muscles in my left bicep than most men have in their entire bodies and the whole package topped off by these pretty baby blues, there's no *try*.

It's all fucking *do*, and it's do *now*, because the world bows to Zeus Berger.

Picking a tough target and following through—this is new. Even if it's only been an hour.

Been a long time since I've had a challenge off the ice.

"Bit of a monster when he doesn't get his way, isn't he?" Manning says cheerfully to Chase with a nod at me while we hunker down with a stack of pizzas at a table so small I could squish it with one ass cheek.

"Suck it, your royal dickiness," I reply. "Night is young, and it's all about the game."

Ares grunts.

Translation: *You make me look like a brain surgeon.*

"Ready to give it up?" Manning says.

"Ain't over till the hockey player sings, and Ares isn't even humming yet," I retort.

My brother's straddling a chair that was built for a pinky-up, champagne-drinking, leg-crossing man a third of his size. He looks at me pointedly and whistles Darth Vader's Death March while the chair legs creak.

Things might not look good, but fuck if I'm calling it just yet.

Also, I sent my agent a shot of me in this dress, and he thinks we've got a chance at a sponsorship from Spanx. Always gotta look at the bigger picture.

Especially since I'm getting up there in hockey years. Fucking *thirty*. And no, I don't want to talk about what happened in the play-offs. Who asked you?

Fireball's six feet away with her sister, silhouetted against the sunset through the windows and standing like she's lined up for inspection in the military or something—minus the salute—while some fucker who was nothing more than a villain's lackey in one of those superhero movies yammers her ear off. I'm getting parts of the conversation—*long days on set, makeup melting under the lights, dickhead director*—and I'm wondering how she's keeping from yawning.

Even Gracie's eyes are starting to glaze over, and that

chick's been getting her rocks off gawking at the famous dudes in this room all night long. She practically wet herself over the ventriloquist.

If that's all it takes, you know this actor's boring as shit.

"Hey, Mullins," I yell at the actor dude. No fewer than a dozen stuffy golf pricks here to mingle with the rich and famous give me the nasty eyeball of *why hasn't security escorted the loud-mouthed cross-dresser out of the building?*, and Mullins himself—what's his first name? Dan? Josh? Chris? They're all Chris, right?—doesn't use any of his smooth acting moves to pretend he's any less of a stuffy goat hole.

"What, ho?" he replies with a haughty smirk instead.

"Ain't tapping that, and you ain't tapping this either." I grab my coconuts and heft them. Fireball looks at me, and she's got those dark eyes that don't give anything away, but I swear on my left nut, she just cracked a smile. Little. Microscopic. Like Mullins's dick. But it was there. "Personality counts."

"You can't even spell *personality*."

"P-E-R-Y-O-U-R-U-G-L-Y."

Manning chokes on whatever he's been guzzling out of that flask.

"Dammit, Zeus, do we need to have the your-you're discussion again?" Chase says.

"His dick's the size of an apostrophe. Didn't think he wanted the reminder."

Mullins turns to face us. Greg. That's his first name. *Greg*. Like *dregs*, except with a G and without the S. He's got Hollywood biceps, a nose with less personality than my belly button, and I swear he's wearing makeup.

Fireball's still playing it cool, watching like she's a bored robot with boobs. Her sister's visibly sucking her cheeks in while shooting looks at the royal puckhead across from me.

"I'll be happy to kick your ass on the course tomorrow," Mullins says.

"Categorically speaking?" I know the word's *metaphorically*, even if I don't know if it's really the word I want—maybe I mean *figuratively*? Oh, who the fuck cares?

I just want to see if I can make Mullins twitch enough that he'll get his nose high enough to drown if someone pulls the fire alarm and makes the sprinklers go off in here.

Not that I'm considering such a childish prank.

Bet you a thousand bucks Ares is thinking it too, though. And he knows how to get away with that shit. He'd probably point at Fireball's sister in that skirt, with her dark hair all wavy and her eyes the same exotic brown, say *Smokin' hot*, blow on his fingers like they're candles, and have everyone patting his head and telling him he's a good boy for watching out for fire.

"Zeus here's had too many hits to the head," Mullins says with a smirk to Fireball.

She doesn't answer him.

Nope, the lady steps away from him, pulls a chair from the next table, swings it around so the back's against the table, straddles it, and grabs a slice of my pizza. "Why are you baiting him?" she asks with her mouth full of a massive bite.

The demigod in my skirt roars to life, because I dig a chick who clearly likes to eat as much as I do. "You defending him?"

"He just doesn't seem like your type. Like he's clearly not capable of shoving you against a wall and banging you until your nuts fall off." Her nose wrinkles, and she looks down at the pizza. "Sausage? Just sausage? Where's the pepperoni? And the jalapenos?"

Ares shudders. Even Chase—who works with some weird-ass organic food shit—looks like he just bit into shoe leather disguised as chocolate cake.

"Ain't having anything interfere with the taste of my sausage," I tell her. Yeah, I know. I got smooth moves. Why other dudes hate me.

Also not confessing to the spice in pepperoni making my eyes water, and don't even say the j-word around me. Shut up. I'm from Minnesota. Ketchup's fucking spicy, okay?

"In other words, your pizza is compensating for your genitals," she muses.

"Be nice," Gracie hisses.

"That was nice."

Ares grins. Chase better not, because he's dating my sister, and I'll knock his lights out if he makes moon-eyes at random chicks with spunk. Manning leaps to his feet and offers his chair to Gracie, which makes Fireball's eyelid twitch. Pretty sure she's castrating him in her mind.

"He's not interested," I tell her. "Has a girlfriend back home. She's a sheep."

Manning nods as he pulls another chair to the table and settles next to Gracie. "I usually offer to share her.

She turned Zeusette here down flat, though, so don't underestimate her taste."

Fucker's got game. Like that about him.

"I'm sure she wasn't the first," Fireball says.

Ares and Chase are both snickering now. Gracie sighs. "Do you have sisters?" she asks Manning.

"My family is biologically incapable of siring female children." He flexes a bicep. Might as well fluff his feathers and strut around like a fucking peacock too. "Seven generations. All uncles and brothers."

"You know what? You probably *do* understand my childhood."

"If you look at my sister's breasts one more time, I'll happily remove your eyeballs for you," Fireball says around another mouthful of pizza.

I've said the same thing to various dudes for my own sister, but fuck, when Fireball says it, the stick in my skirt strains harder. It wants some playtime with the badass pilot chick.

"You're a betting woman," she says to me.

"Fuck, yeah."

She pulls out a pocket knife, expertly snaps it open, and slices a triangle of cardboard off the pizza box. "Bet you I can flick this into that dude's toupee without him noticing."

"And here we go," Gracie sighs.

Manning offers her his flask. She takes a hit, shudders, and hands it back.

Fireball flicks her cardboard and hits the royal flirty-pants right in the center of the forehead. Surprise registers, and three wallets smack down on the table.

THE PILOT AND THE PUCK-UP

"Fifty bucks says you can't do that again," Chase says.

Ares grunts, digs into his wallet, throws a handful of bills on the table, and points to the wall of fame, featuring rows and rows of pictures of white dudes holding golf clubs like baseball bats while their teeth try to blind us all. "Freaky grandpa," he says.

We all look at the center picture, where an old geezer with silver hair sprouting out his ears is grinning like a drunk monkey with a club stuck up its ass.

"Fairly certain a cardboard triangle won't solve that one," Manning muses. Whatever's in that flask is giving him a permanent case of cheerfulness. If the prince thing doesn't work out, he could be a morning news lady. "Two hundred to whoever can plunk a sausage into the punch bowl."

I don't whip out my wallet, because I would've popped a seam if I tried to squish one more thing in this dress and keeping track of a purse all night would've been a bitch and a half. Instead, I give Ms. Fireball the trademark Zeus Berger *you come on over here and pucker up for me, baby* head bob. "You hit Mullins between the eyes, I'll take you back to my room and we can giggle about boys and smear green shit all over our faces."

"You hit Mullins between the eyes, and I'll let your friend here leave with both his kneecaps intact. Hands on the table, your royal grabbiness."

"Don't like him that much," I say.

"Afraid I'm going to kick your arse in the rink this year, you mean." Cheery McCheeryPants stretches back and pulls a teenage movie theater move, arm going behind Gracie like Fireball isn't ripping into that pizza box with too much relish even for my tastes.

That pocketknife is wicked. Kind that'd leave a mark and then some.

The force of her glare alone is gonna leave a mark. She's so fucking hot.

A dark-eyed angel of doom.

"You got any brothers?" I ask her.

"No."

"Damn. Was hoping for a date." Don't ever let it be said Zeus Berger can't play the role of a damsel in a fucking Spandex dress.

"I have a brother," Gracie offers with a pointed look at Fireball.

"What you have is the good fortune to be related to me," Fireball replies as if she didn't just flinch.

It was a small thing. Like the size of a sugar granule. You don't make it in the NHL if you don't watch for the little things, and I saw that flinch.

"You break the princess's kneecaps, we can't binge watch *Gilmore Girls*," I say to Fireball.

She turns the full force of her no-nonsense gaze on me. Her eyes are the color of a dark Irish stout, her lashes thick enough that a Minnesota horsefly would get lost in them, and if I'd had half the control of my stick that she has of her facial muscles, we would've won the Stanley Cup last year.

That demigod in my skirt ain't playing anymore. He wants this chick, and he wants her *now*. My rocks are so tight they make my girdle feel like a loose blanket, and my entire brain is narrowing to focus on one thing, and one thing only.

Shoot.

Score.

I set my elbow on the table, hand up in the air, palm open, pushing the pizza boxes out of the way while she's still sawing. Yeah. Sawing pizza boxes while she stares me down.

I wiggle my fingers at her, an invitation to arm wrestle. "Bet you a naked trip to the lake you can't last two seconds with Poseidon here."

She snorts. "Like you'd last two seconds in the lake."

"I can last for three fucking hours."

She grabs the first cardboard triangle, lines it up, and aims at the chunky old golf dude with the toupee. A quick flick of her fingers, and *boom*.

That thing sails through the air and plunks right on top of his head.

"Who *are* you?" Chase says.

"Just a simple country girl who likes to fly airplanes."

Gracie sighs.

Fireball sends the second cardboard triangle soaring straight to bop the creepy grandpa golf dude on the nose.

At least four men in the room gasp like she beaned Baby Jesus and set his manger on fire.

"*Ms*. Berger," that twat-waffle of a manager says at my back.

Fireball stands and takes a wide-legged stance. "That was me. You want a fight, pick on someone your own size and leave the women alone."

Half of Gracie's face is twitching. "Make sure you grab

your nuts too, Fireball," she says on a sigh. "That'll show him."

"I'm suddenly terrified we're secretly related," Manning deadpans to her with that grin. Dude's cheeks are either made of steel, or he's been somehow surgically altered so he's always smiling. Starting to get freaky here. "You've never had a DNA test, have you?"

"Oh, I have. After what she pulled at my best friend's wedding last year, I was hoping I could prove I was adopted."

"Ms... Your name, please?" The manager is glowering at Fireball like he thinks he can actually take her out. Fuck, I'm not so sure she wouldn't have beat me at arm wrestling.

"Fireball."

"Your real name."

"You discriminating based on names now?"

Chase grins. Ares grins. Manning—oh, fuck. Manning's sneaking out the back door with Fireball's sister.

I imagine what she's gonna do to his nuts, and I grin.

"Madam—if I may call you that—we have certain standards here, and—"

"And you have a rock star in the corner sucking helium and challenging your cronies to a biggest nut sack competition, four football players trying to steal your Bud Light sign, and I don't know what that woman in the green dress is shoving into her cleavage, but I assume if *Ms.* Berger and I were yanking on our penises instead of being strapped into bras, we could probably moon your eighteenth hole without anyone batting an eye."

I stand, because why the fuck didn't I think of mooning the eighteenth hole first. "Butt cheeks to the glass," I tell Ares.

Lame, he telegraphs. *Let's put our Willy Winkers in the beer.*

He might be quiet, but don't let him fool you. Dude has ideas.

"How much is your club making from hosting this fundraiser?" Chase asks. He's the only one still at the table, leaning back in his chair like he fucking owns the place.

Fireball looks for her sister, and there's that flinch again.

Her dark gaze slides to me.

Like it's my fault.

"You know what?" she says to the manager. "Never mind. We're leaving."

Without so much as a how-you-doin', she grabs me by the back of my dress, pockets her knife, and tugs me toward the door.

Ares lifts his phone and snaps a picture. Chase barely catches himself before he topples backwards, jaw flapping like he's a fucking trout.

Heh.

Fucker didn't think I could do it.

Ares gives me a thumbs-up. *Royal prick's getting a copy right now.*

And I let Fireball drag me out of the clubhouse.

Being me is a damn good thing to be.

Even in a fucking girdle.

4

Joey

We're four steps outside that stuffy-ass schmooze-fest when I spin on Zeus freaking Berger and startle him into stepping back. "Where'd your buddy take my sister?"

"Whoa, princess—"

Princess? I have that fucker pinned to the wall by the throat in less time than it takes me to make grown men cry. "Do not *ever* call me *princess*."

He grins.

Probably because he knew calling me princess would piss me off.

Possibly also because his throat's so thick that even with my fingers stretched as wide as they'll go, I can't reach from one end of his jawbone to the other, and his neck's solid as steel.

What the *fuck* is up with that pulsing in my lady brain? She's usually smarter than this. More independent too.

And she's getting all worked up before we notice the brush of something else solid as steel pushing against the top of my abs.

Holy dog. If that's real—no, *concentrate, Joey*.

"Where. Is. My. Sister." I don't make it a question, because men don't respect questions. They respect demands and balls, and, honey, I got both.

"Probably took her out to admire some sheep." Even with the coconuts, dress, and pink wig, Zeus Berger is nothing short of complete masculinity. It's raining testosterone in this hallway. Only explanation for the wetness in my underwear. "Told you, sheep are more his speed. Besides, she's a big girl. Nothing wrong with letting her admire some livestock."

Back home in Podunk, Alabama, yeah, Gracie can take care of herself. But wielding Gomer Smith's pet duck like a weapon when he tries to sneak a pinch of ass—Gomer, I mean, not his duck, though I wouldn't put it past the duck either—isn't the same as being hit on by men with money, fame, and mastery of at least a third of a dictionary.

And don't go thinking we're all dumb hicks down in Alabama.

Nope.

Gomer's simply the only one dumb enough to brave hitting on my sister.

"Admire livestock? That's the worst euphemism I've ever heard, and if he hurts her—"

Zeus's grin gets bigger. "You gonna kick his ass? Can I watch?"

Fuck if that yard of beef in his skirt doesn't grow three inches and fossilize right there under my rib cage. And what's up with my nipples trying to slice their way out of my bra? I gave my virginity to a dildo when I was twenty-one after too many over-confident blowhards fumbled around petting my pussy more for their own pleasure than for mine.

Yeah, I'm technically a virgin. Blow me. Point is, it's a rare man with a pulse who can crank my engine, and I don't understand why Zeus Berger is doing it for me.

"I know six different ways to kill a man," I tell him.

"You are so fucking hot."

The doofus is still grinning, yeah, but his eyes are hooded blue flames that keep dipping to my lips, and this fucking inconvenient arousal is interfering with my focus on my sister. Pretty sure my clit just tried to outdo his boner, and I have an ache in places between my thighs that have never ached for my dildos *or* my vibrators.

I don't know why or how he's doing this to my body and I'm equal parts horrified that I'm considering asking to see the sausage in his skirt and at the same time jonesing to grab life by the balls and see if a ride on his mega-rocket is everything it's promising to be.

He's not trying to prove his manliness by fucking my breastbone—yeah, the stilettos make him that tall—and even though we both know this grip I have on his throat is probably the same as him being cuddled by a teddy bear, he's letting me keep the illusion I'm in control.

I like being in control.

I'm very much not in control right now.

"Tell you a secret?" he says in that overconfident hockey god growl.

"No."

"I'm not actually a woman."

"Yeah, well, I hardly qualify as one myself."

"Jupiter begs to differ."

I'm embarrassed to admit it takes me a full three heartbeats—*fast* heartbeats, just so we're clear—to catch on. "You named your dick *Jupiter*."

He gives one of those *of course I fucking did* shrugs. "Didn't want him getting jealous that he wasn't named after a god too."

"He has rings?" I ask, which honestly shouldn't be making my lady brain pulse harder, but there she goes, insanely curious if he's naturally ribbed for my pleasure.

He wiggles his oddly attractive brows at me. "Don't you want to know."

"A spot?"

I'm insulting his junk, and he's grinning wider by the minute. Hard not to like the guy, which is pissing me off more, because I don't want to like Zeus Berger. He's the physical personification of every battle I've fought in my professional life to get where I am today.

"You need a telescope to see it?" I guess again.

He traces one long, thick finger down my forearm, which sends my nerves into hyperdrive as a pleasurable shiver licks its way up to my shoulder and down my breasts, making my nipples catch fire and pop mini-boners of their own.

"It's okay to be nervous," he says. "Me and Jupiter, we're both big guys."

Damn well better be. If I'm gonna screw this ogre's

brains out, it's going to fucking count. Not that I'm going to—oh, hell, who am I kidding?

Thirty seconds in control of his joystick, and I probably won't need my toy drawer for two months. Can't pass up an opportunity like this. "You know there's a reason they call me Fireball."

"Because you go down smooth like whisky?"

The idea of going down on him—if that bulge in his dress is real—is one more challenge I might be up for. Which is further proof I've lost my ever-loving mind. I smile at him. "Don't you want to know," I parrot back.

His blunt fingers are drawing Z's over the back of my hand. "So how are we going to play this? Me toss you over my shoulder and carry you out of here? Or you toss me over yours?"

The only time a guy's ever thrown me over his shoulder and carried me anywhere was during a military exercise where I had to play the wounded victim. He tripped, sprained his ankle, and I ended up carrying *him* to real medical help.

"You're very sure of yourself," I say.

"Fuck yeah. Optimistic too. Wanna pet my dragon?"

That grin. That *smirk*. He's playing with me. He doesn't think I'll do it. Doesn't think I'll take him up on his offer. Doesn't really mean it.

Just like every other jackass who's thought it would be fun to say he fucked with Joey Diamonte's mind.

I slide my fingers down his neck, over his thick collarbones, and down to fondle the coconuts on his chest. "You pet mine, I'll pet yours."

"Don't want to pet yours. I'm gonna fucking eat it."

Highly unlikely. I grip him by the strap of his dress and go in search of a room.

This won't take long.

And then I'm going to find my sister.

5

Zeus

Hot damn. Suck this, you royal pansy who thought I couldn't do it.

Fireball's about to fuck my nuts off.

This chick—yeah, she's way out of my league. Brains. Self-confidence. Owns her own airplane.

Defies fucking gravity.

She drags me down the narrow hallway lined with pictures of pretentious golf dudes, trophy cases, and framed awards until she finds a door that opens.

Office. Desk. Picture of the manager and his poodle. Window overlooking the course. A big tee clock that neither one of us better sit on.

Her hair's the only thing loose about her, flowing over her shoulders like a curtain of silk. Her body's so smokin' hot it sets off all the fire alarms in my system. She's got the focus of a tiger. Not often I feel like the prey.

Considering she can't be bigger than five-seven, maybe one-forty soaking wet, I should be the lion to her gazelle. But those dark eyes are telegraphing an unmistakable message that she's about to own me.

"You get one chance, Berger," she says as she makes quick work of the buttons on her white blouse and drops it to the ground, revealing olive skin over taut muscle and two beautiful tits held in place by a utilitarian white bra. I don't even care that she's in grandpa pants that go all the way up to her belly button. Blood pumps into my dick like a fucking dam burst.

"Supposed to be my line, Fireball," I reply. "Or should I call you…?"

"Lose the dress. Fireball's all you're getting."

She's using all of my lines against me. *Get naked. Call me the Brute. Let's fuck.*

Yeah, the chicks I bang know my name. But they don't know *me*.

"Your dress?" she prompts.

"Honey, women don't tell the king of the gods what to do." I don't know if I *can* get out of this fucking thing by myself. One wrong move, and it's popping seams.

I can get rid of these coconuts though. I heft them out of the bra, and *hoo*—fuck, I forgot I wasn't breathing all the way. Back's tight too.

She chuckles out a delightfully evil laugh as she peels her breasts out of that ugly-ass bra. "Honey, you don't get to touch *these* unless you do what I tell you to."

My fingers itch, my cock begs to be tagged into the game, and my tongue twists itself in a fucking knot. I've seen boobs. I've licked boobs, I've sucked on boobs, I've fondled boobs. Me and boobs? There's never been a shortage. I know boobs.

But the thought of not knowing *these* pretty titties is making that demigod in my jockey shorts threaten to go on strike.

I'm about to call her bluff—she'll be begging me to lick her nipples in three-point-two seconds—when she cups her breasts, puts her thumbs to her pert rosy buds, and lets her eyes slide shut. Someone's taking a cracker to my nuts, because the sight of this woman touching herself is about to make those puppies under my stick burst.

I spin in a circle trying to grab the hook on this bra Madame Cosette strapped me into. Fuck it. Gonna have to settle for pulling my arms out of the straps.

Except my arms are the size of a normal man's thighs, and *fuck*, the strap's stuck too. I'd burn the fucking thing off if I could find a lighter, because I'm starting to think that's what it's gonna take.

She shoves me back against the desk. The tee clock bounces to the oriental rug under the desk. My coconuts clatter on top of it. Some other office shit moves and shuffles, but I don't notice, because she's climbing up on the desk, straddling me like there's not a huge-ass window right behind us. "Poor baby needs help?" she purrs.

Yeah, she's fucking *purring*.

And I don't give two shits that she's mocking me, because those firm titties are bouncing just enough to hold every iota of my attention, her legs are framing my hips while she thrusts her goods against the demigod in my skirt, and halle-fucking-lujah, she just released the hook on my bra.

My mouth's gone dry as a desert and can't stop salivating all at the same time. I don't know which way's up, what color the sky is, or how to count to ten, but my straining dick knows she's north and it wants to sit in Mrs. Claus's lap.

Shut up. You'd be brain-tied too if this chick had her tits in your face.

She's straddling me, yanking my dress down to scrape her fingers over my pecs, rubbing her pussy against the happiest god on earth, and *fuck*, Mt. VuZeusius is about to blow.

I grasp her waist, grit my teeth, and count my ABCs to get control of that thunder growing down under, because Zeus Fucking Berger does *not* lose his shit before the third period.

"Didn't paint you for a puck bunny," I rasp out.

"Pink hair turns me on, even if you're due for a good weed whacking." She rubs me harder with her magic pussy, and *shit*, I need to get a grip. We're both still in our pants—okay, me in my underpants—my dick's about to punch through this dress, and if her pussy's half as hot and wet and silky as those fuck-me bedroom eyes of hers are promising, this little trip to the principal's office is gonna be one for the record books.

"Not my coconuts?" I grunt out, because grunting's where I'm at. I can't talk. I've got a dick ready to blow and the ref hasn't even dropped the puck yet.

"Which one was Athena? This one?" She takes a nail to my left pec and starts tracing a spiral out from my nipple, shooting sparks so hot the air's crackling. My bra's hanging open, the dress stretched so thin by the coconuts it's showing off the girdle Madame Cosette insisted I wear too. I need this chick out of her pants, I need to get suited up, and I need to get in this game. Now.

"Or this one?" She bends over me, nips my right pec with her teeth, grinds her hips against my dick, and—

Oh, *fuck*.

Fuck fuck fucking fuckity fucking fuck, I'm coming.

Blinding.

Hot.

Fast.

In my jockey shorts.

I jerk up into her, trying to stop it, but I'm fucking shooting fireworks out the tip of my dick. That volcano's erupting. My nuts are running for cover, my dick's making the party foul of the fucking century, and I can't bear down hard enough to stop it. I'm coming like a twelve-year-old who just looked at Dora the fucking Explorer the wrong way—don't judge, asshole, you know you did it too—and Fireball knows it.

I know ice, and this princess who just froze over me is frosting faster than the lake in my Minnesota hometown in winter. "Did you—" she starts.

"No," I lie. "Baby—"

"You did."

"That's just a precursor." Fuck, there's so much more I want to do to this woman. Fifteen minutes, I'm back in the game. I can eat her until there's nothing left. Finger her with my fat sausage fingers that are bigger than most other men's dicks. Hell, even half-mast, I'm twice the man most other fuckers are.

Her eyes narrow.

I'm losing her. She's gonna leave.

I don't want her to fucking leave. I want her to stay, *here*, until I can salvage this—this—whatever the fuck this is. I launch myself up, grip her by the back of her head, pretend I'm not leaking jizz out the bottom of my dress, and slam my lips over hers.

When in doubt, always go for the kiss.

I think.

Fuck, I'm never in doubt. *This doesn't fucking happen to me*.

She lets out a muffled curse against my lips, gives me the titty twister to end all titty twisters, and I leap back with a yowl.

She scowls at me while she shoves her blouse back on and snags her bra off the floor. I can still see her nipples standing rosy and perky and ready under the white fabric. And I'm pretending I don't have the spoils of war leaking down my thigh. Mr. Party Pooper in my Pants has the nerve to give me an *oh, yeah* nod.

"I've never—" I start.

"You know what? I'm really tired of always wearing the pants in a relationship."

The door slams shut two seconds later, and I'm left waiting for my dick to explain to me what just happened.

Which—newsflash—is like waiting for a Minnesota Lake to boil in January.

Because that fucker in my pants has even fewer brains than I do.

"Fucking king of the gods," I mutter.

And because today apparently can get worse, the door swings open again almost immediately, and—*fuck*.

Ares and Chase look at me. Then they look at my dress. My deflating boner. My legs.

My dripping-in-my-own-shit legs.

"Shut the fuck up *right fucking now*," I growl.

Chase ducks his head, bites his knuckles, snort-snuffles, and leaves.

Ares grunts. *Happens to all of us, man. Smear some on the dick's window.*

I don't give a fuck about messing with the asshole manager.

All I care about is finding myself a plate of cookies and a good, stiff bottle of whisky.

Only Fireball I'm getting tonight, apparently.

6

Joey

LIFE RULE NUMBER ONE: Just because a guy has a big dick doesn't mean he knows how to use it.

I know this, and yet I still fell into the trap of mistaking hormonal impulses for good judgment.

A *hockey player*? Really, Joey? *You fucking know better.*

Still, who would've expected Zeus Berger to be king of the early shot?

And why am I so pissed about it?

Not like he owed me anything. Or that I should be surprised. A guy with an ego like that? Of course he's compensating. Twelve solid inches in his pants—good *dog*, he's huge—and he has as much control over it as a rookie pilot in a windstorm. It's like putting a toddler in charge of a cannon. Letting an elephant steer a rocket. Asking a goat to wrangle a bull.

And I was the one stupid enough to think he'd actually care about getting *me* off.

And I'm also the one who can still taste the meaty, manly flavor of his chest. If men are pigs, his body is the bacon, and god help me, I love a good piece of bacon.

Unfortunately, he's undercooked. His package needs a warning label. *Contents may combust with minimal handling.*

After leaving yet one more blowhard with a bigger ego than his shoe size and less stamina than a squirrel—I don't care that they can jump from tree to tree all day long, don't tell me it takes them more than thirty seconds to get their rocks off—I follow the scent of hairy Viking bodyguards to find Gracie out wandering the golf course with Prince Whoever The Hell He Is. I know Stölland. Nordic country between the Northern Atlantic and Norwegian Sea. Ceremonial military. Exports mead, sheep, and apparently fourth-in-line heirs to the kingdom. It was all on the cheat sheet Peach gave me when she shoved us out the door to come here in her place this morning while she hightailed it to the hospital.

There's a reason she usually does our networking. And don't let her name fool you. Or her appearance. She's blonde, cute, brilliant, and Southern to the core, and she'll skin your bones with her tongue faster than you can say *bless your heart*.

"Gracie," I say into the dusk. "Time to go."

A big dickhead steps between me and my sister near the sixteenth green and gives me one of those overbearing, intimidating glares that I can mimic in my sleep.

"Identification," he growls.

"She's harmless," His Royal About-To-Be-Deadness says cheerfully to the bodyguard.

"No, she's not," my sister replies.

The light's fading, so I can't see the nuances of either of their expressions, but he's definitely smiling and she's definitely giving me the *back off* glare.

"Join us, Ms. Fireball," the prince says. "Care for a spot of mead?"

"I'd care for taking my sister back to the hotel."

"All by your lonesome?"

"No, I thought the club manager might join us. Such a winning personality."

The prince's smile widens.

Just like Zeus Berger. So freaking amused by the world, and probably just as likely to be a disappointment.

"Gracie," I say again. "Let's go."

"She's just getting her steps in," the prince tells. So much fucking cheerfulness. And how the hell does he know about Gracie's steps? Does he know about her competition with Peach too? What other secrets has he gotten out of her? And why is he speaking for her?

I suck in a breath through my nose, because even I realize I'm not getting my sister out of here by being a dick.

Unless Prince Butthead has hypnotized her, in which case I fully intend to beat the shit out of both him and his royal bodyguards.

"I have M&Ms back in the room," I tell her.

She steps around the thick-necked royal guard and now that I'm thinking about necks, I'm thinking about

Zeus Berger and his useless mountains of muscles and hair-trigger dick again.

I might've just growled.

Being horny and disappointed and worked up over the sixteen different ways today could've gone better tends to do that to a person.

Gracie looks me up and down and sighs. "It was just a walk. He didn't compromise my non-existent purity or infect me with any horrific diseases or trick me into buying into some royal pyramid scheme with the promise that I, too, can be a princess if I just get six of my friends to sign up as duchesses and countesses below me. He's polite enough to throw down with Miss Manners herself. You brought me here to have some fun. *Please* let me have some fun."

I brought her here because Peach didn't give me a chance to object after dropping the bombshell that she had to skedaddle to take care of her meemaw after some accident with a zoo hippo. *Gracie, go with Joey and make sure she doesn't burn the golf course down if one of them rich boys tries to touch her rack.*

Gracie's been my responsibility since our mama left when I was eight. Our daddy did what he could to do right by both of us, but he didn't know any more about raising girls than I did. Always figured Gracie would've been in therapy by now.

But even though she's never been to a city bigger than Huntsville, never met a celebrity more famous than that local kid who made it to the semi-finals on *America's Got Talent* with his burping puppet routine, and even though it goes against every hard-ass, over-protective instinct I possess, I hold up my hands in surrender.

Because Gracie's all the family I have left in this world, and I don't want to lose her over a stupid argument about a stupid guy.

Can love a person all you want, Joey-girl, but you can't make them love you back. I might've been eight, but Daddy's wisdom stuck. He kept doling it out until we lost him two years ago. *People leave, baby girl. All you ever really have is yourself.*

I don't want Gracie to leave.

I don't want to give her any more reason to leave.

Plus, I know she still knows how to use her elbows, knees, and right hook, and we had a refresher birds, bees, and baby diapers discussion just before we left the hotel for this reception tonight.

I expected her to charm her way into Levi Wilson's company. I know Levi. I trust he has a healthy enough fear of me to not try anything with my sister.

This prince guy?

Not so much.

But even I know I can't stop her. Sometimes, an alternate approach is necessary. I don't *like* alternate, bullshit, prance-around-the-problem approaches. But I'm not bullheaded enough to ignore them.

Mostly.

"Okay. You're right." I hand her the keys to my rental car. "Don't stay out past midnight. Don't let him drive you. And don't sign anything without consulting an attorney."

"It's a walk on the golf course, not a business arrangement."

"He's a fucking prince. Everything's a business arrangement."

"Not the crown prince," Manning says with all the jovial cheer of Santa Claus. "I'm expendable. And not nearly smart enough for business decisions."

Before I can growl out a response, Gracie's hugging me tight. "Go back to the hotel. Take a hot shower. Wash off the rich golfer cooties before you have to do it all over again tomorrow. Eat a steak or two. I'll be back before you know it." She drops her voice to a whisper. "And I'll convince him he needs to book himself and all his brothers on a flight with you to see who pukes first. Imagine the photo opportunities."

Yes, yes, fine. She knows me well, and she probably *can* handle herself.

Doesn't mean I have to like it.

7

Zeus

IF I DON'T HIT something—literally, metaphysically, statistically, whateverly—I'm gonna blow in a totally different way.

Ares, who could've been a fucking Boy Scout with all this prepared-for-anything shit, keeps a bag of spare clothes in his truck. He got me cut out of my dress and set up with clean jeans and one of the crazy-ass shirts that he's started wearing recently. This one's green with the outline of a cell phone and "I lick birds" written on it, and he's pulling that straight-faced shit that means he thinks it's fucking hilarious that I'm wearing it.

Instead of finding a gym or a batting cage or a strip joint—fuck, I'd take a liquor store and the frozen dough section of the grocery store—Chase and Ares are pushing me into a fucking karaoke-slash-game bar in the uppity district of Copper Valley where this golf shit's happening tomorrow.

Haven't been to Copper Valley much other than an away game or two every year, but I like this city. Smaller than New York, bigger than Nashville, with professional hockey, baseball, and football teams. Lots of smarty-pants dudes in big industries that are trying to save the planet with environmental whoop-dee-doo shit that's probably pretty cool if you're into science and math. I'm a fucking environmental disaster just for breathing.

If you count Ares, there's two of me. So probably good that there are people trying to reverse the effects of us walking on this earth.

Ten years ago, if you'd told me the three of us would've been ushered to a private booth, given a magic pass to jump to the front of the karaoke line, and comped all of our arcade games in this hoity-toity, grown-up Aladdin's Castle, I couldn't tell you which one of us would've peed ourselves first for laughing our asses off.

But with Chase and his billions and me and Ares and our hockey fame, fuckers bend over backwards to give us shit so we'll tell our friends and come back for more.

One thing I'm not telling my friends?

The woman who bested my control is twenty feet away, cradling my favorite arcade balls in her hands and racking up a Skee-Ball score on par with my best games.

Fuck.

When instinct kicks in, it's fight over flight every time.

Until today.

Fireball isn't facing us but probably still knows we're here. She's just got this *aura*.

It's saying *I know you're there, Zeus Berger, and you can fuck off unless you want a piece of this.*

Yeah, I fucking want a piece of that.

Not because I'm an *I want a piece of that* kind of guy. But because I can do better. I *will* do better. It was the damn girdle. Or maybe my own coconuts had me too turned on.

What? I'm a dude. I like big boobs. Had my own to play with for a while there. Think the stick in my pants cares if they're real or not?

I clench a fist around the napkin-wrapped silverware on our table and breathe. I'm not fucking running. Zeus Berger isn't a chicken. And I don't leave women unsatisfied, and I don't blow my load early.

That was a fluke. Maybe I'm sick.

Yeah.

My dick caught pre-jaculitis. Needs some pampering. Or a good beating.

After it's out of the penalty box.

Fireball turns her head and locks gazes with me.

She's got these eyes shaped like nuts—almonds, not peanuts or walnuts or those weird-ass pistachios—and that poker face that belies the fact that she's a sex shark. She turns back to the Skee-Ball lane, slings her ball, and *fuck*. She hits a corner pocket. Lights spin, a bell rings, and *High Score!* flashes on the marquee above her lane.

Maybe it was Fireball. Maybe she's got some secret magic pussy power and it put a hex on me.

Whatever it was, I'm not leaving here without my ego put back intact.

"Evening, gentlemen," our server chirps over someone

slaughtering some country song on the karaoke stage. "What can I get you?"

Chase orders something for all of us, because I'm fixated on Fireball and Ares is watching me like he knows how my brain works.

Which he does.

Ain't any of us man enough to handle her, bro, he silently warns me. *Even together. She's badass. Don't do it.*

Too late.

I'm already sliding out of that booth and sauntering to the Skee-Ball lanes.

I don't even know this chick's real name, but I need her to know Zeus Berger doesn't fail at anything. Even if it takes me a few tries to get it right.

I scan my arcade pass to start a game on the lane next to her. "Nice score."

She slides me another of those unreadable looks, then scans her pass to start another game as well.

"You left your bet money." I roll a ball down the lane, and it easily drops into the 400-point hole.

She nails the top hole, earning her 500 points. "You followed me here to tell me I left a couple hundred dollars behind."

"Lucky break. We're just out looking for fun. Found you instead."

She takes aim with a second ball and scores another 500 points. My dick stirs.

Fucker's crazy if it thinks it gets any say in anything I do for the rest of the night.

I toss my ball at the thousand-pointer in the corner, and end up with a hundred.

"Pretty good at this," I tell her.

She doesn't answer. Ares steps up on her other side, scans his pass, and meets my eyes over her head. *Losing cause, dumbass. Move on.*

I roll my third ball.

And I whiff while Fireball scores another 400. Big fat goose egg for me, more points for her.

What the *fuck*?

Who is this chick?

Bells are ringing, people laughing, someone wailing on the karaoke machine. And this woman's quietly beating the pants off me in Skee-Ball three throws in.

Go sit down before you do something stupid, Ares telegraphs.

Fireball rolls her next ball, and fuck a fucking cluck duck, she just hit another thousand-pointer.

I drop my own ball and give up all pretenses that I'm interested in playing Skee-Ball. "Anything you can't do?" I ask her.

"No."

The woman has more bravado than I do. Shouldn't be so damn attractive.

Or intimidating.

But the backstabbing demigod in my jockey shorts is surging and straining and asking to tap into the game again.

"You fly in the military?" I ask her.

"Yep."

"Fighters?"

"Special ops."

Of fucking course she was *special ops*.

"So you know," I say, "I don't usually…you know."

She turns her head toward me, and now my neck feels like those lights on the karaoke stage are glowing right on top of it.

"You don't," she replies. Not a question. Exactly. Not belief either. Ares is wincing while he pretends he's still trying to get a good score on his own Skee-Ball lane.

"I believe in mutual satisfaction," I tell her. "I'm not a selfish prick."

"You're not." Now she's mocking me.

"Not in bed."

"Mm."

Mm? What the fuck does *Mm* mean? I drop my voice, because even though Ares probably knows what I'm going to say, doesn't mean either one of us needs him to hear it. "I'm just saying, if you're around tonight, I'd go down on you. Let you sit on my face. Whatever. No strings. Don't even have to take your shirt off. Not that I'd object."

That's right. I'm propositioning a hot chick who could probably castrate me with her fingernails, and probably wants to after…you know. But what the fuck do I have to lose?

One more ball up the lane, 500 more points on her score. "And what do I get out of that?"

My cheek twitches. She's serious. Like she's never had a guy eat her out before. Like she doesn't get off on…well, on getting off.

The woman rubbing herself all over me not two hours ago was looking to get off. Which means either she doesn't believe I can do it, or she's not into oral.

"You give me ten minutes with my tongue between

your legs, and I'll blow your whole fucking world," I tell her.

Her gaze slides to my crotch, then back up to my face. Total resting unimpressed face. "Mm."

Yeah, she doesn't believe I can do it. I start to smile. Forgot how much I like a challenge. I'm no slouch in the sack. Just need the opportunity to prove it to her.

"Ah. Afraid to let go of control."

She fires another ball up the lane, and fuck if she doesn't score another five hundred points. "Is your concern for me, or for yourself?"

Now I'm starting to doubt myself. Not because she's worried about my intentions—I intend to give her the orgasm to end all orgasms—but because if she's this cool and controlled playing arcade games while discussing me licking her pussy, she might actually be a robot with boobs.

Can robots *have* orgasms?

And if so, do they enjoy getting off, or do their chips overheat, or are they programmed to just make dumb puckheads like me think we're doing a good job?

And will she taste like a woman or like joint grease?

She rolls her eyes like she's hearing my brain waves and tosses another ball. Another thousand points.

And there goes the stick in my pants. He likes a woman who can score. Even if he's still on the bench.

"It would be an honor to pleasure your pussy," I say.

Ares sighs. Probably because even when I'm whispering, my voice is as big as I am, which means even with that dude on the karaoke stage trying to stab our eardrums with the rusty end of a pitchfork, about half the restaurant heard me.

"My pussy remains unconvinced." Fireball nails another five hundred points and my dick bangs on the glass of its penalty box.

"I'm a man with something to prove. Won't let you down twice."

"Really."

"Master of mistakes. Master of corrections."

"You always overcompensate for your mistakes?"

"Fuck, yeah." My ego asks me why we're standing here offering it as tribute to this chick when that cute bartender across the room has been eyeing my ass since I walked into this joint. I tell it to shut the fuck up, because two nights ago—fuck, two *hours* ago—we would've picked the easy one.

But I can't walk away from this loud-mouth woman.

Maybe because I don't want any woman telling tales about Zeus Berger failing at being a god of sex.

Or maybe because she reminds me of me. And I hate losing to me.

Already did that during the play-offs. Not doing it again tonight.

One more ball up the lane, and I wonder if I'm getting to her, because this one lands in the 400 hole. She turns to me. Her face is that mask of straight-laced, take-no-shit, give-'em-hell that I want to rattle just for fun.

"You think your tongue has what it takes," she says.

"Damn fucking right." *It* can't come, so unless she soaks her pussy in hot sauce and pepper flakes, there's no way I won't get her off.

"You name it too?"

"Yeah, baby. You can call it the King."

"Hm."

I cock a brow of *yeah, you know I'll be good* at her, because I'm a cocky kind of guy, and even I know you have to shut up sometimes.

With your mouth. My face can still do plenty of talking.

"Lame," she says. "Attila the Tongue would've been more intriguing."

There are exactly two women in my life who ever put me in my place. My mom and my sister. It's surprising how much I'm enjoying this battle of wits.

I give her the bedroom eyes. "Didn't think you'd get it if I said he's really Olickseus." That's right. I know all about Odysseus and more fucking Greek history than any big motherfucker like me should. Thanks, Mom.

"O*dick*seus, I might've gotten," she says dryly.

I grin, because *damn*. She nailed it. I like her.

Apparently I did something right, because the hard-ass softens. She gestures to my mouth. "Come on. Let's see it."

My gaze drifts to her breasts, the stick in my pants threatens to ruin Ares' jeans, and I forget for a minute what we were talking about.

She snaps her fingers in my face. "Your tongue. Stick it out."

"Not so sure that's a good idea. Don't want you getting so hot and bothered you jump me right here."

"Highly doubt that'll be an issue."

"That's just because you haven't seen it yet."

"I don't let anything touch my pussy without inspection first. Stick it out."

Because she's amusing me, I lower my head, open my mouth and stick my tongue out. I waggle it to give her a good feel for just how dexterous that particular muscle is when I'm in control.

And I gleek.

I fucking *gleek*. Right in her face. A big ol' shot of my mouth juice, arcing through the air to sprinkle all over her nose and cheeks. This woman makes me blow body fluids every single fucking time I see her.

I don't get embarrassed. It's genetically and biologically impossible, because I don't give two fucks what anyone thinks of me.

Except for the second time tonight, I'm getting hot in the cheeks, and I'm frozen in mortification.

Swear to god, she has some nukes loaded up in her eyeballs and she's taking aim with them at me right now. She lifts her shirt sleeve and wipes her cheek. Pretty sure I got saliva in her fucking eyeball. She blinks twice.

And then she leans in and peers at my tongue like I didn't just spit in her face.

I get a whiff of bacon, beef, and cheese along with a peek down her blouse. She's not touching me, but she's wearing my spit and studying my tongue and I think I just sprouted three trees at once. My dick fucking split in three and all three Jupiters are trying to get at her.

"Does it do tricks?" she asks.

I can't fucking breathe for all the straining in my pants, and it takes me a minute to remember she's talking about my tongue. "It does all the fucking tricks."

"Demonstrate."

"Here?"

"If you can't at least curl it, there's no point in continuing this conversation."

Over her head, Ares demonstrates that damn curling-sideways tongue trick he used to do all the time to freak Ambrosia out. I'm more likely to fucking gleek at her again than I am to get my tongue to curl on demand.

But fuck if I'll let my body beat me again.

So instead, I touch my tongue to my nose.

That's right.

I'm licking my own nose with my tongue.

My golf game better be fucking spectacular tomorrow, because I need something more to brag about than being able to lick my own nose. I'm Zeus Fucking Berger. I've never in my life needed to brag about *licking my own fucking nose*.

"Mm," she says.

"Yeah, bet you can't do that."

"I don't use my finger to pick my nose, much less my tongue."

She's quick, I'll give her that. But her gaze is still fixated on my mouth.

Like she's considering my offer and she wants to see more.

I slide my room key out of my back pocket and slip it in hers. "Madison Towers Hotel. Room 842. Your move, princess. Offer expires at midnight."

Am I an idiot?

Perhaps.

But she's interested. Better to leave her wanting more than to stick around and ruin it again.

This Fireball chick—she's got game. Got a feeling she *likes* game.

Let's see if she wants to play.

8

Joey

MY BABY SISTER is probably being compromised right now by a royal ass who won't remember her name in the morning. Zeus Berger just gleeked all over my face. Peach is going to go jilted bridezilla or something on me when she finds out I've flubbed multiple opportunities to be a badass businesswoman around some of these nincompoops who can invest what banks won't in Weightless.

I should be getting to bed, because it's late and while I'm not flying tomorrow and don't have to worry about busting crew rest, I do have to put on a good show on the golf course.

Yet all I can concentrate on is the weight of that key card in my back pocket.

Who tracks a woman down and offers no-strings oral sex to compensate for a premature ejaculation problem?

No one. That's who. No. Fucking. One.

Except Zeus Berger, apparently.

And who's stupid enough to accept that offer?

Me, apparently.

My bill at the bar has been settled up already "by a secret admirer," whom I assume is Zeus, which means there's nothing stopping me from walking the two blocks to the Madison Towers Hotel. I'm free to see if Zeus is fucking with me, or if he can actually satisfy this ache in my clit.

I leave the bar and call Peach as I walk back to my hotel with fancy yellow street lamps lighting the way. If I don't talk to someone, I'm going to do something incredibly moronic and I'd rather be yelled at.

"How many of 'em did you outburp?" Peach asks by way of greeting.

Neither the crowd at the mixer nor the bar would have appreciated a burp-off. Sadly. Probably a good thing none of the kids sponsored by the foundation were there tonight. "All of them. How's Meemaw?"

"You mean am I getting my ass up to Virginia to give poor Gracie a break from babysitting you? She says to tell you she's having unprotected sex with both the prince and his two bodyguards, by the way."

My eye twitches so hard I permanently relocate a few eyebrow hairs.

Yes, I want Peach here to do what she does best. I fly. She runs the business.

I'm good with numbers. I know why Weightless is a good risk. I cobbled together my share of our initial investment by being good with numbers. And pool. And reading suckers. But I'm more comfortable betting the company over a game of darts than I am pretending I fit in with the country club crowd.

Hence Zeus Berger looking so appealing.

He doesn't fit in here any more than I do. He's unpredictable. Not afraid to say what's on his mind or take a risk. Hilarious.

And if you tell him I said any of that, I'll rip your nuts off too.

But my point is, I'm calling Peach because I'm worried about her grandmother.

I don't like worrying.

I much prefer pretending like everything will be fine because sheer willpower alone can change the fate of the world. Even though even I'm not that delusional.

But I'm worried about Meemaw. There. I can admit it.

She's always sending these care packages full of cookies and vintage *Playgirl* magazines featuring Tom Selleck look-alikes and hand-painted cards that say shit like *Reach for the stars and don't let any fucking man stand in your way*.

That woman is a gem, and she's the closest thing Gracie and I have to a grandma of our own. "I mean, how's Meemaw?" I repeat.

"Broken hip. They got her on the good drugs. She's seeing butterflies having food fights and asking for Mariposa."

"Who's Mariposa?"

"Hell if I know. I told her Mariposa ran away with Ferdinand."

"Ah, good?"

"Yep. Hell if I know who Ferdinand is either, but you

know Meemaw loves a good love story. Speaking of, any hotties besides the prince there tonight?"

"What do you think?"

"I think you wouldn't know a hottie if he walked up to you and licked your nipples, but me and Gracie are going to keep trying to find you a special friend anyway."

"I have a special friend. Six of them. Thanks."

"Just want you to be prepared if there's ever a battery shortage."

I let myself smile while I lift my hair up off my neck, looking for a breeze. The golf course will be hot tomorrow. And I'm supposed to show up in a skirt.

A fucking *skirt*.

Maybe I should go see if Zeus is going in a skirt too.

My nipples perk up, my clit pulses, and my better sense wobbles on the edge of the sanity cliff.

"Be nice to those kids on the course tomorrow," Peach tells me. "Talk about flying. Try not to outscore all those poor unsuspecting celebrities. We want them taking rides and posting to social media. I'll follow up with all the moneybags once Meemaw's back on her feet. You find one who can tolerate you, though, you let me know."

I resist rolling my eyes as I push into the black-and-silver lobby of the Madison Towers Hotel. An icicle-crystal chandelier big enough to take out both Berger brothers dangles in the entryway. "We built this company from the ground up. I'm not handing control to some dickhead who thinks an investment in us means he gets to tell us how to run the show."

"No? I kinda like the idea of being bossed around."

Even though I know she's yanking my chain, my blood

pressure heads into whistling teakettle territory. "Yeah, that's why you're still single."

"Wait, what? Hold on, Joey. I need to go talk to one of Meemaw's nurses. Call me tomorrow. Be good on the golf course. Let Gracie have a little fun."

"Tell Meemaw I'll kick her ass if she doesn't get better."

I hang up with Peach. Don't let her name fool you. She's smarter than half my hometown combined, and Gomer Smith and his pet duck excepted—every town has one, right?—there are some pretty fucking brilliant minds lurking in the backwoods.

A text message lands from Gracie.

Cute shop – A la Mode – down the street. Stopping for cherry pie. Want anything?

Yes. I want her to come back and not share her *cherry pie* with Prince What's-His-Name. *Sugar will kill you*, I text back.

So will pizza comes back immediately. Along with *—And sausage. Which I thought you didn't eat?*

Hardy-har-har.

I get in the elevator and force myself to punch the button for my own floor. Satisfying myself is always an option.

So is hitting the gym.

Which is what I opt for, because I'm not tired and if I so much as think about putting a finger to my clit, I'll think about Zeus Berger's massive tongue. It's bigger than some of the dicks I've seen. At least as big as my favorite dildo. And the way he reached it all the way to his nose—I shiver.

Nope.

Not going there. I'm here for business. I'm not going to fall into the trap of trying to bang an over-muscled, over-ego-ed hockey twit. Again.

It takes less than ten minutes to change into workout clothes and get to the gym on the second floor. And less than ten seconds after that for my lady brain to melt down and malfunction while my nipples do their marble impersonation and my mouth goes drier than the air at sixty thousand feet.

Zeus Berger is deadlifting an entire fucking treadmill.

He's got it folded in half and on its side, squatting down while he grips the base with his bare hands.

The overmacho show of deadlifting that much weight, I could ignore.

But *dog almighty*. The grip he has to have on that thing to be able to hold the flat edge while he lifts the machine off the ground, the sheer strength he must have in his fingers, is causing a disturbance in my electro-hormonal system.

I don't even realize I should be pissed he's not sitting in his room waiting in case I drop by.

An eerie sensation of being watched makes me aware that we're not alone. Ares is there behind Zeus, spotting him. I don't care that they're identical, there's no mistaking the two. It's an aura thing. A different presence.

Plus, Zeus has one more bump in his nose.

He's not watching me. Nor is Ares. No, that's Chase Jett, who's lounging in the corner, studying me over his phone.

This is what Peach would call an opportunity.

Zeus sets the treadmill back on its side and shifts that penetrating gaze to me. "You want a turn, Fireball?"

Yeah, I want a fucking turn. But not with the treadmill. I want to know what the man's fingers can do to my pussy. "Wouldn't want to embarrass you when I put the water cooler on top too."

His smile makes my underwear wet, and the way his eyes are going dark makes me wonder if he knows it.

"Ares," he says. "Bring the water cooler over."

"Afraid you'll break a nail if you do it yourself?" I say before Ares can move.

Zeus's grin gets bigger, like he's getting off on having me sass him.

Like he knows I'm all talk and that for every millimeter his smile grows, that incessant ache in my clit goes deeper.

Most guys are running for the door by now. Not Zeus.

Nope, he's looking me up and down like I'm a platter of bacon cheeseburgers that he's going to devour one lick at a time. He steps out from behind the treadmill and stalks toward me.

Fuck, even my nipples are shivering in anticipation.

For a man whose dick sprinted to the finish line before the starting gates were fully opened.

"How much do you bench?" Zeus asks.

"You need to know you bench more than a girl?"

"Hoping I can watch."

I can't walk straight for all the throbbing and pulsing in my girl briefs, much less lift a cotton ball with a steady hand. "Not sure tonight's your lucky night."

Ares visibly swallows a grin. Chase outright snickers.

"Shut up and quit sexting my sister," Zeus growls at him.

"That's later. She's getting a play-by-play right now."

"You want to take a dude down, Fireball?" Zeus asks with a nod to the corner. "I'd watch that too."

"Do your own dirty work, Berger."

He's close enough to smell. Man sweat. Beer. Fried cheese.

Two of my favorite things. The third is surprisingly intriguing. I usually go for rum. Yes, in a strawberry daiquiri. Shut up. It is *not* girly. And even if it was, I'm still a freaking girl.

Most of the time.

And I only like man sweat smell because I love getting the better of them. Master masturbator here, remember?

"You done?" Ares says to him. He doesn't add *dumbass*, but I swear it's lingering there in the air.

Zeus grins wider, just like he does every time I insult him, pretty much confirming my suspicion. "Yeah, go watch your cooking show."

"No po-po," Ares says to Zeus before turning his own steady blue gaze on me. "No knives."

He easily lifts Jett out of the corner chair and carries him by the back of his shirt out the gym door.

Jett lets out a resigned sigh and doesn't fight it.

Doesn't offer me a couple hundred million for Weightless either, but then, I insulted his best friend.

Also, I didn't ask him for any money.

"You do a handstand?" Zeus asks.

That mental image, me on my head, his beefy hands

clenched around my thighs, spreading my legs for his mouth, nearly makes me explode on the spot.

"You need a shower," I tell him.

I need a shower. A cold one. With Gracie and Peach standing there in the bathroom counting off my flaws and threatening to give me nieces and nephews with six different rock stars, hockey players, and gynecologists.

Instead, I hook my thumb to the second door leading out of the hotel's gym.

The one labeled *sauna*. "Like in there."

We trip over each other and a stationary bike racing to the door.

"Dick stays in your shorts," I tell him.

"Your pussy's coming out of yours," he replies.

Damn fucking right.

I'm peeling my athletic shorts off before the door's totally closed in the dark, steamy room. My underwear goes flying. I bang my knee on the bench, which is good, because I needed to know where I was going to get on my back.

"I'm gonna rock your fucking world," he growls somewhere to my left.

"I'll believe it when I see it."

Hot hands settle on my knees, already slick from the humidity in here. "Only thing you're gonna see is stars."

"I see stars every day."

"Hit your head often?"

"I fly, dumbass. Right up to the—*ooh*."

His hair brushes my inner thighs, his beard rubs my pussy, and his tongue teases my aching clit. He's not trying to chew it off or smother it to death. Just licking. Teasing. Tasting.

Holy fuck.

"Ooh?" he says, his breath hotter than the sauna and ticklish against my nether regions.

"I've had better," I lie.

He flicks his tongue over my clit again, and my hips buck off the bench.

"Have you now?" he asks my pussy. Without waiting for an answer, he drags his tongue up my seam to tease my magic button once more. Heat coils deep inside me, twisting and winding and building.

I grip his hair and hold him right where I want him. "Every single night."

His fingers scrape down the back of my thighs, slick with humidity, while his tongue swirls around my clit, and—*Oh*, yes.

This is—holy—yes—more—*there*—I'm almost—

BUZZZZ BUZZZZ BUZZZZ!!

"Shit!" I leap off the bench, bang my pelvis into his head, and crouch for my go-bag, but this isn't a drill. I'm not in the military anymore. And I don't have a go-bag.

"What the fuck?" he sputters.

"Fire alarm. Get out." Where are my pants? How many civilians are in the building? Nearest exits and fire extinguishers?

I find fabric on the floor and shove a leg in. My foot connects with something hard, and Zeus howls.

"I told you to get out," I snap.

"I can't fucking get out if you break my kneecap."

"Give me a break. You've taken harder hits on the ice. Where the fuck are my shoes?"

A light illuminates the humid room. I brush a bead of sweat and an errant lock of hair off my forehead, then dive at one sneaker near his feet.

"Holy fuck, Fireball."

My entire body freezes.

Not because he's getting a view of my back and ass.

But because the only thing on my body that causes that reaction is the scar.

"Never see a woman not lose her shit during a fire?" I say.

Because there's nothing to talk about with my appendicitis scar. Yeah, it's ugly, but that's what happens when you're deployed and pushing through the pain to get the mission done.

And no, I don't want to talk about all the thoughts that flashed through my head when they put me on an emergency transport to Germany. Or the look on Gracie's face when I came to and found her sitting at my side.

In Germany.

Do. Not. Ever. Scare. Me. Like. That. Again.

"Go on," I say to Zeus over the alarms. "Get the fuck out."

I yank on one shoe, the rest of my pants, and the other shoe before he's moved. When I stand, I'm suddenly dangling.

Hanging by the back of my shirt.

"Put me down, you—"

"Shut the fuck up, Fireball. Women and children first."

I take a swing and miss by a country mile. Him and his fucking ape arms.

And no matter how much I swing and fight, he doesn't let go.

He doesn't even break a sweat.

And as soon as he deposits me in Gracie's care outside the hotel, he disappears.

Which is probably for the best.

For both of us.

9

Zeus

My life has always consisted of three basic truths.

One: Ares will always have my back, and I will always have his.

Two: cheeseburgers, pizza, and pineapple tater tot casserole are second only to sex. Yeah, pineapple tater tot casserole. Go on. Mock it. You don't know what you're missing. More for me. Punk.

Three: Sex is no-strings. Women don't fuck me for my brain, my personality, or my moves. They fuck me for my muscles, my fame, and my dick.

Which means having my brother silently telegraphing that I'm in over my head with a woman I want to share a cheeseburger with and bang all fucking night long because she's playing hard to get means my entire life is off-kilter.

If she likes pineapple tater tot casserole, I'm done for.

Not that I'll ever find out. Fireball's a one-and-done kind of girl. And I've fucked it up twice. Not the good kind of fuck either.

You want a one-night stand?

Yeah, I did too. And this is the most fucked-up one-night stand I've ever participated in.

We got the all-clear to go back into the hotel forty minutes ago, but we've been hanging back, signing a few autographs, mocking Chase for a phone call he took with Ambrosia, and talking shit with Manning over the pudding pie he's making love to on the street corner. Yeah, I mean pudding pie, because Fireball took possession of Gracie the minute I put her on the ground.

And because none of us are as dumb as we act—usually—we all got out of the blast zone before she blew.

Lady didn't like being carried out of the hotel.

Me?

Ain't often I get to play hero. And I saved her ass good from that false alarm.

Probably good that I'm never gonna see this chick again.

Chase hangs up with my sister, Ares finishes his tattoo peep show for the three lingering women, and Manning rubs his tongue all over the last of the pudding in of his takeout container.

"Need to work on your form," I tell him. "No wonder Gracie left you for her sister."

"As a gentleman, I decline to comment on her level of satisfaction with my form." There's that damn cheerful grin again. "But it's worth noting which sister was smiling when we parted."

I hate that the fucker has a point.

This close. I was *this close* to Fireball coming apart at the seams when that fucking alarm went off. I can still taste her. Still feel her plump flesh on my tongue and her strong, silky legs in my palms. I want to finish what I started.

When we walk into the lobby, three things hit me at once.

First, the place smells like fresh chocolate chip cookies, which are my second favorite food in the entire planet right behind a thick, juicy steak the size of my head.

Second, this is the squeakiest-ass floor I've ever walked on. We sound like a herd of elephants stepping on chew toys.

And third, Fireball and Gracie are in the hotel bar. Fireball's throwing darts and fucking hitting a bull's-eye with every last one.

That good-for-nothing demigod in my jockey shorts stands up.

I tell the fucker to sit down and keep out of it, because he's still in the penalty box.

Ares cuts a look at me. He sees her too.

Chase is watching her with an expression I don't like. He's dating my sister. If he's getting fucking ideas about trading her in for a flying model, he'll find out what the sharp end of my skates can do to a man's jugular.

"You realize I'm far more terrified of your sister than I am of you," he says without taking his eyes off Fireball.

"Being a little smart doesn't make you all smart."

"Mead and cookies, gentlemen?" Manning says.

I take one last look at Fireball. Fuck, I don't even know her real name. After today, feels like I should know everything from her birthday to why she has that scar to if she gets a little orgasm every time she sneezes.

Fuck, that'd be such an awesome superpower.

She suddenly turns and looks at the four of us. Her gaze passes easily over Chase and Ares. The volcano shooting out her eyeballs, nostrils, and ears when she pauses to give Manning a good glare—the *don't even fucking think of asking to try my sister's pudding* glare—suggests her nickname is well-earned.

He blows her a kiss. Ballsy fucker. Told you I liked him.

Her nostrils flare, and her attention shifts to me.

And that's not a glare.

It's not soft, but it's not hard. Not accepting, but not judgmental.

It's somewhere between. Something elemental. Her dark gaze simultaneously tells me that I might not be the puck-up my first performance suggests I am, and also that I've still had my two strikes—fucking fire alarm—and I'm ejected from the game for arguing with the ref over that last call.

I never go down without a fight. I don't walk away from a challenge. I've never met a woman I couldn't satisfy one way or another, and when you're as big as I am, you get plenty of practice with *another*.

But this woman?

She's different. Stronger. Smarter. Harder.

She's got something inside her, something driving her, that I want to touch. Want to see and feel. Understand.

I want to dig until I find her soft spots, because I know they're there.

Fuck, I have soft spots too. Not that anybody cares.

Or that I'll ever let them.

Training camp starts in three weeks. Last year on contract—I'm a free agent at the end of the season. This year has to be spectacular to make up for—just *for*, okay? Fuckers on *SportsCenter* are already tossing around the R-word. I might be heading into old-man land, but I'm not done yet.

So I'm walking away from Fireball.

Let a woman in my headspace once. Long time ago. She fucked me up good. Almost ruined my best junior season. Almost cost me being drafted.

I'm not gonna let another one fuck up the most important season still to come in my life.

I nod to Fireball. *Nice knowing you, princess.*

One corner of her mouth twitches north. Barely. *Same, Zeusette.*

Can't help but appreciate a woman who makes you earn it.

I give my companions the *let's get out of here* head jerk. "What the fuck's mead?" I say to Manning. "Favorite girly drink of the Eskimos?"

"Thousand bucks says it knocks you on your ass before midnight," he replies cheerfully.

"You're on, dumbass," I reply.

Newsflash for him: I've already been knocked on my ass today.

And the woman who did it still has a keycard to my room.

Not often even I'm impressed by my own stupidity, but today's been that kind of day.

10

Joey

He fucking gave up.

He fucking gave up.

Of course he did. I shouldn't have expected anything different. And I shouldn't care.

I *don't* care, I tell myself as I run deeper into the heart of Copper Valley the next morning. I'm simply pissed that I didn't sleep well because I had indigestion from inhaling all the obnoxious, rich-ass fumes at that reception last night.

I snort softly to myself.

Fine. I'm lying.

I care.

And I'm pissed that it's my own fault. I don't know how to be nice to men who show interest. Smiling and petting their big muscles and stroking their egos isn't in my nature. I'm multilingual—straight-talk, Southern, and sarcasm—but *flirting* is so foreign it might as well be alien.

I run a flight adventure company. Next stop is the moon. After that—after that, I damn well need to know *alien*.

I can be nice. I know my fucking manners. Gracie, Peach, or one of my crew needs something, you're damn right I'll make sure they get it.

Even if it's an inexplicable desire to spend time with me.

I grunt and hang a left on Memorial Parkway to cut through Reynolds Park, which is bursting at the seams with trees, bushes, and flowers all seemingly happy to be representing Copper Valley.

This little Virginia town isn't what I call a *city*. Yes, it has a population big enough to support professional football, hockey, and baseball teams. A mass transit system, skyscrapers in downtown, multiple universities, Lyft drivers available twenty-four seven, and restaurants featuring food from every ethnicity on the planet, but with the Blue Ridge Mountains in all their blue hazy glory hovering in the distance, it feels more rural than it is.

Plus there's that unmistakable Southern charm that comes from being barely a stone's throw from North Carolina.

I like it.

See? I like things.

Just not Zeus Berger this morning.

Because he gave up on me last night.

Don't get me wrong. I don't want a *relationship*. I just want…something. Growing a private aerospace business takes commitment, sweat, and balls. Even I can't play hard-ass day in and day out without needing a break now and then.

And knowing Peach is sitting in a hospital, waiting for Meemaw to go into hip surgery, isn't helping.

I don't like it when the people I love are hurting.

Or in danger of getting hurt.

Or leaving.

Fuck, I hate when they leave.

I haven't worked out all my frustration on the run yet, but I head back to the hotel anyway. I promised Peach I'd swing through breakfast to see if there were any moneybags worth talking to, and since I can't exactly fly home to watch over Meemaw's surgeons—the flying part, yes, but getting into the operating room, no—I'll do what I can to not let my business partner down.

And all my plans immediately get flushed down the toilet when I find Gracie laughing over grits and sausage with His Royal Better-Keep-His-Fucking-Hands-Off-My-Sisterness.

Prince Manning executes a quick leap-twist-grab that has a third chair magically appearing at their table while he offers me his seat.

Like I should be honored to sit in his butt warmth.

"Ms. Fireball," he says like he's already had six cups of coffee this morning. "You're looking fresh as a daisy and twice as lovely this morning."

Gracie winces. "He means you're looking strong and determined and capable."

I take his grits, add two pats of butter, a swig of syrup,

all three of his sausage patties, and make myself breakfast stew. "Why are you talking to my sister?" I ask.

"To piss you off."

"Three points for bravery. Which won't save your nut sack. Do you actually fuck sheep, or do you just tell the ladies that so they'll think you can get them good wool coats?"

"I'm beginning to see why Zeus is so taken with you."

I haven't started a food fight since I was twenty-six, but I'm sorely tempted to fling some grit soup at him.

Gracie heaves a heavy sigh. "Joey, I love you. Go away, or I'll tell Peach you castrated a potential customer, and you know she has too much on her mind to deal with that too right now."

I eyeball the prince.

He's maybe six-two. Probably a respectable two-ten, maybe two-twenty when he's suited up for a hockey game. Has a glint of red in his brown hair and beard and a twinkle in his smoky eyes that suggests it's all fun and games.

Period.

Which almost definitely means it's *not*, because no one is that simple.

"You're a gambling man."

"Joey..." Gracie starts again.

Manning stretches back in his seat and studies me. "I do love to squander my family's money for no good reason."

I can sniff out a lie at forty paces, and this prince has *dirty rotten liar* written all over him.

Which is interesting.

He's either mastered sarcasm at a decibel level I can't clearly detect, or he wants the world to think he's a useless lout.

I hate rich fuckers who play this game. They tend to have little appreciation for how hard the rest of the world works. "I have a little nest egg that says I can make you toss your cookies on my airplane."

"I have the stomach of a goat and the inner ear balance of a shark. That would be a completely unfair bet, and I refuse to take your money."

"You'd take that bet if I were a man."

"On the contrary. There's no fun in a bet if it's a sure thing. Any pilot losing that bet to me is a sure thing. Now, if we were to put a wager on the better score today, I'd happily sign up. Because I intend to kick your arse on the golf course, though given your reputation, I suspect it will actually present a pleasant challenge."

A man pauses beside our table and pulls up a chair uninvited. "Getting your ass kicked so early in the morning?" Chase Jett asks the prince.

"She's all bark," he replies.

Probably to rankle me.

Which it does.

Only partly because he's right. Although, there was that one time in flight training that a classmate learned the hard way why you wait for permission to touch another person. Especially on a breast or between her legs.

He didn't graduate.

In case you were wondering.

"I was expecting your partner," Jett tells me.

"Wouldn't that have been lovely for all of us." I bite my tongue to keep from adding that he's a brave man for coming down without his bodyguards, because I don't want to know where Zeus Berger is, or even imply that I care.

I don't care. I don't care that he exists at all.

I need my plane here. Familiar ground. Or air, as the case may be.

"You and Ms. Maloney don't get out much. Why sponsor this tournament?"

"It was this or sponsoring the Bitches Get Shit Done celebrity golf tournament, but it turned out bitches had better things to do than plan a golf tournament. Your turn."

"Zeus threatened to pull my arms out of my shoulder sockets and use me like one of those screaming flying monkey toys if I didn't."

I fucking love those flying monkeys. Used to fling them at Peach all the time, until we got too busy. I don't fucking love how my nipples sit up straighter at Zeus's name. "Seems a good use for you."

Jett grins, and the light catches—is that *glitter* in his chin dimple? I don't want to know. "She's a handful, isn't she?" he says to Gracie.

"You have no idea."

"He voluntarily associates with the Berger twins," Prince Happy says. "He might have a vague clue."

"Peach signed up to sponsor this because I went undiagnosed with dyslexia as a kid and Joey threatened to break her kneecaps if she decided to put their sponsorship dollars anywhere else once that cute little kid reading the prayer to her dog went viral this spring," Gracie announces.

"Who doesn't love a kid who prays to her dog?" I say. Gracie's dyslexia is none of any of these fuckers' business. Even if it bothers me more than it bothers her.

Our daddy didn't know what dyslexia was. Neither did I, but I knew she was smarter than her report cards said, and I knew it was my responsibility to make sure she grew up able to take care of herself.

But she's right.

I did threaten to break Peach's kneecaps if she picked another cause to put our name on. Aubrey Alexander, the seven-year-old who went viral on social media earlier this year when some celebrity re-posted a video of her prayer to understand letters and brought more public attention to how far we still have to go in making sure all dyslexic kids get the help they need, reminded me so much of Gracie my heart ached.

And my heart aches even less than my vagina does.

At least, I wish it did. *Fuck*.

"What do you do, Gracie?" Jett asks.

"I bake the best damn cookies you'll ever taste south of the Mason-Dixon line. If you're half as smart as I hear your girlfriend is, you might ask me what I've been doing with organic and gluten-free ingredients. I'm a bargain right now, but I won't be for long."

Delivered complete with the Gracie Diamonte dimple and eye twinkle that once led to me making an emergency trip home to beat her prospective prom dates off the front porch with a broom.

"Don't even fucking think about it," I growl at Jett,

who's studying Gracie as though he's trying to decide how good her cookies might be.

"That's not how you seal a business deal," Gracie says primly to me.

"That's how *I* seal a business deal."

Gracie slaps a business card on the table and shoves it across to the billionaire. "In case you want to talk without the threat of bodily harm."

"Haven't done all your research on his girlfriend," Prince Cheer muses. He takes Gracie's hand and presses a kiss to her knuckles. "Lovely dining with you this morning, Miss Diamonte. I must be off. Early tee time."

She blushes.

With her natural olive skin, dark curly hair, and that light glowing in her brown eyes, she's a smiling, dimpled rose of beauty, grace, and elegance.

Like a fucking princess

Beauty to my beast.

The prince smiles warmly at me. "We'll compare scorecards over dinner, Miss Fireball. And if I win, I want a ride on that plane of yours."

"Forget winning," Jett says. "I'm paying for a ride on that plane."

I hand him my own business card—with the number to our office, of course, because dog knows no one wants me answering our phones—and shrug as though I don't give two fucks what he wants. "You can call and see if there's room on the flight tomorrow. But we're usually booked at least three months in advance."

With tomorrow being the exception, since we reserved

it specifically for anyone from today who might want a demonstration.

I was supposed to fly in tonight, with Luna—our tricked-out 727 that my crew and I take to zero-gravity a few times a week—and run a demo ride for a few lucky kids drawn by the Dyslexus Nexus foundation and any heavy hitters Peach charmed here this week.

Peach isn't here.

I could be flying a half-empty jet with mostly kids and parents.

Hell, I'd fly it for just one passenger, without complaint, because I love flying, but that won't necessarily pay the bills.

Gracie squeezes my hand when Jett leaves the table to hit the buffet line. "Your plane's going to be full, and you know it," she whispers. "You really know how to play men, and don't pretend you don't. Peach should send you places like this more often."

"Not if we all want to stay out of jail."

She laughs so hard she snorts, and for a brief moment, I give in to the urge to smile at my baby sister.

We might not always get along, and we might rarely see eye to eye, but I've got her back.

And she's got mine.

11

Zeus

The mead was a bad idea.

Fucking *mead*. Manning's honey wine shit went down like ice cream and stayed down like a whole carton of rotten eggs. And I'm not talking a dozen.

I'm talking the mega-pack you get at the fucking big box store.

Stuff had to be five hundred proof, and don't tell me five hundred proof isn't a thing.

Because here on the golf course, with the noon sun beating down like a mofo looking to strike us all dead of heat stroke—who the fuck decided August in the South was a good time for a charity golf tournament?—my head's being held together by the knots I put in my hair last night.

Skipping this round of golf occurred to me.

But I don't blow off my commitments. Switch tee times with Chase, yes. Blow it off, no.

I'm not here because any of the corporate blowhards for my team wanted me to get the good publicity, or because my agent suggested we go after a sponsorship for golf clubs or balls—*heh*, balls—or because any courts ordered me to community service on the links for that little incident with the stoplights and the dildos right before the play-offs last spring.

No, I'm here for my brother.

Wouldn't know it to watch him on the ice, but Ares is the biggest-hearted mother pucker on the whole fucking planet. He could've done something a lot bigger with his life than playing hockey if anyone had taken the time to look past the shit we pulled when we were little to see if his problems in the classroom were something more than him being an overgrown, rambunctious Berger twin.

Not that Ares doesn't like his life.

But not every kid gets to grow up and get paid millions to play hockey if they don't get the education they need. And while I've got a few options for after I—you know, do the R-word thing in a few years—Ares is stuck on the ice until he's forty, at least, because every single fucking asshole on the entire planet underestimates him still.

I could get a coaching gig.

He's still sheltered from talking to the press because of dumbass execs who think he'll sit there and pick his nose instead of answering questions in full sentences.

So I'm here with Panther, a tatted-up, straggly-haired rock star who *is* here because of corporate blowhards—

PIPPA GRANT

his record label made him come—and the royal mofo who set me up with that mead last night. Apparently getting drunk is the best way to stay warm in fucking *Stölland*.

And because Panther doesn't have enough ink on him, and also because he probably makes ten times what I do every year just for singing and gyrating on a stage, I catch him by surprise and sign his forehead with my favorite Sharpie while we wait on the fourth person in our group.

He snaps a selfie of the two of us making monkey faces and fiddles with his phone. Probably posting it to social media with some kind of insult he thinks is unflattering. I'm too hung over to give two shits, and I didn't get the usual rush from leaving my mark.

Fucking mead again.

"Who is this *Joey* person?" Manning says cheerfully with an evil glint in his eyes. Fucker apparently has the alcohol tolerance of a four-hundred-pound goat. Ares was hurting like a bitch this morning too, but Manning, in all his regal princely glory, isn't even wearing sunglasses. "He has two minutes before we start without him. Got a schedule to keep."

Panther grabs one of the balloons tied to the post at the first tee, bites into it, sucks on it, and smiles at the two of us. "Got a schedule to keep," he mimics in a British accent made eight octaves higher by the helium.

The four caddies for the day—all kids helped by the Dyslexus Nexus foundation, all between nine and twelve—snicker.

My head threatens to crack.

"They say sucking helium shrinks your bollocks," Manning says, again with that god-awful cheer.

"Watch your fucking language," I growl. "Kids present."

"You shouldn't say *fuck*," my caddy informs me. She's eleven, with some girly name like Sunshine or Rainbow or Meadowlark. "Cussing also makes your *bollocks* shrink."

I eyeball the blond terror as a warm chuckle drifts from the hill leading to the tee. A chill slinks down my spine, followed by sheer dread coupled with undeniable fucking glee.

Last night was supposed to be the end of this.

"You are wise beyond your years, my young friend," Fireball herself tells my caddy. She sticks her hand out. "I'm Joey. And you're…?"

"Stuck with this lughead today," she says with an eye roll and a head jerk in my direction. "You can call me Bailey."

"Ah, Ms. Joey," Manning says. "Of course." The fucker's glacial eyes light up the way mine usually do when I'm picturing a chick naked, except there's something more there.

Something like maybe he's in on the joke.

Of fucking course he is. Spent all night with her sister last night, didn't he? I glower at him.

His fucking evil grin widens.

"You're Joey?" Panther says in his helium voice while he takes stock of her skirt, her rack, and her sunglasses.

Not in that order.

Joey looks at Bailey. Which isn't like Sunshine or Rainbow or Meadowlark. Maybe that was one of the boy caddies. "We're in for a long day, aren't we?" she says to the girl.

"I was really hoping to get Levi Wilson."

"Weren't we all?" Fireball—*Joey*—pulls her phone out. "I'll see if he can meet you after the ninth hole. Sound good?"

"Like *holy shit* good," Bailey says.

"But only if you watch your language. These men are so impressionable."

The kid's got some *fuckin' A* in her nod.

I don't want to like her—either one of them—but I can't help myself.

Especially where Joey Fireball is concerned.

Joey Fireball.

She's even got a girl mobster name. That's so fucking hot.

She introduces herself to the caddies, we do a round of boring-ass pictures, and then she turns to me, Manning, and Panther. She's in aviator sunglasses that make her a total badass despite the white golf shoes and ankle socks, the white golf skirt, v-neck T-shirt with the Weightless logo, and her sun visor.

"Shall we, gentlemen?"

Panther trips over himself offering ladies first and pointing her to the front tee.

Manning smirks at Panther, who apparently hasn't had the pleasure of truly meeting Joey.

Me? I'm struggling to keep the jackass in my pants from trying a repeat of last night's debut performance. Her legs have more tone than a whole fucking orchestra, her ass should be declared a national treasure, and that hint of cleavage in the vee of her shirt is making me want to jump off the cliff of her boobs and see how far down I can go.

I twitch my hand at Bailey. "You got that bag I gave you?" I ask.

Because there's only one thing that can take my mind off a woman.

"Yes, your bullyness," she says.

I cut a look at her. I'm big. I'm loud. But I don't push people around to get my rocks off.

Not off the ice, anyway.

Can't exactly holler that I'm not a bully to prove it though. Even I'm not that dumb.

"You play sports?" I ask her.

"No, because I'm a *girl*. They don't have good sports for *girls* where I'm from. And even if they did, my grades aren't high enough for me to get off academic probation."

Little spunkmuffin reminds me of my sister when she was little, except Ambrosia never had trouble with her grades. And now I'm getting pissed for both of them.

I grab the grocery sack myself and pull out a lemon while Joey's busy arguing with Manning and Panther about the order of play, which tee she'll use, and handicaps.

Doesn't want privileges for being a *woman*. Says she'll beat the pants off us fair and square.

And after watching her last night, I'm thinking I shouldn't underestimate her.

Wouldn't mind one more chance for us both to get off though.

Hey, what fate giveth, Zeus Berger doth not take for grantedeth.

Which means the only way to not lose to this woman —again—is to change the rules. I'm no slouch on a golf course—club, ball, stick, puck, what's the difference?—but I also know some of these other sportsing dudes, actor wankers, and millionaire douchebags take all this under-par shit seriously. None of us in this foursome are winning squat today.

Which means we need a new game.

"Fu—duck-a-duck the game," I say. "A hundred bucks says I can hit this further than any of you sissies."

"Don't say *fuduck-a-duck*," Bailey says. "We all know what you mean, and it's not polite for a golf course. That dickhead manager said so."

The other three caddies eyeball her like they know who's in charge and probably won't even mutter a *darn* today either.

"Change of terms?" Manning says to Joey, again with the fucking cheer, while he plucks the fruit from my fingers. What the *cluck* is that all about? "Two hundred towards my ride on your jet says I can smash this lemon against that pine tree."

"That little pine tree four feet away?" Joey deadpans. "Or the pine tree that means you're taking out half the audience?"

"I like her," Panther declares in his helium voice while we all glance toward the roped-off audience watching in rapt silence.

People who watch golf are weird.

"It's against the rules to hit anything but balls at anything but the hole," one of the boys caddying for us mutters.

"You want to play golf, or you want to have fun?" I ask

him. And I don't snicker at *balls* or *holes*, even though I want to.

The kids all share glances. They're in yellow vests and official crew name badges, and they all smell like sunscreen.

"Let's have fun," the smallest of the group says.

I hold out a fist, he bumps it with his puny little knuckles.

Bailey puts her hands on her baby hips. "What else do you have in that bag?"

"Firecrackers, paintballs, giant spitwads that me and Ares made last night, and four bottles of champagne we're going to pop the *right* way."

She eyes the grocery sack, obviously not big enough for half that shit. "My mother says honesty is the true mark of a person."

"If you can't be a good example, be a warning."

"Put your club where your mouth is, Berger," Joey says.

She doesn't add *if you think you can score*, but she doesn't have to.

It's hanging there for both of us to hear.

Along with some *and fuck you and the horse you rode in on too*.

Like she's pissed at me.

Like it was my fucking fault the alarms went off last night.

Like she's not the one who had a key to my fucking room that she didn't use.

Those eyes. So dark. So pissed. So fucking sexy.

Maybe she did go to my room. Maybe she heard all of us in there and didn't want an audience.

Manning twitches a brow at me. Panther sucks down another half-balloon. And Bailey lifts her chin. "It's your turn, *Mr.* Berger."

"Call me Zeus, kid."

"Fine, Zeus Kid," she says.

Despite the tension hanging between me and Joey, I'm grinning when I put my lemon on the tee.

Do I want to be stuck all afternoon with the reminder of everything I fucked up last night, and the reminder of just how much I'm still interested in this woman?

Fuck, no.

But you're damn right I'm going to make the best of it. And my caddy doesn't know it yet, but I'm the best damn thing to ever happen to her too.

12

Joey

BY THE EIGHTH HOLE, the guilt is seeping in.

And I fucking hate guilt almost as much as I hate feelings.

It's possible I should go easier on Zeus. He smells like he pickled his liver last night, he's pretending like his knee doesn't hurt after he took his own club to it when all three of the nimwits I'm playing with tried to prove they could toss a club better than I can toss a rifle—swear to dog, I had no idea an old ROTC classmate would be leading a drill demonstration off the fourth tee and challenge me to prove I still had some moves—and his caddy is giving him a beat-down like she's Mark Twain playing the role of Genghis Khan.

Bailey's going to *own* him by the end of this round. I've never met an eleven-year-old so able to eloquently put a brute in his place.

The way he tolerates her with that smug grin of his growing warmer with every insult is adding to both my irritation and my guilt. And it pisses me off more every time I feel guilty.

He walked away last night after he carried me out of that hotel. He's acting like he didn't beg to get his mouth on my pussy. Like he didn't hit on me half the night. Like I'm nobody.

Don't get me wrong—I hardly think I'm the shit.

But I'm not *nobody*.

Nor did I ask to be in this foursome today.

But it's entirely possible he doesn't want to be around me because…well…I'm me.

He's teeing up with a hockey stick and a can of baloney. "Five hundred yards," he grunts to Prince Manning.

"Maybe if you're Fireball," Manning replies jovially.

"I give you fifty," Panther squeaks out. I don't know what that black scribble is on the rock god's forehead, but it goes well with the ink on his arms and almost distracts from the rags-and-holes-inspired clothing that suggests either he has horrible managers who've stolen all his money, or he's planning on some kind of mud wrestling orgy when we finish up here and doesn't want to be bothered to change before the fun starts.

"You keep sucking helium, you might actually be able to sing," Bailey tells the rock god, which cracks the men up.

I'm physically incapable of giggling, but I get a good chuckle in.

Kid's hilarious. I like her.

"And another point for the caddy with the mouth," Manning says. When he's not hitting on my sister, he's reasonably bearable. He hasn't so much as mentioned her, in fact. Which either means he's planning to compromise her and thinks I won't suspect if he avoids the subject, or he's a playboy ass who's already forgotten I have a sister.

Yes, I know. I'm putting all of them in impossible situations where I'll refuse to like any of them. Gracie tells me often enough this is why I'll end up alone in my old age, but I have plans. Master plans.

One day, when I pick a man good enough for her, she'll give me nieces and nephews, I'll spoil them rotten, and they'll gather round to hear stories of the time I took myself to the moon.

"What would helium do to me at zero-gravity?" Panther asks me.

"It would make your lungs expand until they burst," I tell him, channeling some of Manning's cheer. Not because sucking helium in my plane would actually make anyone's lungs burst—even if it would in actual space—but because his royal highness apparently appreciates both bloodthirstiness *and* merriment, and I'd like him to know I do too.

In case he has secret plans he doesn't want me to know about.

Zeus cuts a look at me. "Not if your cabin's pressurized with real air."

Hello. Where did those brains come from? "Hockey player *and* physics expert?"

"Need to know basis. You don't need to know." His lips curve in a wolfish smile teeming with a wicked promise he couldn't fulfill last night, and despite my best efforts to wrangle my hormones into submission, I get a longing pull deep in my core and some heat channeling between my legs.

He lowers his head over his shot, grips his stick like he's on the ice, pulls it back, and lets it fly.

The can of baloney takes off like a shot, but it's not flying down the fairway.

Nope, it's slowly meandering on its side over the grass like a drunken clown car tire. It flops to a halt barely twenty yards down the way.

"Fu—*cluck*," he mutters.

"You're up, Ms. Joey," Manning says. He treats me to a royal smile behind his beard—the copper in his hair is glinting in the sunlight, and even if I hadn't seen him with my sister the last twenty-four hours, I would still suspect his brand of charm gets him as many women as Zeus Berger's overt manliness.

I wonder if Manning has issues performing in private as well.

Okay, fine. I *hope* Manning has issues performing in private as well. Because even if he's proving to be entertaining with his continued insistence that he's going to win a ride on my plane—which he's not, because his golf game sucks—he flirted with my sister.

And even if he might actually be a nice guy—he's been remarkably decent to the caddies, and he did help Panther when the rocker tried to tee up backwards two holes back, and he also keeps waving his guard back every time I get my hands on a golf club—I refuse to let my sister live in the bubble that comes with dating royalty.

THE PILOT AND THE PUCK-UP

I take a can of baloney from Manning and turn to Zeus. "May I?" I ask with a nod at his stick.

I can't see his eyes behind his sunglasses, but I can see the twitch in his left cheek.

Because I'm asking for his *stick*, or because I'm asking to borrow his baby?

"I'm not going to *break* it," I say, and whoops.

Probably a poor choice of words, because now that twitch has moved to his chiseled jaw. Might even be causing some movement in one of those notches in his nose that speak of a man well-versed in hockey fights.

Gracie would be laughing her ass off if she were here.

And if she knew the full story. Which she doesn't, because I'm a hard-ass when I have to be, but I'm not cruel.

It's also two-faced of me to jump a guy while I'm sabotaging her efforts to *take a walk* with another, and I refuse to confess my transgression.

Zeus thrusts the stick at me. I take it, our fingers brush, and *fuck*.

Most of my adult life has been spent with egotistical asses. Part of the pilot world. You get used to it.

You also get used to feeling like one of the guys.

But Zeus Berger—despite everything—is still a big enough, bad enough dude to make me feel like a woman.

It's the strength in his hands that causes that ripple of awareness to shoot up my arms, I tell myself.

Nothing more.

I mount my baloney can—similar to the shape of a can of tuna or a hockey puck—on four tees, step back, and get a feel for the stick in my hand. I've spent plenty of time on golf courses—was a personal goal to be able to golf as well as the colonels and generals I reported to back in my military days—but not as much time holding a hockey stick beyond some pick-up street hockey games with brooms and tennis balls. The wood's smooth, the weight different than a driver, so I shift my stance to compensate, pull the stick back with the same motion I saw Zeus do—or as close as I can get—and I let the stick fly.

The blade connects with the can, and it flies down the center of the fairway.

"Yeah!" Bailey crows.

"Holy *fuck*," Helium-Panther squeaks. We're going to be carrying his ass off the course before too long if he doesn't lay off the balloons, and I've had to forbid him from sneaking any more helium to the caddies.

I hate playing mom, but one of us has to do it. Should've been fucking Manning's job. Or one of his lurking bodyguards.

"A good fifty meters, yeah?" Manning says. "Right good shot for a puck without ice. Berger, I do believe the lady could school us both in the rink."

"Can I get your autograph?" Bailey says to me. "You are so cool."

"You want mine, kid?" Panther asks.

"No, just Joey's."

Zeus is watching me, and it's making my skin itch and my lady brain perk up. As if *she's* forgotten last night. And as if she thinks he might be worth giving another chance.

She either knows something I don't, or she's been kicked in the head one too many times too. Might want to check the setting on my vibrator when I get home.

"Of course," I tell Bailey.

Not a chance in hell are we going there with Zeus Berger again, I tell my lady brain.

Manning grins. "All this female bonding is making my bollocks itch." He lines up his own baloney can, takes aim with Zeus's stick, and sends his makeshift puck flying.

It stumbles to a halt a good ten yards short of my can, which gives me an inordinate burst of satisfaction.

"Thrusters are gonna fire your ass," Zeus grunts.

Manning nods in agreement. "Only want me for the publicity anyway," he says cheerfully.

I should've been born a fucking princess. I could've exhibitioned the shit out of being a royal stand-in for a few astronauts the way Manning is for Copper Valley's hockey team.

"I can't even throw a can that far," Panther says. He's coming down off his helium, and he almost has the gritty rock-and-roll voice back. He shoves his can of baloney at Bailey. "Here. You do it for me."

Bailey lines up with Zeus's stick, almost takes Panther's head off when she pulls it back, and lets that puppy fly.

"Holy *fuck*," Panther says again, and without the helium addition, he sounds as reverent as though he were stroking a guitar.

I've seen the guy's music videos. Don't let the helium fool you. He oozes sex when he's ripping out a guitar solo, and the tats don't hurt either.

Zeus squats down to Bailey's level. "There's no girls' hockey team in your town?"

She gives him a look that would probably be accompanied by a bird if she were three or four years older. "If there was, you'd be carrying *my* golf clubs."

"Cluckin' right," he grunts.

He stares at her another moment before jerking his head at the fairway. "Load up and go grab your cans. Stuffy McBust-Our-Balls is coming."

The club manager is being a dick.

On that, we can all agree.

"I'll get yours," Panther says to Bailey. He flashes a rare smile. "If you'll promise to not hit me with that stick."

She puffs her chest up and shoves the hockey stick at Zeus.

He shakes his head. "Keep it."

And then the big old goober pulls a Sharpie from his back pocket and flips it to me. "Sign that for her, Fireball. If she says please."

And once again, Zeus Berger has managed to take me by surprise.

Dammit.

13

Zeus

Wanna know the last time four hours was such hilariously fun torture?

You're gonna have to figure it out on your own, because fuck if I've ever had this much of a good time being this miserable.

And I've made a reputation being a hilariously fun fuck-up, so you know this has to be epic.

Joey Diamonte isn't just handing me my ass, she's handing me my nuts and my mangled, chewed-up, useless stick too. She almost hit a hole in one with her lemon. She cost me my favorite hockey stick. I can't use the damn thing when someone else outshot me with it. And she's about to cost me my pride, because I can't fucking quit this woman.

"Designated flyer," Panther declares as we stand arguing on the last tee.

"Whoever's flying, Fireball's going last," Manning says. "We only have the one drone, and I don't want her plucking it out of the sky before I get my turn to try."

She doesn't reply. No smile. No smirk. No coy *Oh, it's all beginner's luck.*

Nope, she's got this straight-faced, *Let's get on with it*, no-bullshit attitude as she swigs water off a bottle her caddy handed to her and checks a message on her phone.

All of the caddies are in love with her. Watching her with hearts in their eyes.

Except Bailey.

The little spitfire's got *I'm gonna be her someday* written in her every move. Wouldn't have pegged Fireball for the kid-friendly type, but there's something to the way she's talking to these kids that has some primal instincts deeper than my nut sack wanting to see her soft underbelly.

My instincts can go drown themselves in the fucking lake. Me and Jupiter and Attila the Tongue—Joey's so fucking brilliant—and every other bit of me doesn't do this obsessing over one woman shit.

Especially when she's so good at handing me my balls.

I shove the remote at Panther and point to Manning. "Go on, you whiny baby. Take your shot."

Panther hits a button, and the drone whirs to life. "See this, Fireball? I'm a fucking pilot too."

"All of our mothers are going to hate you tomorrow," Bailey tells him.

"Yeah, well, I—" Panther stops himself.

Pretty sure he was going to say he fucked all their mothers. What I would've said. If there weren't kids present.

"The world really should be run by women," Bailey tells Joey.

Her lips twitch in a smile. Can't help wondering if she's just as happily miserable as I am.

Probably not on the miserable side. She's barely acknowledging I exist.

Not that she's ignoring me. She's just treating me no differently from anyone else here today.

Like I haven't seen her tits. Like she wasn't riding me in that office last night. Like I wasn't two seconds from setting her world on fire in that sauna when the damn smoke alarms went off.

Women ignore me all the time. They either want me or they don't, and there are plenty enough who want me that I don't give two thoughts to the ones that don't.

Until there was Fireball.

I met her while I was wearing a fucking dress. Lost my shit before we even got started having a good time. And she's kicking my ass on the golf course. We're not even playing real golf, and she's winning.

I can't decide if I need to ask for her phone number or get the fuck off this course and try some kind of weird-ass hypnotherapy to forget she exists.

"Get it up there good and high," Manning tells Panther. "Don't make it too easy on me."

"I'd never go easy on your pansy ass," Panther grunts.

The drone floats up in the sky. Manning finally plops a golf ball on the tee and lines up. He's got all the form you'd expect of a royal ninny—hips and shoulders and club all in a good line, the right *thwack* when his club connects with the ball, chin in the air as he watches it fly.

Damn good shot.

Nowhere near the drone.

"Damn," he says. He's the happiest fucking disappointed prince I've ever met. I put on a good show of being a happy-go-lucky dumb-as-shit fuck, but he's got me beat by a mile.

"Panther one, His Royal Buttwipe zero," Panther crows.

"I could make them all throw up," I hear Joey murmur to Bailey.

"That would be so cool."

I wouldn't fucking puke in her plane.

"You're up, you big brute," Manning says to me.

Panther's veering the drone all over the place—dude's so drunk on helium, he probably shouldn't even look at a golf cart. "Come and get me, you big fucker," he says to me.

I line up my shot, eyeball that four-propellered drone, shift my stance, and give that ball the Zeus Berger treatment.

Except I *miss*.

I take a big old bite out of nothing but air, and come up swinging still more air on the other side. My knee twinges, my shoulder protests, and my ego all but curls up in a ball and dies.

"Better show him how it's done, Fireball," Bailey says.

"Everyone whiffs now and again." Manning's choking back a laugh like I'd like to choke *him*. Panther's high as a fucking balloon, which means the princely puckhead is the best candidate for me to choke. "Have another go at it."

My temper's hitting danger zone levels. This time yesterday, I would've stuck my coconuts out and told him I missed on purpose, but I can't work up the smirk or anything remotely close. I need to get off this course and blow off some steam. Zeus Berger doesn't make a fool of himself. Not on the ice. Not in the bedroom. Not on a golf course.

I swing my club again, one-handed and short-tempered, and this time, it connects with the ball and sends that fucker floating a mile up in the air. It barely misses the drone, and it's hooking to the right—toward that damn lake they just had to put on the last hole—but it's sailing like a ball that got its ass kicked and its teeth knocked in.

That's more like it.

It bounces and rolls to a stop just shy of the rough surrounding the lake.

"Missed me, missed me, now you gotta kiss me," Panther sings like a fucking five-year-old.

"Kiss this—" I start, then I remember there are kids around. I hitch my pants back up—kids probably only got a flash of my ass—and flick a look at Joey. "Your turn."

For the record, I don't add *If you're man enough*.

And she doesn't smirk.

Not on her face.

But I can *feel* it. She's taunting me. Somewhere behind those cool-ass aviator sunglasses, somewhere deep in her soul, the woman is mocking and teasing and taunting me.

She takes a driver from her own caddy, lines up on the men's tee, tells Panther to step back before she clocks him in the nuts, and takes aim at the drone.

Her club arches back, those beautiful boobs go out, then it's all feline grace as she drives that stick down, smacks the shit out of the ball, and sends it spinning straight into the drone.

Straight. Into. The. Fucking. Drone.

"No fucking way," Manning says reverently.

The drone spins ass over teakettle a few times, listing in the air while the ball veers to the right. It doesn't bounce as far as mine when it lands, but me and Joey, we're headed the same way.

"You hitting a ball?" I ask Panther.

He's sunk to his knees already, and now he flops onto his back. "Life is no longer worth living."

"That's the helium talking," Joey says. "You'll feel better once there's oxygen in your brain again."

"You killed my spaceship."

"For a hundred grand, I'll take you up in my spaceship. Double it, and I'll toss in a bouquet of balloons."

"Fuck, I spend that on haircuts every month."

Even I can't help but stare at his shaggy mane.

"I believe you Americans call this *getting ripped off*," Manning says.

I amble toward the golf cart. "C'mon, Fireball. Bring a club. I'll give you a lift."

She insisted on walking the course—of course she did, because she's a badass who'd probably flap her arms to fly hole to hole if she could—but I also think she believes none of us have noticed her checking her watch and her phone. Like she's got somewhere to be.

Might as well make that appointment happen for her,

because it's clear I'm getting nowhere else with this girl, and I got an appointment to get to myself.

My ego's in need of some licking and my liver's in need of some pickling.

I can find that at a bar downtown easy enough.

Joey doesn't immediately move to the cart. Instead, she gives me a long, steady, silent interrogation that seems to ask everything from my driving record to my favorite book to how many times I've been in love.

Heat's creeping over my scalp again, but this time, it's not the sun, it's not my temper, and it's not even that sensation that I should probably hang out at home a few more minutes in case I need to drop a load, which, for the record, you should never do in public when you're the size of a semi-truck.

But locker rooms are fair game.

No, I'm getting itchy at my roots because I *know* she's weighing and measuring me behind those cool-ass pilot sunglasses. Like maybe the lady *has* known I'm here.

And she's not looking for the meat.

She's evaluating the man.

I'm about to pop off and tell her to walk her own ass when she silently climbs in the cart. She doesn't argue about me driving. Probably because I'll just drop her off on the way to my ball, and it's faster for her to hop out than to switch drivers.

Faster than arguing about it too.

The cart groans under my ass, like most of these ant-sized contraptions do. Joey's side lifts two feet in the air. She grips the roof for balance. I put the cart in gear and steer us toward our balls.

"Nice game," I say.

"Mm," she replies.

I'm starting to figure this chick out. And I'm not gonna let her *Mm* ruffle me this time.

Much.

"You play golf a lot?"

"No."

"Hockey?"

"No."

"Hard-ass?"

"That's not playing."

Water's sparkling at the edge of the rough, mirroring that bitchin' hot sun. I'm dripping—hard to stay cool when you're the size of an elephant—and she's barely breaking a sweat. We're getting close. She'll hit her ball right up on the green, probably sink it in two shots, and we'll be done.

Goodbye, Joey Diamonte.

Thanks for the memories.

"Was it good for you at all?"

She turns her head toward me, and now my neck feels like the sun is glowing right on top of it.

I need to shut the fuck up. *Now*. But my fucking mouth has a mind of its own too. "The second time. Before…you know."

She's still not saying anything.

Of course not. She was fucking *special ops*. She defies gravity. She's trained to be a badass. Can probably orgasm on command and withhold it for weeks at a time too, in case she was ever captured and put in a brothel for…for… fuck, I don't know what for. And it doesn't matter, because now I'm sweating at the thought of six Joey Fireballs in my own personal brothel.

Jupiter's straining too. Him and me, we had a talk last night. I'll stay out of the girdles if he swears to never pickle sneeze before we get our girl off.

Not sure he got the memo.

"I slept fine last night," she says finally, which I'm pretty sure wasn't what I asked, but now I can't remember. "Thank you for your concern."

Fuck fuck *fuck*.

I get it now.

She knuckle shuffled her nubbin. And now I'm thinking of her digits on her skittle. The over-named deity in my pants needs to hit the penalty box again before he snots my jockey shorts.

"You busy tonight? We could try it again." Fuck, what do I have to lose? Can't fail much more than I already have.

And it's not because I *like* her.

No, I'm offering because I'm practicing being a gentleman. And learning new tricks. Not often I get to practice my moves on a chick who gets me hot enough to be a danger to ice fishing.

"Do you honestly have this much trouble finding women to warm your bed, or are you simply lazy and taking the easiest available option?"

"There's nothing easy about you, princess." Fuck fuck *fuck* again. "And I respect that about you. I do. You got balls. Not that they take away from your tits. I mean you got girl balls. The tough kind. I like girl balls."

She's staring at me, which, *yeah*. Of course she is,

because I'm babbling like a fucking fourteen-year-old girl swooning over fucking *Prince Manning*.

But this is Fireball, and you never know what she might be thinking. So I cut a glance at her to see if it's an *I'm considering it* stare or if it's an *I'm letting a loony bin drive me around on a golf cart* stare, and—"*Fuck!*"

There's a fucking spider.

It's a foot wide if it's an inch, dangling in the cart between us.

I swerve, and the fucker swings toward me, its giant legs reaching out to grab my face. I scream and swerve again, and now it's fucking going to eat Joey's head.

"*Fuck!*" I yell again.

Joey's yelling something too, but I can't hear her for the rushing in my ears. That fucking spider is laughing. It's laughing like a cartoon villain and shooting poison out its webhole, covering us with horrific spider venom, swinging and hollering some *Yippie-ki-yay, motherfucker!* while I try to clobber it with a club that I don't have a good grip on because *there's a fucking spider trying to steal my golf club*.

"*Kill it! Kill it!*" I holler at Joey.

Sweat drips down into my eyeballs and I can't fucking see and there's a spider and—

And we're suddenly lurching to a stop, and Joey's diving out the side, and there's a splash, and the spider's gone.

It's fucking *gone*.

I launch myself out of the cart and stumble into water and mud up to my knees. "Get it off! *Get it off!*"

That fucking spider's on me. I can feel it. It's there.

So I do the only thing a man in my position can do.

I dive into the lake—head, shoulders, knees, and dick all going under the water—with a manly shriek of terror.

Because *it's a fucking spider*.

Those fuckers are assholes. And they can kill. And there's nothing normal about an animal that spins fucking yarn *out its ass* and catches other animals in its ass-yarn so it can fucking suck their blood out.

That's *wrong*.

And—oh, *fuck*.

Joey.

I sputter back to the surface of the lake and spin in a circle. "Joey? *Joey?*"

She's hip-deep in water on the other side of the crashed cart. People are yelling and running for us. Her white T-shirt is smeared with mud, breasts dripping wet, nipples straining the fabric and showing off their natural, dark rosy glow. Her skirt's hitched up to the top of her legs, and *fuck me*, those legs, the angle of her elbows as she stands with her fingers on her hips, aviators bent and finally showing those dark, exotic eyes.

"Is it dead?" she asks.

All business.

All *you're a dumbass* business.

Okay, maybe that wasn't her calling me a dumbass. Maybe that's me.

Because I am definitely a fucking dumbass.

Something lands on my neck. I slap it. Something else brushes my bare calf, and I twitch.

She pinches her lips together for a second before

opening them again with a *pop* that makes my dick twitch too. "Excuse me. I need to find a phone."

And that's the last I see of Joey Diamonte.

The badass pilot golf queen who very well might be the woman of my fucking dreams.

14

Joey

My phone is dripping wet.

Peach was texting that Meemaw's surgery was taking longer than expected, my flight engineer was texting about a potential problem with Luna, and I haven't heard from Gracie in over an hour.

She went hiking *by herself* in an unfamiliar mountain range and she hasn't texted in over an hour.

The logical, rational part of me knows that Gracie's probably fine, there's not a doggamn thing I can do to fix Meemaw's hip, and my flight engineer is more than competent, as is our mechanic. Luna's delayed, not done for.

And I'm pissed.

I'm pissed that Zeus Berger keeps taking me by surprise. I'm pissed that his offer was intriguing. *Again*.

I'm pissed that I want to turn around, march back to the lake, and make sure he's okay.

He's ten feet tall, six feet wide, and weighs as much as a freighter. He doesn't need me saving him from a spider.

Still…the only good spider is a dead spider. And don't give me that shit about spiders eating bugs. The only thing worse than a spider is a spider dressed up like a clown. Or a clown dressed up like a spider.

I shudder.

Can't beat that fucker to death with my shoe. But you're damn right I'd try.

I'm squishing up to the clubhouse when two people rush out the back door.

I bite back a curse. Jett on his own is a mild annoyance, because I'm warming up to him. Do I *want* another partner at Weightless?

Not really.

But Peach and I can't get a business loan for the type of money we need to expand and make us competitive for NASA contracts, government research grants, and to fulfill demand for more tourist flights.

So we need a private investor.

Who can tolerate me.

And Jett's best friends with Zeus Berger. Which means he probably has a high tolerance level for nearly any kind of bullshit.

And with him?

His girlfriend. Aka Ambrosia Berger, sister to the twin brutes.

"What happened to Zeus?" Ambrosia asks.

Too many shots to the head with a hockey puck?

Second-hand helium exposure? He used up his ration of intelligent brain cells for the day and had to dip into his ration of Cro-Magnon brain cells instead? "Baby bunny dashed in front of the cart," I lie.

No, I don't know why I'm lying for him.

And no, I don't plan on thinking about it anymore.

They both stare at me for half a second like I've proposed letting a bag of okra fly an airplane. "A bunny," Ambrosia repeats.

I don't blink.

Good life skill to have. And I practice all the fucking time.

Ambrosia's lips twitch as though she's trying not to laugh. Chase isn't as successful at hiding his amusement. She thumps him on a back a few times as he breaks into a coughing fit.

"You mean a daddy longlegs?" she asks, which sends Chase into more choking spasms. "Because that was a classic Zeus-seeing-a-spider reaction."

"Definitely a baby bunny," I say.

I'm a complete moron. I'm trying to save face for *Zeus Berger* by lying to the man who might possibly be the only billionaire in the world I could tolerate doing business with.

"A baby bunny," Chase repeats, still snickering. "Must've been some bunny."

I didn't get a good look at the thing, because first of all, it dropped from the ceiling right on the heels of Zeus's proposal of him letting his beefy tongue loose on my pussy again, which *she* was fully in favor of from the minute the first syllable passed his lips. Second, I almost got whiplash when he suddenly jerked the cart around—I'm going to be *so* pissed if there's any reason I can't get in my cockpit tomorrow—and third, because when I see a spider, I don't fucking stop and wonder if it's *some impressive spider*, like Jett's implying.

I either hit it with a shoe or get my ass as far the hell away from the fucker as I can.

Apparently not with the same finesse as Zeus, however.

No one on the whole entire *planet* can do anything with Zeus Berger's style of finesse. Except perhaps his twin brother, who's now down by the scene of the spider crime as well, patting Zeus's shoulder.

The gesture doesn't appear to be appeasing the big oaf, who jerks away, grabs the half-sunk golf cart by the back poles holding the roof on, and lifts the thing out of the lake.

He lifts. The golf cart. Out of the lake.

By himself.

My jaw slips.

"You should've seen him take on the world's largest ball of twine," Ambrosia says. "He was sixteen then. Before puberty. The twine won. Still does, actually. He and Ares don't know we know they go back and try once a year or so."

I eyeball the woman again. She's normal sized, with dark blond hair, light eyes, and if she had three lumps in her nose, I imagine it would be a miniature version of the schnozz her brothers sport. Their curvy lips are oddly similar—though hers are also of a more normal size—and I can't help but wonder the kind of defense mechanisms she must've learned to survive growing up with her brothers.

"He didn't hit puberty until sixteen," I repeat.

She grins. Mischief takes corporeal form and dances naked across the country club lawn, and yep.

That's how she survived.

By being smarter, quicker, and funnier. And while yesterday I would've said it probably didn't take much, spider incident excluded, my suspicions are growing that Zeus Berger is hiding some brain under that brawn.

Also?

When Zeus Berger went through puberty and why he's afraid of spiders isn't my concern. *Zeus Berger* isn't my concern.

But business isn't at the top of my brain like it should be, and I'm thinking of *scoring* some anti-gravity time between my legs.

"You need a towel or something?" Jett asks. "Bathrobe?"

A breeze kicks up, and I belatedly remember that I'm soaking wet and slathered with mud. Yet my lady brain is deciding that manly shows of strength are what get her jet engines fired up, and she's taking more headspace than anything.

I tell her to shut up.

She's usually good about listening. Not today though.

I shake my head at Jett. "No."

"Beer?"

Ambrosia cuts a glance at him.

"No," I echo.

"We haven't met," Ambrosia says to me. "I'm Ambrosia Berger."

"Joey Diamonte. Call me Fireball."

"You're with...?"

"Weightless. We're a private aviation company specializing in simulating a zero-gravity experience for the casual space enthusiast."

"Like you're floating in space?" she asks.

I nod.

She gives Jett a playful shove. "Why haven't we tried *that* yet?"

"I don't like you that much," he replies with a broad grin.

"Know why they call it the zero-G club?" I say, because there's absolutely *no* doubt what they're talking about. I'm not the business brains in our operation, but I can still sniff out a high-paying customer willing to pay extra for some perks.

These two want my weightless cabin to themselves.

Ambrosia tilts an interested brow toward me. "Why do they call it the zero-G club?"

"Because there's *zero* chance he's getting to your *G* in the thirty-second bursts you're weightless."

Part of me wants to kick them both for the sexual tension nuke that just sparked off the heated look they're sharing. Because you know what happened the last time I got turned on?

Yes. Yes, you do know what happened. Or more precisely, what didn't. *Both* times. So you know *exactly* how irritating it is to be waylaid by two people who might've just gotten each other off with a *look*.

"She's right, you know," Ambrosia says. "You couldn't do it."

Chase's grin is growing by the minute. These two are clearly warped. And I'm so fucking jealous my pussy hurts.

"I could do it *twice*," he replies.

"I can almost guarantee I'll make at least one of you puke," I say. That's right. I'm the wet blanket. The wet part literally, the blanket part more metaphorically. And odds are good they won't puke, despite my plane's name and my love of its reputation. Too much puking is bad for repeat business. "Also at least one staff member is in the cabin at all times, even on private flights."

"What's it cost to get trained to be that staff member?" Chase asks.

"Couple hundred million dollars."

He's grinning even bigger now as he takes stock of me.

I don't twitch a single muscle. I'm not bluffing, so he can't call me on it. He wants my jet to himself, he's going to fucking pay for the privilege.

His grin gets wider.

"She's almost as devious as you are," he says to Ambrosia.

"You wish."

A giant shadow darkens our table. I look up, and there's Zeus, leaning over us. Me, specifically, his blue eyes flaming hot, his chiseled jaw ticking, his biceps bunched as though he's barely keeping himself from grabbing a golf club and snapping it like a toothpick, and I have the craziest desire to ask him if he's named his biceps like he named his cock and his coconuts.

"I bet you a date I don't puke in your fucking airplane," he growls at me.

Any sane person being treated to Zeus Berger's Brute Stare would flinch at least a little. Even half the military guys I used to work with. But I don't want to flinch, I don't want to blink, and I certainly don't want to let *anyone* think dinner and a movie is the equivalent of a two-hour trip on my plane.

Because it's not.

But his bet is still tempting. I want to know how far he's willing to go to prove himself. If it's about his ego, or if it's about my satisfaction.

Although the bigger part of me doesn't care, because that slick heat gathering between my thighs is begging me to accept.

She knows what she wants.

Since the minute I set foot on the Georgia Tech campus to pursue an aerospace engineering degree, I've been one of the guys. I talk shit, I participate in big dick contests—don't ask, you don't want to know—and I don't apologize for anything.

Flight training in the military made me even more hard-assed, and there's no room for *feelings* in ninety-five percent of my life.

But there's *something* here between us.

There's a yearning, deep in my core, and it's howling out an answering call to his proposition, coming from parts of me that have never known a real man. My pussy's offering herself as tribute. My mouth is dry, my nipples are tightening impossibly harder, and there's not a meteor shower in the entire galaxy that could match the stars streaking through my center.

"You'll have to call the office and see when we have availability for the next flight," I say coolly.

Like I'm not four seconds away from grabbing him by his muddy collar and dragging him into the locker room to see if he can finish the job he started last night.

Any of them.

There's only one way to know if his rocket misfiring last night was a fluke or standard operating procedure.

And I probably have heatstroke and whiplash if I'm seriously considering giving him the chance without making him earn it.

But he has to earn it. Yeah, I've got six open spots on the run tomorrow out of the Copper Valley airport. Got the report from my office manager thirty minutes ago. However, if he's not willing to make the call to find out, he's not getting in my pants.

"You get your mitts away from my sister before I twist your ears all cattywampus and tell your mama on you." Gracie pushes her way between Zeus and me like she's bigger than five-four and a buck ten. She gets right in his breastbone, poking his stomach and letting her temper fly. "Just because you got the size of an overgrown boar doesn't mean you get to use the manners of a pig. Were you raised in a barn, you big ol' doofleschnitzel?"

And there's Dad's half-German heritage coming through along with our backwoods raising. I'm torn between wanting to hug her and wanting to demand to know where she's been that she couldn't text me back for the last hour.

"Gracie. Down girl. I've got this."

"Shut up and let me have my moment," she replies.

Yes, this *is* the same woman who accidentally stuck her finger in a beer bottle while trying to tell a pop star how much she loved him yesterday. Don't mess with her family.

And honestly, it's fun to watch the bafflement flash over Zeus's solid brow line and rigid jaw. She's a bunny rabbit nipping at a horny bullmastiff's ankles. And she shouldn't be underestimated when she's spun up like this. Ask me later about the chicken dumpling incident the one and only time I ever entered anything in the county fair.

"Gracie," I repeat, "let him go. You know I like them healthy before I make them toss their cookies."

"Is he paying you for the privilege, or is he making that old rookie mistake of offering to do unspeakable things to your private parts in exchange for a joyride?"

"Rookie mistake?" Zeus growls. "How many fuckers—"

Behind him, Ares snickers. "Pay the girl, dum-dum head."

Zeus is going a shade of purple in his cheeks.

He slants those crystal flame eyes at me. "Of fucking course I'm paying for the fucking *privilege*. In case it wasn't fucking clear."

I belatedly realize that weird noise is Ambrosia clucking her tongue. "Three fucks? Zeusy-boy, your temper's showing."

He doesn't break eye contact with me, and truth be told, that hard, determined glare is sending interest spiraling harder and hotter through my pussy.

He's as big as *two* linebackers. His size alone would

enable him to push and bully his way through life, but that glint lighting in his expression isn't *I get what I want because I'm the biggest badass.*

It's *I get what I want because will is stronger than power alone.*

Got a hell of a lot of respect for *will*.

I jerk a thumb at Jett and take Gracie by the arm without blinking in this stare-down I have going with Zeus. "Your buddy has all the numbers. Excuse us. I have an important appointment." With a shower. And probably a mechanical special friend.

You want me, his gaze says.

Yeah, but you have to earn me, and dumping me in a lake ain't gonna cut it, buddy, I reply.

Because he might be more than he seems, but I'm still trying to not do something stupid.

15

Zeus

ARES HAS BEEN mother-henning me to death since we left the golf course. *Eat a cookie. I go spray for bugs. Grunt. Scratch. Snort. Go jack off in the bath.*

No fucking way. My dick's in the penalty box again.

And I'm gonna go find the biggest fucking spider on the planet and stare that mofo down until even those creepy eight-legged butt-yarn mutants know who's the king of this fucking jungle.

Dammit, now I'm sweating again.

I bang out of the bathroom naked, because hotel towels are for pansy-assed *normal* size dudes, and it ain't like Ares has never seen my junk before.

"God, Zeus, can't you *pretend* to have some modesty?" Ambrosia digs her fingers into her eyeballs like she's trying to claw them out. She's in the corner in a chair while Ares sprawls over my bed, watching some cooking show on Food Network.

"Nobody invited you," I tell her.

"I'm on spider patrol."

Ares snickers and chomps on one of those little chocolate mint things. Dude's addicted. Has the best breath in the NHL.

"Quit being a dick," I tell my sister while I root around in my bag for clean clothes.

"You like Joey Diamonte."

"Didn't I just tell you to quit being a dick?"

The thing about Ambrosia—Bro, *See-uh*, whatever the fuck she wants to be called these days—is that she ain't scared of shit. Not spiders. Not jail. Not tattoo needles. Not the Easter bunny—don't think I won't fucking cut you if you repeat that—and not me or Ares.

Which means it's damn hard to get her to shut up when she's got something on her mind. "You need lessons in courting a woman," she informs me.

"I know how to fucking court a woman."

"Not this woman. She's got bigger balls than you do. *And* she totally tried to cover for you. She told us you were dodging a baby bunny."

I turn and give my baby sister a full frontal, because it's really all I've got.

Also, what the fuck does it mean that Joey tried to save face for me? That she likes me? That she really did see a baby bunny?

That I'm a pansy-ass moron for wondering if she likes me?

Whatever. Point is, chicks don't cover for me. Most of 'em never find out I'm afraid of fucking *spiders*.

They never care enough.

"Chase's dick is bigger," Ambrosia says.

"The fuck it is."

"Fine. But it's still better."

Ares turns the TV volume up until all we can hear is Martha Stewart trying to out-Dogg the Snoop.

My brother's always got my back. I dig out the third bag of chocolate mints I've got hidden under my underwear and toss it to him. He catches it single-handed, grunts, and nods.

"Take them out of the wrappers this time," I say over the TV.

He flips me off.

When your fingers are the size of bratwurst, it's fucking impossible to wrangle the little shit sometimes.

Or so we like to let people think. Unreal what kind of stupid crap they'll do for you when they think you can't do it yourself.

Case in point? Ambrosia flops onto the edge of the bed —only part there's any room—and tackles the chocolate wrappers for Ares.

"You going on her plane?" she asks me.

I grunt.

Because there's no fucking room. All booked up until almost Halloween, the reservations agent told me. Well past the start of hockey season.

I reserved the whole fucking jet for an off day in early November.

By then, I'll be back in Nashville, through training

camp, traveling for away games, hitting practice like a beast, doing a few puck bunnies every week, and Joey Fireball Diamonte will be a distant memory.

A blip in the Zeus Berger memory bank.

"I'm just fucking with her," I tell my sister.

Ares pounds a finger on the remote, sending the TV into blackness. He growls at me. "Lie."

"Even you aren't too big for biology," Ambrosia says with that smirky grin she's had ever since she started sleeping with my best friend a few months ago. "Face it, you big lug. We're *all* wired to want a mate. And you want her."

"So? She's hot."

Both my siblings roll their eyes.

Probably because they remember that time I thought the neighbor's dog was hot, but until you're a ten-year-old kid in a man's body, shut the fuck up and don't judge.

"You like her," Ares says.

"I like you too. Doesn't mean I have to sleep with you."

"Fine," Ambrosia says. "You think she's nothing more than pretty boobs and a big brain. Guess you don't really want one of those seats Chase got for her flight tomorrow."

Mother*fucker*.

When I'm done playing hockey, I'm gonna be a damn billionaire too. Chase gets all the fun.

Ambrosia's smirking again. I missed her smirking ass too much the last few years to get mad about it though. If she has to be annoying, at least she's happy. "When's your flight booked?" she asks.

"November," I grunt.

Ares gives me a high-five brow wiggle. Ambrosia pumps a fist in the air with a squeal of joy. "I *knew* it!"

"Shave," Ares tells me. "Dress nice. Smell good. Hold doors."

"Somebody been trying to teach you manners while I wasn't looking?" I demand.

His cheeks go pink. He grunts, tosses three wrapped candies in his mouth, and flips the TV back on.

Huh.

"Don't even try to change the subject." Ambrosia waggles a finger at me. "He's right. Get dressed. Something nice. And we're taking you for a haircut, and you damn well better have a fresh stick of deodorant somewhere, because you're going to need all the help you can get."

"I don't want a fucking *girlfriend*."

She just smiles.

Nothing good ever comes when my sister smiles.

But if she's helping me work my way to proving to Joey that I can do her like she's never been done before, then fine.

Ambrosia can stay and help.

16

Joey

I DISTRACT Gracie from her inquisition about Zeus Berger on the ride back to the hotel with stories about Bailey the caddy, and I'm in the shower when Peach calls Gracie's line to let us know Meemaw made it out of surgery with flying colors despite the delay.

She also wants an update on my conversations with Chase Jett, which Gracie apparently texted her about in the midst of smack-talking about how many steps she got on her fitness tracker while hiking today.

That's the good news.

The bad news is, no relief for that unfortunate throbbing in my clit still taking up half my mental space. I'm wrapped in a robe with my hair drying in a towel while I answer more of Peach's questions. Gracie's walking in place, since she knows I'm talking to Peach, who's probably also walking in place on her end of the phone.

"Hot damn, Fireball," Peach says as I finish giving her the run-down of my golf game. In which I do *not* mention Prince Manning, because Gracie's listening, and I don't want her to know he's flying with me tomorrow too. On his dime. "You do business shit even better than I do."

"I insulted three potential customers and all but told an investor to fuck off."

"You're weeding out the wusses. Good job."

"Tell her to quit walking," Gracie hisses.

"Aw, is your baby sister getting all het up over losin' to a girl?" Peach says. "Bless her heart."

Peach loves Gracie more than I do, if that's possible. When Gracie launched Facookies—the online storefront for her bakery back home where people can order sugar cookies with anyone's face printed on them—Peach all but begged to play Gracie in a series of social media ads. Because there's nothing like a sweet Southern woman saying, "I'm gonna eat all y'all's faces off," to inspire butt-loads of cookie sales.

It was also Peach's idea for Gracie to branch out into Dickookies and Pussookies too.

Yes, it *is* exactly what you're thinking.

I pretend I don't know my baby sister is making a shit ton of money off putting people's genitals on cookies. She pretends her profits are up because of high demand for Facookies alone.

And we all go to bed happy, most nights with me considering myself the sanest of the lot of us.

Though with Zeus still floating in my brain, I'm not sure I qualify as *sane* today. Horny? Yes. Conflicted? Undoubtedly. In need of a vacation? Most likely.

I fucking hate it when I need a vacation.

I don't vacation well.

"Anything else we need to cover?" I ask Peach, because I'm hungry, I'm tired, and I need to make sure my crew's ready for tomorrow before I hit the sack.

"Just that I got a little update that Zeus Berger himself reserved a private flight in early November. You plannin' on mentioning that he drove you into a lake today? You know that's the kind of thing normal people talk about with their girlfriends."

I blink at the notes on my tablet in front of me.

Because *November*?

That's definitely not related to his bet.

Is it?

November makes it seem like…like he'll be thinking about me for the next few months.

Or like he made the reservation just for show, and he'll cancel it tomorrow. Or he won't cancel, and he just won't show up.

There's no way Zeus Berger plans his booty calls three months out.

And why is *booty call* the first thing that popped in my head? Maybe the last twenty-four hours have really been about him getting into my jet.

Shit.

If he just wanted to get in my jet, he wouldn't be betting me a date. I can't hide behind that one.

"Is she talking about Zeus?" Gracie demands. "Put her on speaker."

"Yeah, put me on speaker," Peach echoes.

"There's nothing to talk about," I tell them both.

Gracie snatches my phone and pounds the button to put it on speaker. "I had to separate them," she tells Peach.

No point in fighting it. They love to gossip. Instead, I cross the room to look for a pair of sweatpants and a T-shirt in the drawer I claimed.

"Like they were fighting, or like they were tongue-wrestling?" Peach asks.

Dog. Attila the Tongue.

Yeah, he was totally doing it for me before those fucking alarms went off last night.

Interest flares to life once more in my pussy—as if it's actually died down at all—and I suppress a shiver.

"Like he's trying to talk his way into her pants," Gracie says.

"Joey Diamonte, you are a *stud*," Peach crows.

"Are you serious?" Gracie fires back. "She's *so* much better than some overgrown puckhead."

"Lighten up, Gracie-girl. She ain't fixin' to *marry* him. She's lookin' for a ride on the Brute train."

"She is *not* going to sleep with him any more than *I'm* going to sleep with a prince." She gives me the little-sister stink eye.

"You ain't thinking she's some kind of virgin, are you, Gracie-pie?"

I am most definitely some kind of virgin. Not that it matters. Sex doesn't inspire me.

Not that there's anything wrong with sex. It's just not my primary motivational factor, and when it threatens to become such, I take care of it.

Maybe my problem is that I can't jack off with my sister in the room.

"I'm thinking she has better taste than to sleep with Zeus Berger," Gracie replies.

"What's wrong with him?" I ask.

Like an idiot. Because now Gracie's staring at me as though an alien has possessed my body, and I've known Peach since my second week of flight training, and I know she'll hear the interest. She has the ears of a bat and the nosiness of her Meemaw.

"You *like* him?" Gracie squeaks.

I don't know that I *like* him—he still fucking walked away last night—but I feel like I should at least defend him. "He was here to play in a tournament to raise money for kids starting life at a disadvantage. Even I can respect that."

And—spider and his alternate methods of playing golf aside—he's oddly endearing in his own way.

Plus, I can't tell you the last time a man asked me on a *date*. Even if he had to bet his way to getting there.

Peach is right—I'm not going to marry the man—but he's definitely more than meets the eye.

Which shouldn't matter, because I'm not going on a date with him. Even if he is mildly intriguing.

You don't get where Peach and I are—running a successful flight adventure company at our ages—by having a life.

But we're almost there. Weightless is profitable. We pay our staff well, benefits included. Another year or four of hard work, maybe some investment money to expand, and we'll be able to relax knowing we're all set for a very comfortable future.

That our families are set for a comfortable future too.

My dad was my fucking hero. After my mother walked out, he single-handedly raised me and Gracie on a handyman salary in a place where everyone already knew how to fix their own shit, which meant he was often out of work. But he still made sure we had what we needed.

Doesn't mean I ever want Gracie's kids to lie awake at night worrying about where they'll go if she can't make a mortgage payment.

"You like Zeus Berger," Gracie says. Not asking this time. Accusing.

"Always had a thing for guys in pink wigs and minidresses."

"Did we all just take a trip to an alternate dimension, or did she just say hockey's biggest badass was wearing a dress?" Peach asks Gracie, who's now *running* in place, even after hiking all day. "No, wait, don't answer that. She's playing those mind tricks to distract me again. Joey, I will never forgive you if you don't tap that while you got the chance."

Gracie shudders as she lifts her knees higher. "I'll never forgive you if you do."

"Moot point," I tell them both. "I'm never seeing the man again"

"He asked her on a date, Peach," Gracie says. "When's the last time a man asked her on a date?"

"We counting that time Bullwinkle Jones bet her she couldn't shoot that can of Bud Light during the Okra Festival a couple years back?"

"Nope."

"Huh. Don't have a clue then. Meemaw's gonna be so

excited to hear Joey's got herself a boyfriend, even if he does dress up better than she does."

Gracie sucks in a smile.

Peach cackles like she knows it.

"Hanging up now," I tell Peach. "It's dinner time."

"You take those kids and those moneybags on the ride of their lives tomorrow, honey-pie. Then bring the money home to mama."

I hang up. Gracie looks on the edge of keeling over, but she's still jogging in place. "She's cheating," she says. "I know she's cheating. She was in a *hospital* all day. And she's *so* not right. How is it possible to hate and love someone so much all at the same time?"

Probably the same way it's possible to be completely disappointed and yet still so completely interested in an egotistical ape on skates. "It's nature's way of making sure we're too stupid to truly take over the universe."

Gracie laughs and collapses on the nearest bed. *"Thirty thousand steps,"* she says to me. "Thirty thousand. And she's *still* beating me."

"She's just seeing how far you can go."

"Freaking *forever*," Gracie declares. "Quitters never win. And I'm going to freaking win if it kills me."

Yeah, that's my sister.

"Thai, Indian, or sushi?" I ask, just to see her nose crinkle.

"Hamburgers. With extra pickle."

She's so very predictable. With excellent taste.

And I love her for it.

17

Joey

EARLY THE NEXT MORNING, after no more hockey player, billionaire, or prince sightings over dinner and a trip to buy me a new phone, I drop Gracie at the airport so she can get back to her regularly scheduled life.

She has cookies to bake, and monstrosities to frost and ship. *Dickookies*.

I have a plane to fly.

I head to the other side of the airport complex to hit the secondary flight line studded with hangars for private jets, freight operations, and other non-commercial air travel. My crew brought in Luna, our 727, late yesterday after she had one of her sensors replaced. I park and make my way out to her with my first officer and flight engineer right behind me.

"Morning, ma'am," Boomer calls to me.

I nod to Boomer and return Monkey Butt's salute. Yes,

I could tell you Monkey Butt's real name, but he's been Monkey Butt for thirty years, and even though he's almost old enough to be my father, I will never be able to call him anything else.

I do wish he'd quit saluting me, but I know a losing battle when I see one.

Usually. Which is why I'm aggravated with myself for letting Zeus Berger still be taking up some of my headspace.

He's gone. He was good for a little fun, a little disappointment, and now I need to move on.

And get my brain back in my airplane.

Which is way more dependable than some half-cocked offer of a date from a guy whose ego was bruised.

Boomer, Monkey Butt, and I climb aboard Luna for our normal pre-flight checks. Today's run is relatively early. For crew rest reasons, we won't be able to head home until tomorrow. Late this morning and all afternoon are open for answering questions from anyone on the flight today, with my crew on standby if anyone on the flight with a couple hundred million lying around who can stand the idea of letting me outrank him in this company wants to talk to them. Not standard operating procedure, but then, this isn't a standard flight.

It's an incentive flight for the kids, a promo op for Weightless and the celebrities, and a chance to show off to everyone else.

But first, I get to do my favorite thing in the entire world.

I get to fly.

"Going for that perfect parabola today?" Boomer asks with a grin.

"We're certainly not going for half-assed," I reply. It's our pre-flight routine, Boomer and Monkey Butt playing the funnymen to my straight-laced hard-ass.

For the first time in a long time, I wish I could be the funny man.

Funny isn't something I've had time for in... Never mind.

It doesn't matter.

We're finishing up the pre-flight checklist when the head of my flight crew steps onto the plane behind the flight deck.

"Got some heavy cargo today." Nyla's dark eyes are wide and she's breathing a little fast. I can't tell if it's embarrassment, interest, or something else entirely. Her navy-blue flight suit is clean and pressed, her hands steady as she passes me the manifest, so I give her a lingering look—the *everything okay?* question that every one of my crew knows is code for *No questions if you need to not be on this flight today.*

Safety first.

Always.

She gives a smart nod. "Surprised, but I got it under control, boss." She points halfway down the manifest. "Just wasn't prepared for *that*."

I follow her finger, and *are you fucking kidding me?*

I must've made a noise, because now Nyla, Boomer, and Monkey Butt are all treating me to my own *Everything okay?* look.

"Medical forms?" I ask Nyla.

"Called and double-checked them myself."

An unwelcome and poorly-timed tingle of interest flares to life between my thighs. "Make sure they're on opposite sides of the plane."

"Already done. And I confiscated four helium balloons from Mr. Richardson."

"Richardson?" I scan the list and find a John Colbert Richardson.

"The Panther," Monkey Butt says reverently.

Boomer perks up. "*That* Panther? We're taking The Panther weightless?"

I smile, because Panther grew on me yesterday. "Put the balloons on board. If he makes it through the first seven parabolas, give them to the kids and let them taunt him."

"Speaking of the kids, I had to separate one from the Berger twins. Ma'am, this is one interesting bunch of passengers."

I scan the list again.

It certainly is.

And for the first time in a long time, I'm looking forward to the post-flight briefing almost more than I'm looking forward to the flight itself.

18

Zeus

THIS PLANE IS FUCKING HOT, and not just because Joey's a sexy beast in that dark blue flight suit. I'm strapped in across the aisle from Ares, with that little punk kid from yesterday chewing my ear off about all the mistakes I made in the play-offs last season—like I don't know them myself—and I can't stop thinking that Joey's up there in the cockpit—heh, *cock*—making us fly.

Before we took off, she and two dudes in matching flight suits came out to welcome us aboard and tell us some technical shit about what to expect from our joyride in the sky today. She was military stiff and professional as a freaking professional professionaler. Like she gets paid to look like the badass mofo in charge.

Like she didn't remember at all that I bet her a date I won't get sick in her plane today.

I don't go for badass chicks who can ignore me. I like 'em giggly and starry-eyed and eager to get off on a little Zeusitude.

But I cannot get Fireball out of my head.

I've been fighting a woody the size of a redwood in this one-piece matching suit they made us all put on—*in case of unexpected motion sickness, so you don't get your clothes dirty*, Joey's head minion had said cheerfully when we checked in. Should be easy to keep the stick in my pants hanging loose with Bailey detailing exactly how it was my fault we lost that last game to Chicago, but nope, that wood's stubborn and proud and once again asking to tap into the game.

It doesn't understand patience.

Fuck, *I* don't understand patience. This isn't normal.

But I'm going to prove to her that Zeus Berger doesn't fuck up without making it right.

Except all I seem to be able to do is fuck up.

"Earth to Zeus," Bailey says. The kid's just as badass in her flight suit as Joey is, except in a terrifying eleven-year-old way. "I just said you hold your hockey stick like a toothless llama."

Her mother cringes.

"I don't use llamas as sticks," I grunt.

Bailey dissolves in a fit of laughter. Zeus ten, Bailey seven hundred million. But I'm on the fucking board now.

And the kid deserves a laugh or two. Heard her mother talking to another kid's dad about grades and lack of funding in their district for help for her learning disabilities. Pisses me off.

As does the lack of a girls' hockey team in her town.

Across the aisle, Ares smirks at me. Behind him, Chase and Ambrosia are smirking too.

Panther kicks my seat. "Sounds like I'm not the only one who could use a hit of helium."

"Fairly certain our dear friend Zeus needs something more physical to feel better," Prince Manning replies cheerfully.

"Can we *not* talk about that in front of the c-h-i-l-d-r-e-n?" Ambrosia says.

"You know how to make friends?" I say gruffly to Bailey.

She gives me that *duh* look, like she's not afraid of me at all. I fucking love this kid.

"Don't be an ash-hole," I tell her.

"I learned that when I was four," she replies. "Along with *don't take shift from bullies*."

Shift.

Heh.

Her mother's cringing again, but this kid is funny. She's going places.

One of the crew steps to the front of the seating area, which is overlooking the empty white cavern in the center of the plane where we're supposed to go weightless. "It's time. Who's ready to walk on the moon?"

We all unbuckle. I adjust Mount Woodmore in my pants. Ares tugs his suit out of his ass. They weren't exactly prepared for us, but we were both grateful there were two suits this big.

And fuck yeah, I want to know what it's like to walk

on the moon. Don't quite believe it yet—I'm one heavy mofo—but sure, I'll let Fireball give it the ol' college try.

We're split into two groups. Ares and Chase get to go in the front section. I'm told to lay on the floor between Bailey and Manning with Ambrosia behind us. Panther's whistling something near the center. Bailey's mother keeps lifting her head to eyeball me, like she's afraid I'll squish the kid or something.

"Martian gravity," a male voice over the intercom says, and *holy fuck*.

My stomach dips briefly, and then I suddenly feel—like I'm not a gargantuan beast of a man. Not like I'm *little*, but like part of my weight disappeared.

Bailey shrieks next to me. She climbs to her knees, then her feet, and she jumps. She floats back to the ground—not slow, but not fast either—eyes wide, still shrieking with laughter.

I get to my feet too, and when I jump, I land like—huh. Like a normal guy. I'm not going to shake the whole motherfucking plane out of the sky.

We jump around a few more times before the crew orders us to lie down again. This on-our-backs thing seems pointless. The crew's up walking around. But I'll set a good example for Bailey.

For once.

After a minute, the voice comes on the intercom again. "Moon gravity."

The crew signals us to our feet. Bailey's shrieking harder. "Ohmygod, Mom! Look! I'm on the moon!"

I jump again, and it's like half of me wants to float, but I'm still coming back down to the ground.

Like I'm a feather. A gorilla-sized feather. I could be a ballerina. A *Zeus*erina.

A manly-ass Zeuserina.

"Rather unexpected," Manning says with a grin while he lifts his legs from beneath him and twists in the air.

"I'm a fu—freaking balloon," Panther crows.

This is the most fucking awesome feeling short of sex or hockey in the whole fucking universe. My feet are still big, but they're not going to crush anybody's toes or fingers. My arms are floating like they're made of air.

I'm light as a fucking fairy princess. And drunk on moon gravity.

And too soon, it's over.

"Down on your backs," the short, bossy crew member calls. She's been watching me the whole trip like she'll boot my ass out the back without a parachute if I try any monkey business.

Probably shouldn't have checked in and told her I could fly the fucking airplane in my sleep better than anyone in the room, but it's so fucking easy to bait these people sometimes.

Bailey's giggling next to me. "That was so flipping cool," she whispers. "Joey's the *best*."

I'm about to agree when the plane suddenly feels seven million pounds heavier. I'm not a fairy princess anymore. Now I'm a wooly mammoth getting pulled through the floor.

"Almost two G's," the crew lady says with a grin, still standing by the white padded wall and gripping a rope. "Not living until you're pulling at least four."

Fuck, there's a pressure in my gut that's not happy cotton candy. More like sour milk.

I've taken plenty of hits on the ice. Taken some pucks in some unfortunate places. Been sat on by some beefy dudes once or twice. But this—this is new.

Uncomfortable. Not like that bra and coconuts and girdle were uncomfortable the other night. More like *so this is what it feels like to be squished to death by an elephant* uncomfortable.

I try to peer at the next section to see how Ares is doing, but lifting my head makes it swim.

Fuck.

I close my eyes and breathe until the deep voice comes over the intercom again. "Zero gravity. We're weightless."

Fuck, *yeah*, we are. My ass is suddenly floating.

Floating.

"Holy fuck," I sputter.

Bailey smacks me in the arm. "Watch your mouth and don't talk like that in front of my mother." She giggles, and the little turd-monkey flips.

In midair.

Hair floating. Completely impervious to gravity.

"Whheeeeeee!" she crows.

I'm looking for some kind of balance, but *holy fucking shit*. It's like swimming in the ocean without any water. Like—like I'm a fucking astronaut. I float to the top of the plane and bump the ceiling. Not because I'm too tall, but because I don't weigh a single fucking ounce.

Me.

Zeus Berger.

The biggest dude ever to play hockey—except maybe Ares, depending on which of us took a shit last—and I'm floating like I'm no bigger than a fucking oxygen molecule.

Ambrosia's shrieking with laughter and pushing herself from one side of the plane to the other.

Ares grins at me from the front of the plane. He's floating too. Floating with his hands behind his head like he's in a fucking hammock.

Fuck yeah, that grin says. *Life doesn't suck*, that grin says.

We're two lucky motherfuckers, I grin back.

Chase gives my sister a look I pretend I don't see and that makes me glad the crew knew to separate those two.

Horny fuckers.

"On your backs," the crew calls.

Gravity starts to kick in. We get settled back on the ground, and in about thirty seconds, we go from floating to having something sitting on our chests again. This G business isn't a joke. I wonder how Joey's feeling in the cockpit. Does she get to float? How intense is it?

If I was flying this thing, I'd have a nonstop hard-on. Killing gravity?

That's fucking hardcore.

After a minute or two, the pressure on my chest eases, though my stomach's still twitching and my head's floating off-center, and suddenly gravity disappears again.

And I'm floating. Again.

Shit, I could live like this all the time. I'm not an ape up here. Not an ogre. Not too big or too heavy or too *anything*.

I'm just a dude who's fucking defying gravity.

"Hey, your royal assssss—ah, *high*ness, you're getting shown up by a girl," I holler at Manning, who's chatting with my sister about how much Willow, his stepsister and one of Ambrosia's best friends, will be jealous to have missed this while they both float like we're in outer space.

He spins in the air—more of a barrel roll than a somersault—and still manages to show me his ass. "Eat this, Berger," he says cheerfully.

I flex and wiggle—muscle ain't doing shit for helping me move without the gravity to fight against—and I manage to look like a hippo trying to lick its own ass in space before we're ordered back on our backs.

This is weird shit—floating like a speck of dust one minute, and weighing eight hundred pounds with all that extra force pushing down the next. How many times are we going? Twelve? Fifteen? Fuck, I didn't pay attention.

I was too busy sending brain signals out to the plane, telling Joey all the places I'm going to take her and all the different ways I'm going to make her scream my name when I win our bet and we're back on the ground.

But I don't want to eat right now.

Not food. Not pussy either. *Fuck*, it's hot in here. And there's a friggin' elephant sitting on my chest.

But I'm not going to fucking puke.

No fucking way.

I'm taking a badass pilot out to dinner and then for a special brand of Zeus Berger—oh, *fuck*.

Fuck *fuck FUCK*.

It's hot.

Stomach.
Roll.
Head.
Floating.
Barf bag.
I need a fucking barf bag.

19

Joey

AFTER TWO HOURS of owning the sky a few miles above our strip of the Atlantic Ocean, Monkey Butt lands us back at the sunny Copper Valley International Airport in the shadow of the eastern side of the Blue Ridge Mountains. My muscles are all strung taut, and I'm coming down off the adrenaline high that perpetually hums in my veins beside the intense concentration we keep in the cockpit.

None of us break mission talk until we're parked.

"Nearly perfect on that sixth run," Monkey Butt says.

I slap him on the shoulder. "Damn right. Beautiful headwind." I look at Boomer, who's grinning like a kid on Christmas morning despite the weathered lines deepening by the day on his forehead. "Any casualties?" I ask. As our flight engineer, he monitors all comms with the back of the plane.

"Two of the moms, Panther, and one of the Berger twins."

Oh, *no*.

I barely keep from cringing.

If it was Zeus—no. Nope. Doesn't matter. I've already given the man too much thought. Him getting sick—meaning no date, not that I agreed to his terms in the first place—isn't just the final nail in the coffin, it's an extra three tons of dirt dumped on the ground to keep that corpse good and buried.

He probably threw up on purpose so he wouldn't have to follow through.

Except even I can't convince myself it's Zeus's style to continue to embarrass himself for the sake of a woman.

Which means…

Fuck. I don't know what it means.

"Anyone else?" I ask.

Boomer glances at the closed cockpit door and double-checks that our comms are off. "Nope. And Nyla says Chase Jett and his girlfriend have been looking you up on their phones and whispering ever since we leveled off on our way back."

Putting an airplane through the kind of acrobatics it takes to simulate zero-gravity is like taking a brain surgery test while running a marathon at ten miles an hour. Boomer, Monkey Butt, and I have been known to clean out the Weightless snack bar and crash out for two hours after any given flight.

Hope Peach has some time for a phone call.

Expanding Weightless, with an investor I can tolerate —*fuck*, that would be cool.

"Aw, she's smiling." Monkey Butt gives me a friendly punch to the bicep. "Isn't that cute."

"Shut up, you big butthead."

I know, it's too soon to smile. You don't grow up dirt floor poor and make the mistake of counting your chickens before the hogs are let loose to trample the chicken coop.

But it was a damn good flight. Shrieks and giggles from the cabin are still coming through the flight deck door, along with deeper chuckles and fast voices. Satisfied customers.

And Jett isn't stupid. Any man who can make himself a billionaire before he's thirty—especially a man who started with just as much nothing as I did—will do his homework. Probably already has.

I strap out of my harness and join Boomer and Monkey Butt in leaving the flight deck. I barely step out the door before I'm tackled about the middle.

"Ohmygosh, Joey, this was *so flipping fabamazesome*. I'm gonna be an astronaut one day, and I'm going to play baseball in space and be a kickaaaa—labama *rock star*. Can I get a picture? And your autograph again? And one of those cookies with a picture of the plane and one with your picture? I swear I won't eat your face, but I might eat the plane. If I have a spare."

How can you *not* smile at this kid? I pat her back and smile wider at her mother's *what can you do?* shrug. "Pictures in the lobby in fifteen," I tell her. "We'll have a tablet for ordering cookies too."

Damn right I pimp my sister's business.

But not the genital cookies. I see nothing, I hear nothing, I know nothing.

Her mother mouths a *thank you*, and they depart.

"They didn't let me have my balloons," Panther says dryly.

"Maybe skip the haircuts and come back next month," I reply, and yes, I'm smiling again, because it's impossible not to smile at a plane full of satisfied customers who've just had the experience of their lives.

I fucking love my job.

"Ms. Diamonte, you've surpassed my wildest expectations." Prince Manning bows over my hand and kisses my knuckles as though I'm the royalty on this plane.

"Good. Stay the fuck away from my sister."

His grin spreads wider when he straightens. "Hope to do it again someday. Might bring my brothers. Did someone say *cookies?*"

I level my very best *you don't* ever *get to touch my sister's cookies* glare at him.

His eyes twinkle like he's fucking Santa Claus. I know without a doubt he didn't put a finger on my sister. I also know he's getting his rocks off by fucking with me.

Because I'm a fun target, or because he's plotting something, I don't know. And I shouldn't care.

Except he's been hanging with the two massive puckers stepping up behind him as he exits the plane.

Zeus stops before me. He gives me a quick once-over, his hooded eyes lingering on my lips and making me flush from my toes to my fingertips and everywhere between.

Never in my life has a man been able to fire my engines with one look.

It has to be the sheer size of him. The muscles, the height, the thick growth of stubble on his cheeks and chin. That grip he had on the treadmill. He's so inherently *male*, despite all the cracks I've seen in his machismo.

He lifts those blue eyes to meet mine, and he gives me a single nod. "Well played, Ms. Diamonte."

"Enjoy your flight?"

He doesn't answer. I honestly don't expect him to. I'm not making fun—even the passengers who toss their cookies tend to love the experience, because how often do you get to float like you're in space?—and I hope he realizes it's an honest question.

His eyes flicker. It's not annoyance. Or pride—there's not enough bravado.

No, it's something else entirely.

Something…vulnerable?

He blinks, and the vulnerability is swallowed into his intense *I will devour you in one bite and burp out the air in your lungs* hockey-god glower. "I'm done fighting fair. We're taking this to my turf. You. Me. Hockey sticks. Two o'clock. Mink Arena."

"Didn't realize this was a fight."

He bares his teeth. "This is so much more than a fight."

My nipples pucker so fast my lungs go lightheaded. My pulse might've just pushed the throttle full-force to head into a forty-five-degree climb too.

Before I can tell him where he can shove his stick—yes, fine, I *do* want to know what his stick could do to me. Shut up.—he follows the prince off the plane.

Behind him, Ares makes eye contact with me, and a subtle grin tugs at his lips. The two of them are physically identical, but the way they carry themselves is so very different. One's verbally brash, the other lets his size speak for itself. He has his flight suit unzipped, showing off a pink T-shirt stamped with a picture of mountains and the phrase "Nipples Have Lips" scrolled across it.

Boomer and Monkey Butt both shift closer to me, which is as abnormal as a third full moon in a single month. Both because they know I don't need their protection, and they sure as fuck aren't the types to cower behind me.

"Have fun up there, big guy?" Boomer asks.

Ares nods. He smirks again, gives me a smart salute, and follows his brother in ducking off the plane.

Chase Jett holds out a hand. "You have lunch plans?"

Lunch plans, nap plans, and then fashionably late plans.

If I meet Zeus at the hockey rink.

Which I will, because how often do I get a chance to learn to play hockey from a pro? Need to add *handling a stick* to my repertoire.

Fine, fine.

I admire the guy's pucks, okay?

"Flight debrief," I tell Jett.

"Hm."

He doesn't say anything else. I don't offer.

But I'm holding my breath when he and Ambrosia leave the plane. She pokes him in the back, and I hear him mutter, "Timing, Ms. Bossypants."

So there's to be a power struggle if he's going to consider propositioning us.

Excellent.

Peach will be so pleased.

We finish seeing off our passengers. As soon as the bus pulls away to take them back to the small private terminal, all of us—Boomer, Monkey Butt, the six crew members cleaning up the plane, me—sag against the walls.

"One for the record books," Monkey Butt says with a subtle smile.

"What's going on with you and that Berger brute?" Boomer wants to know.

My lips go rogue and sprout a smile that I can't stop, which pisses me off because I've worked damn fucking hard to not be a smiley-ass kind of woman. "I have no idea what you're talking about."

"The one who puked took a beating from that Bailey girl," Nyla tells me. "Kid doesn't take crap from anybody."

"Sounds vaguely familiar," another of my crew murmurs.

"She was nice to him when he tossed his breakfast though."

Those two. They're like long-lost cousins.

I'm actually going to miss them both when we go home tomorrow.

20

Zeus

That flight—*dude*.

Just *dude*. You want eloquence, go talk to fucking Manning.

Not that he could come anywhere close to understanding how it felt for a guy my size to be totally and completely weightless, but he's got bigger words than *dude*.

When we're all off the plane, we don't stick around for pictures. I get Bailey's mom's phone number—shut up, I got your mom's phone number too—and we load up.

No reason to find another new and creative way to fuck up my last chance with Joey—not that I'm convinced she's gonna show—and Chase needs to run something to ground.

Whatever the fuck that means. It isn't screwing my sister, because while I down a cow's weight in pizza and verify the rink is iced over and open at the Arena, she and Ares play thumb wars.

Ambrosia's got freaky strong thumbs. My sister scares the shit out of me sometimes.

I leave them all behind at the hotel, and now I'm skating around the ice, lining up pucks, two sticks in my pants—hockey sticks, not the demigod sitting over my planets who thinks he's getting playtime today too—while I wait for Joey Fireball.

Not much I've done right the last two days. This is my last chance to show her there's something Zeus Berger is fucking *fantastic* at.

Maybe my last chance to bang her brains out until she can't remember her own zip code.

Shut up. I'm managing my expectations here. Fireball's not the type to forget her name.

And shut up again. We're thinking positive here. She's gonna show. And there's gonna be some damn banging.

But if she's not coming, there's nowhere I'd rather be than on the ice.

Until today, this was the only place I ever felt completely normal. Yeah, I'm still bigger than all the other puckers in the NHL—Ares excepted, like always—but not many of them quake in their skates when they see me coming. Aren't many afraid to take a swing at me either. When I'm cutting ice on my blades, I'm not a behemoth who can't squeeze between two tables at McDonald's or fit in a sports car. Not that I need a fucking sports car—nothing to compensate for here, *shut up again*—but it'd be nice to not be so fucking *big* all the time.

On the ice, I'm quick, I'm respected, and I'm fucking grace with a stick. *Both* my sticks.

On Joey's airplane?

I'm an average Joe. Not some Bigfoot ape.

Don't get me wrong. I got a good life. Don't mind being the biggest badass out there. But living large, benching cows, and plowing through the buffet at Golden Corral gets old.

Hard to believe, but there it is.

Sometimes, Zeus Berger wants to be *normal*. Tell anybody, and I'll tell them about what your mom did to me last night.

The door opens onto the ice, and I watch Joey Fireball hold on to the wall while she steps into the rink. The staff here got her set up with skates that fit, but she's clearly not in her element.

Her feet aren't steady. They're wobbling like she's on bobble-feet.

She's got this ballsy determination written all over her face though. This chick's gonna fucking *own* this rink.

Only question is how long it'll take her.

"Didn't think you'd come," I say while she tests her balance without the wall.

"Never turn down an opportunity to practice."

"Practice beating my ass, you mean?"

"No, I mean my hockey game's rusty."

Rusty my ass. Gotta have some skill to start with to get rusty.

Unless she's a mega-shark. A mega robot shark with balls and boobs.

I'm grinning, because I can't help myself. She fucking

came. She's talking shit. And even with those pink glittery ice skates—I'm tipping the manager here for finding *those* for her—she's so badass my nuts hurt.

Her dark hair's still tied back. Not tight, like she's trying to give herself a facelift with her ponytail, but not hanging loose either. She's in black athletic pants and a tank top. Only clue she can feel the coolness of the rink are those two perky nipples straining against the white fabric.

Her foot slips. She corrects it without so much as a flicker of a scowl. If anything, she smiles. Half self-deprecation, half *bring on the fucking challenge*. It's not just the knucklehead in my pants who notices. Got something caught in my chest too.

Takes one hell of a person to *enjoy* not being good at something. For all she annoyed me on the links yesterday, beating the pants off all of us, she didn't brag or rub it in. Just took care of her business, made sure the kids were getting attention and her own brand of praise, and the hell with the rest of us.

"Decided I'll take it easy on you," I tell her while I glide over my home turf.

"Like I took it easy on you in the plane?"

She's fucking *flirting* with me. I'm gonna score the *shit* out of today. "Yeah. Something like that."

She makes her way slowly out to meet me at the blue line.

"Skate much?" I ask.

"Just want you to think you can win a round."

Fuck, she's hot. Funny too. "You're full of shit."

"Am I?"

She is. And those plump lips are twitching up in the corners, like she's enjoying trash-talking me.

Lady's on my playing field now. And I can out-trash a trash-talker with four teeth and half my tongue tied behind my head.

I slide a hockey stick out of my pants and offer it to her. "Ladies first. Unless you need me to show you how it's done."

She eyes the stick with more interest than disgust, which is one more good sign. Like she's contemplating pulling something else out of my pants.

I might have to play hard to get. Wonder what she'd think of that.

"If I'd known you were going to pull that *Ladies first* shit, I would've made you puke more," she says while she takes the stick.

"Only puked to make you feel like you were doing a good job."

"If I'm doing a good job, you sign up for another ride."

Yeah, I'm totally flying in her jet again. First chance I get.

Even if I puke again.

To go weightless? *Fuck*, yeah. "Now you're stalling. Afraid I'm gonna kick your ass?"

She's almost smiling as she rolls her eyes, swings around on the ice, lines up like a four-year-old taking an oversize golf club to a water balloon, and swings the stick at the nearest puck.

And hot *damn*, that little puck shoots across the ice, straight at the goal, where it swooshes the back netting when it lands.

Her lips part, her eyes widen, and a full smile blossoms and almost knocks me on my ass before she goes poker-face again.

"No," she says. "Not really worried."

I treat her to the infamous Zeus Berger *I'm going to fucking eat your face* glower.

She smiles.

A sparkly-eyed, cheek-to-cheek, ear-wiggling smile.

My dick threatens to split my zipper, my brain goes tongue-tied, and there's that squeezing in my chest again, like someone's trying to rub one out of my lungs.

I point to the pile of pucks. "Go on. Do it again."

She presses those rosy lips together, but she's still smiling when she bends her head to take an order for once.

And she scores another fucking goal.

I yank the other stick out of my pants and toss it in the air behind us. "Who the fuck *are* you? Are you sharking me?" I poke her in the arm to make sure she's real and not a hologram.

Yeah, yeah, fine. And because I want to touch her.

Never met a woman who could keep up with me before, let alone one-up me. "You punking me? Who sent you? Did fucking Giovanni send you? You weren't flying that plane, were you?"

She laughs.

There's no one here. No one but us. Me and Joey Fireball. And she's laughing.

It's fucking music.

I point to the pucks. "One more time."

Fuck if her smile doesn't light up so bright I need sunglasses. "Ladies first."

Oh, no, she—yeah. Yeah, she did.

She's not owning the ice.

She's fucking owning *me*.

And she knows it, if that deep chuckle rumbling out of her is any sign.

"Fuck me," I mutter. "Where the hell are you from?"

"Goat's Tit, Alabama."

"No shit?"

"Just outside it, actually. We weren't good enough to be townsfolk."

"You don't talk like you're from Alabama."

"Your brother doesn't talk at all. What's your point?"

I growl. It's instinct. Nobody gets to fucking talk about my brother.

Nobody.

But Joey doesn't blink.

No, she smirks. The lady's pushing my limits on purpose.

Probably because I'm pushing hers.

She's almost smooth as she skates back from the pile of pucks, her eyes sparkling brighter than her pink glitter skates. "Your turn."

I snag my stick, maneuver it to pick a puck out of the pile and skate it around Joey. I could push a puck over the ice in my sleep. Been doing it since I was three, and I'm a fucking master of control.

Yeah, yeah, I'm showing off. Fluffing all my rooster feathers for her. She's got grace—or something—when she's flying. I have my own fucking grace on the ice.

I pull up short and slap my puck dead-center toward the net.

It slides past the left goal post and bounces off the backboard.

"Son of a *bitch*."

Joey squeaks and puts a knuckle in her mouth. Her feet slip, but she corrects and stays upright. Knowing the muscles she's clenching to stay balanced makes the demigod in my pants hard enough to crack ice.

I pull another puck over, swing my stick, fire, and miss again.

I fucking miss again.

Shit. This isn't good. The play-offs—and now this.

Joey chokes on air.

I swing around. "You cursing me? If you're gonna fuck up my whole season—"

"I'm a pilot, not a witch doctor."

She's fucking unreal is what she is. Not smiling anymore, but there's a dry warmth from the quirk of those dark, exotic eyes to the set of her slender jaw.

This woman doesn't smile enough.

Doesn't let her hair down. Cut loose.

Relax.

"Hit another one." Loud is my middle name. I—right. *Fine. November* is my middle name—thanks, *Ambrosia*, for spilling the fucking beans—but it *should* be Loud.

But my point is, I'm talking so soft right now my voice is barely reaching the ice below me. Because I can't be any louder. She's got my lungs in knots and fucking goose bumps—goose *mountains*—breaking out all over my skin.

I want her to score.

I want her to fucking hit the net.

I want her to kick my ever-loving ass on this ice.

And I *don't know why*.

She holds my gaze long enough for me to pick out the stars lurking in her dark eyes. To get a glimpse of the universe working inside her. She's not asking if I want a beating.

She's asking something more.

Something bigger.

Something I don't understand and can't comprehend but that makes that swelling in my chest puff up faster than one of Panther's fucking balloons popping.

With a shrug, she breaks eye contact and taps her stick on the ice. She's not winning any awards for her stick work, but watching her handle the wood makes the pipe in my pants ache so hard it's in danger of permanent dick-brain damage.

She pulls a puck from the remaining six or seven, and she slaps at that puppy.

It doesn't fly fast—doesn't fly at all—but it's straight and it's as fucking determined as she is. She bends toward the puck like she can will it to keep sliding.

To keep going.

To reach that goal line.

I'm holding my breath.

I can feel *her* holding her breath.

And the puck keeps sliding.

Inching.

Almost…There…One…More…Foot…And…

And it stops.

Just inside the goal posts.

She thrusts both hands in the air and almost takes me out. "*Yes!*"

My stick clatters to the ice. "Who are you?" I grip her hips, holding her while she lets me skate her backward toward the door. Because I'm done. She wins.

And I'm still planning to kiss this chick until one of us can't breathe.

Probably me. "What the fuck *can't* you do?"

One corner of her lips twitches up. Stars, moons, and whole fucking galaxies are dancing in her dark eyes. "That's classified."

"You play hockey in Alabama?"

"No."

"You some kind of spy? A girl James Bond?"

"Yeah. That's me. Call me double-O-Aces."

"What else do you play?"

Her smile's growing in direct proportion to the aching need growing in my dick. "Badminton," she says. "Curling. Toe wrestling."

"There's no fucking way you could beat me at toe wrestling."

"I'd agree you probably have an unfair advantage, since your toes are likely the size of a normal person's fingers, but you should never underestimate a determined woman."

"You are so fucking sexy."

"You truly have had too many pucks to the head, haven't you?"

We stop against the boards. She's not fighting.

No, somewhere she lost her stick, and her fingers are resting on my forearms, hot little ribbons against my skin.

"So fucking sexy," I whisper. I brush her cheek with my knuckle. The fog of our breaths hangs suspended between us. Swear on my skates, her nipples are trying to grab me.

Or possibly cut me—hard to tell what this woman's intentions might be.

But it's her palms that get the job done, gripping my ears and pulling my face down to hers and kissing me like I'm the fucking trophy for scoring three goals.

Her lips are full and lush and talented, her tongue hot and quick, her hands—*fuck*, her hands are strong and determined and so fucking soft at the same time, I'm about to lose my shit all over again just from the stroke of her fingers down my face.

Me and kissing? It doesn't happen.

Not like this.

The chicks who hit on me usually want me for the world wonder in my pants and for what I can do under their skirts and for the glory of getting to say they banged Zeus Berger. They don't want to *kiss* me. They want to fuck me. Good trade-off, because usually, I just want to fuck them too.

I don't want to fuck Joey.

I mean, I want to fuck Joey. Jupiter's raring to go, those subplanets hanging out under him are heavy and tight and throbbing enough to make me feel like I took a puck to the nuts. But fucking isn't *all* I want to do with Joey. Not even close.

Not when she's scraping her fingers down my neck, nowhere near my dick or my ass, not fondling my biceps or pecs or abs. She's not looking for a handful of a hockey god.

She's touching my fucking neck and eating my mouth like it's a big juicy steak after months of nothing but bean sprouts. Moaning those little sounds that make my pulse rocket and my dick strain and my brain short-circuit.

Kissing Joey is better than hockey, better than pranking the shit out of anyone, better than being weightless.

Which is more terrifying than a roomful of fucking spiders, that's for damn sure.

I want to shove her against the boards, strip her out of that tank top, and suck on her frosty tits until she forgets her name. I want to eat her from the inside out. I want to taste that spicy pussy again. I want to make her scream my name so loud the whole fucking city knows they're never going to have sex as good as Joey Fireball gets sex at my hands. And mouth. And hands. And fuck, I'll toss in an elbow and some toes if she's into that kind of thing.

I'm gripping her hips so tight I'm probably cutting off circulation to her legs, but her fingers have found their way to my hair, and she's pulling on it and igniting nerve endings in my scalp that are more likely to take a beating than ever see some lovin'.

And I'm once again two seconds from blowing my load early.

Fuck.

Fuck fuck fuck.

I break the kiss with more effort than I've ever had to put into benching anything, and I once benched a fucking cow. Her eyes are black as space, her lips swollen and rosy, her breath coming every bit as fast as mine.

"That all you've got?" she asks.

Fuck.

I growl as I dive back into kissing her, teeth gnashing, tongues going at it like we need a fucking wrestling mat. Her mouth's hot and juicy and if I give half a thought to her sucking my dick, I'm gonna blow so hard I'll shoot her through the boards. Her hands grip my ass, Jupiter pops a hole in my jockey shorts, and my focus narrows to one single thought.

I'm fucked.

I'm going to prove to this woman—somehow—that I'm not just an air-headed, oversized puck-up.

I'm a big, mean, scoring machine. I'm gonna blow her mind. I'm gonna blow her mouth—with a fucking awesome dinner, pervert—and then I'm gonna blow her pussy until she's begging for mercy.

Because I'm fucking Zeus Berger.

And I can.

So long as my dick doesn't pull another pre-game quick shot.

I lift her up against the boards, my skates anchored, cradling her ass with one arm while my other hand snakes between us. I thumb the smooth fabric over her center, she moans and thrusts into my touch, and *fuck*, I need to get in her pants.

Jupiter's wailing out some "I'll make love to you"—I like boy band shit, suck my dick—but he's not tapping into this game.

This one's for Joey.

THE PILOT AND THE PUCK-UP

And if anyone interrupts us this time, I'll fucking tear his limbs off and feed them to my manager's pet hamster.

Joey's skates are cutting into my back where she has her ankles hooked, but fuck if I care. I slip my hand under her waistband, under her soft cotton panties, and go sliding through smooth skin and rough hair until I find that magic button.

She gasps in my mouth, grips my ears again, and melts in my fucking hand.

I stroke her pussy.

She jerks against my fingers, her tongue gliding over mine, skates digging in. Might be taking out a kidney.

I thumb her nubbin and thrust two fingers into her slick, tight heat, and even though that hole in my underwear is choking the life out of my dick's head, I'm still about to come.

Not because I'm petting pussy.

Fuck, I know pussy as well as I know boobs.

But because Joey Fireball's losing control.

For me.

That's right. I'm king of the fucking sex gods. With the sexiest fucking woman on the planet riding my fingers and feasting on my mouth and clamping her legs so tight around me I can barely move my hand to tease her clit and jerk my fingers in and out of her tight little pussy.

Fuck, the superhero in my pants wouldn't last three seconds inside Joey Fireball. She's tight as balls, hot as the fucking sun, and slick as black ice.

She jerks her tongue out of my mouth, bangs her head back against the plexiglass, and moans while she clenches and spasms around my fingers. I put my thumb to her magic pearl, and she gasps and moans louder, hips bucking uncontrollably while she comes all over my hand. Her skates slice my back. Her legs grip me so tight she's bruising my lower ribs.

And she's still coming.

Still squeezing my fingers.

Still riding me like I'm the best fucking bull she's ever had between her legs and she's gonna keep coming until we both die of sexposure.

Yeah. Oversexposure.

It's a fucking miracle I'm not shooting cannonballs out my dick right now.

Or maybe that's the lack of circulation in my head.

It's also a miracle I'm not blowing my load through my fingers right now. Can fingers orgasm? Because my fingers are in fucking heaven. They're shooting joy sparks all up in her pussy, getting off on getting her off.

Joey goes limp in my arms. "Oh my fucking dog," she pants.

Like I'm every bit the sex god I think I am. "Good?" I should be smirking, because I know it was good. I'm *always* good.

But this is Joey Fireball.

And I'm terrified she's had better fingers. Because of course she's a big O expert.

She smoothes her hair back—not that any of it's out of place—and meets my eyes, and *fuck me*.

That's not bravado. Not badass. Not balls.

My hot pilot chick has gone soft. "Why would you do that for me?" she whispers.

Like no one ever has before.

But that's impossible, because…because…because she's Joey fucking Fireball.

Except… "Who wouldn't do that for you? I'll kick his fucking ass."

Those eyes. *Fuck*, can a man drown in space?

"I intimidate men."

"You'd intimidate a T-Rex." I grin, because it's the truth. "That's fucking hot."

She doesn't blink.

Of course she doesn't.

But that intense, no-bullshit, you-just-rocked-my-world gaze has a bonus quality to it that's making my ribs tight.

"Can you do that with your dick?" she asks.

Get.

Back.

In.

Her.

Pants.

Now.

"Fuck, yeah," I tell her.

"Before you blow your load," she amends.

"I only do that when I'm playing a chick."

"You mean a hooker troll?"

"The hottest fucking hooker troll in the world."

She laughs, and I fumble to unbutton my pants. No sense wasting opportunity, and a double-O, on the ice—she's gonna remember my name for-fucking-*ever*.

Which is good, because I'm never forgetting hers.

I've almost worked Jupiter free when a whistle erupts behind me.

"We're playing *that* kind of stick hockey today?" Manning's cheerful voice carries across the ice.

"I'm going to feed that royal ass his nuts," Joey growls.

I'm going to stand back and watch.

Because if I'm not getting back in her pants, watching is all that my nuts are currently good for.

21

Joey

Hockey doesn't come naturally to me. I grew up in a place where three snowflakes would shut down the entire state. The extent of my experience with hockey was chasing a tennis ball down the street with a broken broom.

But I'm so fucking pissed that his royal cheerfulness just cock-blocked me that I'm going to mop the ice with his face.

I think.

Probably.

Just as soon as I come down off this happy cloud Zeus's fingers put me on.

Holy *shit*.

I came so hard, I thought my vagina was going to flip inside out.

He sets me down on the ice, where my rubbery legs

almost give out on me. He catches me under the armpits with a grin that nearly fries my motherboard. "You got this, Fireball."

Know what he has?

He has a bulge in his pants that can probably be seen from the International Space Station.

And it's making my very satisfied pussy pop another lady boner.

Zeus Berger is more than hot air.

It's been a long time since I've cared if a man ever pops my cherry, but if I leave this town without screwing that man's brains out, I'm going to be a bitch to live with.

And I'm already a bitch to live with.

I lean around Zeus and point to Manning, who's accompanied by Ares, Jett, and Ambrosia. "I get the Bergers. You get the leftovers."

"Hardly sporting," he says with that shit-eating grin.

"Fuck sporting."

"Tough chicks on my team," Ares says.

"I'm gonna eat you for breakfast," Ambrosia tells Jett.

He smirks in a way that suggests she already did.

They pile onto the ice, every last one of them steady in their skates.

"Don't you dare fucking miss another goal," I growl at Zeus.

He adjusts himself and grins at me again. He's pushing six-nine, broad as a house, but when he smiles—I shiver.

That smile packs the punch of a hundred men.

Because Zeus Berger doesn't do *anything* small.

He pushes away from me with a grace impossible to ignore. His Nashville T-shirt is stretched to its limits over his thick arms and barrel chest, and his skin's hot despite the cool temperature in the rink.

And his fingers—I shiver again.

He might've just ruined me for dildos.

He retrieves both our sticks while Ares collects the pucks, eyeing each like he's considering taking a bite.

Jett and Ambrosia circle each other, flirting and laughing. Manning checks the goals.

All of them are clearly in their element on the ice.

I'm going to land on my ass before this game's even started.

Zeus turns back and watches me as I once again get my bearings. He's a leopard in the rink, just as likely to pounce and play as he is to pounce and eat. His feet aren't still—I suspect the only time this man is still is when he's asleep, and maybe not even then—and his eyes are locked on me as though he knows I'm thinking about him.

Or possibly as though he knows I'm going to bruise my tailbone and probably get squished by my own teammates and land in the wrong goal before the next fifteen minutes are over.

I'm bad at a few things.

Knitting. Baking. Putting up with bullshit. Driving. Yeah, I've got a lead foot and I can't park for shit. Shut up. I can make your ass puke in an airplane too.

Point is, I know where I'm good and where I'm bad.

And those three goals aside, I'm going to suck eggs on this hockey rink.

Doesn't mean I'm not going to try though.

I'll own sucking before I whine my way through not trying.

Zeus skids to an easy stop next to me. "Four on two isn't very fair," he says.

"He looked at my sister wrong," I say, because hell if I'll admit to knowing I'm going to suck. Also, I need the rage—which I'm struggling to actually locate in this post-orgasmic bliss still making my legs wobbly—to fuel my game.

I punctuate my statement with another slip on the ice. He steadies me, heat shoots from my armpits to my love muffin, and I grip his arm.

I don't want to play hockey.

Not ice hockey. Tonsil hockey, probably. I could go for a score.

He's grinning again like he knows it. "Fireball, we've got a problem."

"Too many clothes and an audience," I grunt in agreement.

He snickers, my pussy tingles, and my nipples point out they haven't gotten any attention at all.

It's official.

Zeus Berger has finally made me the equal to every man pilot in the world. I, too, want to fly, eat, sleep, and screw.

Not necessarily in that order.

Fine. Definitely not in that order.

"The problem," he says, "is that you suck on the ice. And I'm not losing to that royal fucker today."

I straighten my spine, my skates slip, but he's still holding me up. "I'm not sitting this out. So you're just going to have to make up for my suckage for once."

His gaze drops to my lips.

I manage to not let my feet get away from me this time, but *hoooo*, doggie, my legs haven't wobbled this much since my first check ride in pilot training.

"Think I got a solution," he says, his voice low and rumbly.

"We break their kneecaps?"

That thing I mentioned about him not doing anything small?

Yeah. He goes big with the admiration too. His eyes are so lit up with it, they're practically smoking.

Or maybe I'm getting my A-words confused.

Because anyone else might call that *affection*.

He pulls me away from the wall. "Something much easier."

"Clunk their heads together?"

"Nope. We get *my* head back between your legs."

My pussy leaps in agreement. My nipples strain against my bra. And before I can count backwards from Sunday, he spins me out, sneaks behind me, sticks his head between my knees, and stands until I'm sitting on his shoulders.

I shriek—*dammit*, I hate when I do that—and grab a fistful of his hair to steady myself. He tucks my calves behind his arms. "Quit squirming or we're both going down," he says easily, as though it's no big deal to add another half of his body weight and three more feet of height *while he's on ice skates*.

"Yo, Ares," he calls. "You bring the rubber chicken?"

Ares pulls a rubber chicken out of the front of his pants.

"Swear to God, I am *not* related to you two," Ambrosia declares.

Zeus zips us both closer to her while Ares drops the chicken and smacks it with his stick. "Are too," he taunts his sister.

"Saw you born," Ares calls.

"Better you than me," Jett calls as he tries to steal the chicken, Manning rushing up behind him to help.

Zeus easily claims the chicken—the *pucken?*—and suddenly we're flying around the ice, him pushing a rubber chicken with his stick, me hanging on for dear life.

And laughing.

Because *oh my god*.

I'm flying.

Flying.

On Zeus's shoulders.

While rubber chicken hockey rages below.

This is one for the books.

22

Zeus

We've officially adopted Joey.

She probably doesn't know it. Probably *shouldn't* know it. But we have.

Once you play rubber chockey with us, you're ours.

Consider yourself adopted by extension. Welcome to the rubber chockey club.

Guess we have to keep Manning too, but so long as he keeps his hands off Joey's sister, we're fine.

We're hanging at Ducky's Burgers, a hole-in-the-wall joint two blocks from Mink Arena, eating the shit out of these juicy burgers the size of my fist and fries fresh from the potatoes while Joey and Chase and Ambrosia bicker about the future of space travel.

I could argue with them, but these fries are hot and salty and the next best thing to pineapple tater tot casserole, so instead, I'm just listening.

And playing that triangle tee game.

Joey solved it in four seconds. Because she's Joey.

Me?

I get like six pegs left every time.

It's her fault. Every time she opens her mouth, I quit paying attention to my burger, my fries, and the tees, and I just listen.

She's smart. She's tough. She's probably a terrible singer.

But I can't stop listening to her voice anyway. It's music to me.

"Fine," she says to Chase. "Believe what you want. But don't come crying to me when Peach and I put a colony on the moon and suddenly you want a piece."

See? Fucking music. She's got balls and she knows what she's worth and she's not letting anyone—not even my best friend, who can be fucking ruthless—undersell her.

"Shut up and just make her a real offer," I tell Chase.

He gives me one of those looks that means I'm probably gonna find some massive blow-up Halloween spider in my living room when I get back to Nashville, but I don't fucking care.

He wants in on Joey's company. I know it. He knows it. Ambrosia, Ares, and even Manning know it. He's dicking around now, seeing how far he can push her.

"It's like carting around a preschooler," Chase says to Joey.

"I'm the whole fucking preschool class, and it's fucking dessert time."

Preferably with both the fucking and the dessert. Or maybe fucking as the dessert.

With Joey, I mean. Not with Chase.

"Stay out of it, Zeus," Joey tells me. "I can take care of myself."

Huh.

Lady might've just told me no fucking, because she'll fuck herself. Not so sure I like that. But— "Sure. I like to watch. But I get bored when I can't play too."

"There are medications for that." She scribbles a number on a napkin and slides it to Chase. I catch a glimpse, and the number of zeroes makes my eyes water.

That's a fuck-ton of money.

Yeah, Chase has it, but me and Ares together won't ever make that much playing hockey combined. Total. All our years added up.

This chick is making me so hot and hard I could fucking Zamboni the shit out of a rink with just my dick right now.

"That's insane," Chase says.

"Your loss. You don't want it, I can count at least six other investors who do."

"And then you have to deal with six jackasses instead of just me."

He can be six jackasses all by himself. Which I *don't* say out loud, for the record, even though I know Chase, my brother, and my sister all know I'm thinking it. Ares and Ambrosia snicker like they agree. Chase gives me those squinty eyeballs that mean I'm finding more than a giant spider in my living room if I don't shut my pie hole.

Don't care.

Except I do care that Joey's looking at me.

Like, *looking* at me. Maybe through me. Like she heard me say it too, and when those hard lines around her mouth soften into something that's not a smile, but is definitely amused, I feel like I just put a biscuit in the basket at the buzzer to win the whole fucking Stanley Cup.

That redwood in my jockey shorts is once again reaching for the heavens.

And by *heavens*, I mean Joey's special lady cave.

"You're forgetting one very important detail," Joey says to Chase.

"Highly doubt it, but go ahead. Amuse me."

"Weightless doesn't need to expand. We're solid just as we are." She takes the napkin, crinkles it up, and drops it in her ketchup-mustard mix that's just as disgusting as my jock strap after a game. "Bet I could beat the shit out of all of you playing rubber chockey on the moon."

Ares shoots me a look. *Dude. You are in so over your head.*

Fuck, yeah, I am.

"But don't you *want* to grow?" Ambrosia asks. "Zeus said there was a three-month wait for private flights. And there's so much interest in research on the effect of zero-gravity on plants and humans and—"

"Bet you fifty bucks I can eat more ice cream than you," I say to Joey.

She tilts those dark eyes at me, and there it is again—that subtle amusement at my expense. "Is your brain capable of freezing?"

"I was born with my brain freezing."

Ares nods. We share a fist bump. Hell froze over the day we were born. Except we weren't born in Hell. Minnesota was just butt-ass cold that day.

"It's too late to ask you not to encourage him, isn't it?" Ambrosia says to Joey.

"He encourages himself."

"That's freakishly accurate. Are you sure you just met a couple days ago?"

"She can tell them apart too," Chase says. "It really is fascinating."

"You can't?" Joey asks.

"Sometimes I don't want to."

Ares grabs him in an affectionate headlock. I tilt my head at Joey. "Got a banana split with your name on it."

"You are so gross," Ambrosia mutters. She flicks Ares's ear. "Let him go or I'm pulling out my kazoo."

"Bad hum," Ares mutters. He drops his hold on Chase.

Manning's just taking it all in, grinning.

"What's so funny, fucker?" I say.

"Just like being at home," Cheery McCheeryFace says. "Except I'd still like to take dear old Fireball's sister out for dinner and dancing."

Joey doesn't go all *Alien* baby on him. No lasers sprout out her eyeballs and castrate him on the spot. She doesn't even flinch.

Much more than anyone but me would notice, anyway.

She smiles at him.

Warm, friendly, and fucking terrifying. "That's fine. You're boring."

His grin's so wide now his eyeballs are disappearing in

the crinkles. He's one big mass of well-groomed beard, thick eyebrows, prominent honker, and disappearing eyeballs.

He nods to her. "The psychological games. Excellent. Works well with sheep too."

Joey leans over his plate. His royal guard—ever vigilant, but quiet enough I usually forget he's there—leans toward the table.

She plucks the last of his hamburger off his plate—four normal human size bites there—shoves it all in her mouth, flips him off, and turns to stroll out the door. "Later, y'all," she says.

I think.

Hard to tell with her mouth full.

But I know one thing.

That woman's not leaving without me.

23

Zeus

I catch up with Joey outside a pie shop down the block. "Hey."

She looks up at me like she's never seen me before, and I can't deny what that pang in my chest means.

This chick's getting to me.

"You're rather relentless."

"You're special."

It pops out before I can think. Or stop it.

And now she's looking at me like not only has she never seen me before, but I'm possibly from an alien planet.

Which I'm realizing isn't necessarily a bad thing. She likes space and shit. Maybe I'd be more appealing if I was an alien. I should slather my body in purple face paint, dye my chest hairs green, and see if it helps.

"I'm special," she repeats.

She's still chewing her hamburger. I love how much this woman loves food. I can eat a whole fucking sheep—wool and all—in a single day. I go out with some skinny chick who eats like two pieces of lettuce and a protein shake, and we just sit there while she cringes at me shoveling it in.

Just because I'm a big fucker doesn't mean I don't pick up on shit.

Means I don't date much either.

What's the point?

"You…" I'm losing words. You want poetry, talk to Ares. He can one-word haiku the shit out of trash-talking on the ice. You want to be fucking told how it is, you come to me.

Until you're a badass, hot as fuck pilot chick who can both outclass and probably out-burp me.

That's mad skill right there.

"I?" she prompts.

She's pretty? I like her hair? Her brains make her boobs look good? I'm out of my league with Joey Fireball.

"You wanna go look at some stars or shit?" I blurt.

Her lips part, and a chunk of hamburger falls out. She snaps her jaw shut, swipes her mouth, and visibly swallows.

She's no longer staring at me like I'm an intriguing alien specimen.

Nope, this is all *who the fuck does this moron think he is?*

"Or go bench some bellhops," I add quickly. "Or get a wool coat and try to light it on fire while we tie Manning up and make him watch. Dude loves his wool. Gets freaked out when I make my biceps dance too. He's jealous."

She tilts her head and looks up at the sky, then slugs me in the arm. "Do whatever the fuck you want. I'm going to look at the stars."

24

Joey

Zeus Berger: The Romantic.

Didn't see that coming.

Didn't see me liking it either, but here we are. Stretched out on a couple blankets he commandeered from the hotel, an hour or so south of the city, breathing in the warm night air, listening to crickets, and bullshitting while a carpet of stars twinkles in the vast eternity of space.

He's not touching me. Not physically. But even if he were silent as the moon, I'd know he was there.

It's not just his presence. The impossibility of overlooking him for his sheer size.

It's something else. Something putting a quiver in my belly, a pull in my pussy, and utter stupidity in my chest.

"Your favorite animal is a lemur," he guesses.

"Can't guess it if you can't spell it," I reply.

"It's got an *um* in it."

He's so full of shit. He can spell it and we both know it. Or at least come close. It's a weird word. I'd spell-check it, and I'm not ashamed to admit it.

"Your favorite is a koala," I guess.

"Fuck, yeah. I love animals that start with a Q. Especially when they're in the cat family."

I try—and fail—to stifle a snort of laughter.

His teeth glint in the darkness. "You as bad at coloring as you are at driving?"

"You as bad at baking as you are at spelling?"

"I can bake the shit out of chocolate chip cookies."

"Uh-huh."

A pebble drops on my face as Zeus crashes his shoulder into mine. On the blanket. While we're both on our backs.

I shove him, because if I don't, I'm going to straddle him, and this thread holding us together is too weird. I don't do emotional shit. I do concrete, take-care-of-myself shit. "What the hell?"

"Missed. Dammit. You want a Milk Dud?"

He's back on his own blanket, silhouetted in the darkness as he rattles a box.

Of candies he's trying to toss into his mouth.

Making the little things extraordinary. *Fun.*

"Got any Cadbury Mini Eggs?" I ask.

"Those M&M-wannabes they sell at Easter?"

"Yep."

"Fuck, no. It's August."

"You're dead to me now."

He snorts. "Whatever. You want my Milk Duds. I know it. You know it. The fucking stars know it."

"I've never wanted a dud in my life."

"Missing out. Probably wouldn't try pineapple tater tot casserole either. Loser."

"Punk."

"Hard-ass."

"Baby."

He laughs—*holy dog*, Zeus Berger has a laugh as big and rich and surprising as he is. I smile in the darkness and breathe in the night air.

Been too long since I stopped to watch the stars, much less took the time to really enjoy another human being's company. Peach and I have been so busy researching opportunities and updating our long-term business plan —Weightless took off much faster than we expected—that neither of us has taken much time off the last several months.

Okay, *years*.

Peach brought most of the money to the table to start the company. I scraped my share together with loans, minimalist living, and sheer gut. I don't like not pulling my weight, so when I start out behind, I work my ass off to catch up.

Having Peach out while Meemaw recovers from hip surgery isn't going to help.

Not when we're playing with an investor who's serious enough and has big enough pockets to put Weightless on an entirely new playing field.

Zeus's shoulder brushes mine, his arm cuts off my view of a third of the sky, and I make out a finger pointing upward. "You going there someday?"

"Fuck, yeah."

His arm drops beside mine. Close enough that I could grab his hand and squeeze it. Or he could grab mine.

He doesn't.

Neither do I.

But I think about it.

"Big dude like me couldn't fit in a spaceship," he says quietly.

He's not wrong. His height would disqualify him from NASA's space program. Even with private space flight, he'd take up as much room as two passengers.

I roll to face him, squishing my boob against his arm and perking up my nipples. "Do you want to go to space?"

"I'm fucking going on your airplane again."

I don't mention him puking, because despite being a badass unafraid to call him a baby—which we both know he's not—I don't rub people's shortcomings in their face. Life's too short to be a shithead—the cruel kind, not the take-care-of-yourself kind—and you never know who you're going to need tomorrow.

I never know who Gracie's going to need tomorrow.

And possibly I can confess, since it's dark and I'm feeling mellow, that I like having guys on my crew who will step up and have my back when a big-ass hockey dude looks like he might eat me.

"Didn't think you could do it," Zeus adds gruffly.

"Motion sickness is easily managed when you know it's a potential issue. Hell, even Peach still tosses her cookies up there now and again."

"I meant make *me* weightless."

His voice isn't just quiet.

It's vulnerable. Exposed. *Human.*

Like maybe he doesn't always want to be a big badass.

Like maybe sometimes, he just wants to be normal.

A whole fucking rose bush explodes in my chest in a blooming mass of flowery emotional shit. My lungs gobble up the sweetness. The jet engine driving my pulse fires up.

Not good.

So not good.

I hold myself completely still until I'm sure my voice won't wobble.

Sometimes, I'd like to be normal too. "Never doubt a kid from the sticks."

He rolls to face me. Our noses are inches apart. I could grab him and kiss him again. Swing a leg over his hips.

Or, you know, his ribs.

Because neither of us is *normal.*

"You always know you wanted to go to space?" he asks.

"Nope. Used to want to be a lady."

He doesn't laugh. Like he knows it's not actually funny.

Gracie and I grew up crammed into a one-bedroom bungalow patched together with duct tape and tar. We had Dad and two dogs that were less *ours* than they were simply not anyone else's. There was love, but there wasn't much else. Heard the song "Fancy" when I was nine, decided I'd be a lady too some day. Until the day I found my true calling.

Maybe it's the night air. Maybe it's the stars. Maybe it's this weird magnetic pull that keeps bringing me back to

Zeus. Whatever it is, I'm suddenly whispering secrets I've never told another soul outside my family.

"I won a trip to D.C. my junior year of high school. It was the first time in my life I'd been on an airplane. Swore it wouldn't be the last." That drive to be something more than a poor kid from the sticks was always in me, but being airborne for the first time took it to a new level. "I've worked my ass off since then to live a life in the sky, starting with the college scholarship courtesy of the military. Flight training too. I wanted to be an astronaut. Knew it would take a long time. But then I heard about private space flight companies not long before I almost died of appendicitis, and I didn't want to wait any longer."

"Your scar."

"I got better."

He breathes out a chuckle and traces the path of my arm from my shoulder to my wrist. Goosebumps erupt over my entire body.

Even my toes. Fuck, my toenails too.

"Your family come fly with you?"

"Just Gracie." Dad was too sick by the time Peach and I were ready for our first flight. I asked him to go anyway—*it's almost your time anyway, what's it matter if it happens while you're almost touching the stars?*—but he declined.

He was sick and dying. It shouldn't have felt like he abandoned me. Like it meant he wasn't proud of me. But those fucking emotions—they get in places they're not supposed to and tell you lies convincing enough to border on your fears about the truth.

Zeus pulls my favorite trick and stares at me in the dark.

"Your family come to your games?" Because I'm not going there.

He doesn't push it. "When they can. Just retired, so they're probably coming to more games this year." He snorts again. "Probably follow in their footsteps before long."

"You're going to go watch your kids' hockey games and drive like you can't see the road?"

"My mom can kick your ass at driving."

"She'd have to catch me first."

"And I don't have any kids."

"That you know of."

"You know what I know?"

"Dog himself probably doesn't know what you know."

"I know if I had kids, I'd fucking know it. And I wouldn't have fucking *one*. When I have kids, I'm having quadzeuslets. Live large, play large, procreate large."

Quadzeuslets.

That's the most fucking terrifying thing I've heard all day. "Oh my dog."

"Not having kids." Again, there's a rawness to his voice that tugs at every fiber in my chest.

"Why?"

"Because who the fuck wants to have quadzeuslets?"

With him, he doesn't say. Out loud. Except it's hanging there between us.

I saw him with Bailey. His heart's just as big as the rest of him. He's loud. He's outrageous. He's everything the world expects him to be.

Until someone smaller and weaker needs him to be something else.

Walls. Down.

I want to hug him. And I never want to hug anyone.

"My mother left us when I was eight," I whisper. "Didn't stick around to watch us grow up. Never checked in on us again. I don't know if she's dead or alive. I just know she didn't want us anymore."

I can't do this anymore, Josephine. Take good care of Gracie. You've always been better at it than I was anyway.

Gracie barely remembers her. And Gracie still believes in forever.

Me?

I believe in stars. Constellations. The moon landing. The physics of the universe.

I don't understand them all, but I know they're not going anywhere. And they're bigger than I am.

I poke Zeus in the chest. "You'd be a better parent than my mother was. Don't fucking sell yourself —*mmph!*"

He muffles my order by capturing my lips with his mouth. I grip the soft cotton of his T-shirt and hold tight while I part my lips for his tongue.

There's nothing small about Zeus, and kissing him is no different. He *kisses* big. Not that I have much practice, but our mouths aren't melding.

No, kissing Zeus means our entire bodies are having an experience. His lips touch mine, my nipples pull a point-and-click, my lady cave gets herself all dolled up inside, the hairs on my arms dance a jig, and I can't keep my tongue to myself.

Not that I have any lingering aspirations of being a lady.

I've just never understood the appeal of tongue-wrestling.

Until Zeus.

There's something about his meaty tongue caressing my lips, stroking my tongue like it's his favorite vacation property and he's here to have a party, that makes me want more.

Crave more.

I don't want to kiss him.

I want to inhale his essence. Imprint my mouth on his lips.

Claim him.

This big, bold, fearless man—yeah, I want to climb that mountain and conquer the beast.

And for the first time in my life, I don't care if that means I let him claim me too.

Just for tonight, I tell myself.

One time, I can let someone in. I know he's leaving. I know this is temporary. I'm not getting attached.

He rolls me onto my back. I wrap my legs around his waist and strain to rub my rosebud against his hard stomach, but I can't get a good angle.

He's just *so big*.

And suddenly I don't care, because he's doing something to the pebble standing in for my nipple that's making heat streak across my chest and lightning course through my veins straight to my yippidee-doo-dah.

My dildo has never done *that*. Hell, neither has a vibrator.

I gasp, breaking the kiss, and thrust my nipple into his hand to offer it as a sacrifice to the sex gods. I'm beginning to understand the hoopla about a man participating in making orgasms.

"Holy fuck, you're sexy." Zeus follows the proclamation with a lick to my neck. "Can I eat your boobs?"

I'm already squirming out of my tank top. "I'll fucking kill you if you don't."

"That's the hottest thing a woman has ever said to me."

"Shut up and get naked. If you pull that trigger early again, I'll strangle you with your own condom."

He rips through the center of my bra with his teeth —*holy fuck*, that's unbelievably sexy—the cups spring back, and my breasts pop free. He licks one from the underside, up over the nipple, and follows it with a pinch that I can feel in my clit. I buck against him again, because I'm aching so hard I need to rub it on something.

He reaches between us, fiddles with something south of where his fingers *should* be, namely fiddling with my hooha—and suddenly—*holy fuck* again.

Something harder and longer and thicker than a lava lamp slides between my legs and bumps that hard, needy nub in my pants. A carefree, sex-starved, badass fairy princess takes over my personality, panting and moaning and dry-humping that solid piece of meat like the fate of the entire fucking universe depends on this one big O.

And that's before he does that thing with his tongue to my other breast.

I grip his hair and shove his head back to my chest. "*More.*"

His teeth scrape my nipple, my nerve endings ignite, and I buck off the blanket. His wondercock glides along the fabric hiding my pussy.

Must. Get. Naked.

Must. Not. Break. Connection.

Which isn't a problem, because his fingers are creeping into my pants, slipping under my underwear, and hitting— *"Oh yes there more THERE holy dog in heaven MORE."*

"Fuck, Joey."

His thick fingers flick my clit, slide down the seam of my pussy, and thrust into my aching, ready depths. One more flick of his thumb to my clit, and I'm coming so fast and hard I can't tell which constellations are real and which ones just spontaneously big-banged into existence in my brain, but there are stars.

So many stars.

Planets. Suns. Moons.

Solar systems.

All in this eency-weency slice of space where Zeus is teasing my climax harder and longer and deeper with those talented fingers, making my world so small he encompasses the entirety of my existence while also making me feel like I own the whole fucking galaxy.

The last of the spasms roll out of my body, but I'm not going limp-armed and noodle-legged.

No fucking way.

Not when he's still poking my leg with that yard of beef.

I'm the space cowgirl who's gonna ride that megarocket to the edge of the whole universe. "Roll over," I order.

I push, and he rolls. I strip out of my pants and follow him.

He's already sliding on a condom when I straddle his hips. "Joey—"

"Shut up and fuck me."

He pulls himself up, cradles my head in his massive hands, and claims my mouth again. His tongue, his teeth, his lips—*fuck*, this man could teach me a thing or seventeen about kissing. Because while his mouth is worshiping mine, his strong hands are stroking my head, my hair, that spot between my shoulders that's always too tight.

His thick stubble scratches the skin around my mouth. The sensation borders on exquisite pain, and I want more, so I kiss him back harder.

Deeper.

I let my fingers trail down his neck to his broad shoulders, the curves and angles of solid muscle a puzzle that's already solved itself and is just sitting there waiting to be explored. He has a scar over his left pec, rough hair sprinkled over his chest, his nipples are hard tips that are just as sensitive as mine. I flick them with my thumbs, his cock pulses thicker between my thighs, and he moans into my mouth.

Yeah, I'm totally doing that again.

And again.

And again, until he grips my upper arms, breaks the kiss, and swears out another *fuck*.

"Flex," he orders.

I squeeze my biceps.

And I swear on my jet, his dick grows another inch. "You could kick my ass in arm wrestling," he says reverently.

The hell I could. His arms are so big, he's developed muscles for holding up his muscles. I slide his meat between my thighs. "I'd let you win."

"You're such a trash-talker."

I get the feeling that's as much a turn-on to him as a sweet-talker would be to a normal woman.

And I dig it.

I don't like feelings.

We got too close to them already tonight.

And despite that spiral of apprehension at the bruising my cherry might take at the hands of his monster cock—pretty sure he's twice the size of my biggest dildo—I want to do this.

I want Zeus Berger to be my first.

His fingers trail down my spine. "You're so fucking sexy," he whispers.

I wonder how many other women he's called sexy, and I quickly banish the thought.

There's no room for jealousy in a one-night stand.

Or a three-night stand, or whatever this is. I'm going back to Huntsville tomorrow. He's...doing something that's not going to Huntsville.

I rub my pussy over his cock, angling for his swollen head.

He grips my arms again. "Joey—"

I freeze. He's going to tell me to stop. That he doesn't want to do this. That it's all a big misunderstanding.

"I'm kinda...big."

I blink.

"Understood," I say brusquely. He's not *big*. He's super-sized. If all men's dicks were this size, dildos wouldn't be made for half-size packages. He's like the jumbo hot dog in a world of cocktail weenies. "Are we doing this or not?"

He hesitates.

I'm about to fling myself off of him—and possibly off the nearest cliff in utter frustration, because *so this is what it feels like*—when he speaks again.

"You're so fucking tight. So fucking sexy. But I don't always...fit."

My heart's made of fucking iron. It doesn't bend. It doesn't break. It's impervious to cannonballs and hissy fits and sharknados.

But that fucker's melting in my chest right now.

Because Zeus Berger's dick is sometimes too big.

"You're going to fucking fit if we have to get a shoehorn," I growl.

Even in the dark, I can see his jaw slip. The vibrations of the chuckle looming in his chest are more potent than anything batteries can produce. His thumbs caress my arms, and *fuck*, more parts of me are melting again.

"A shoehorn?"

"Or a dickhorn. Whatever." *Fuck*. Now I'm getting all hot and bothered and popping a lady boner in my clit over the idea of a dickhorn.

Which, oddly, is why I'm totally comfortable with the idea of bumping chubs with Zeus.

He kinda gets me.

But even in the dark, I can tell he's watching me with too much intensity. "You've, ah, never been with a big dude. Have you?"

Oh, hell. My lady boner's deflating. She's losing her

steam. My nipples are drooping too. This—this isn't sexy-time conversation.

"Fuck, yeah," I lie.

And he knows it.

His grip on my arms tightens. I can *feel* every cell in his body going on lockdown.

Only his cock seems to miss the memo. It's still pulsing between my thighs like it wants to go home, and it knows home's close, but some dickhead—no offense to Zeus's penis—has it on a leash.

"It was never worth the bother, okay?" I blurt. "Sex doesn't motivate me. It doesn't drive me. And there's no way I was fucking up my life plans by screwing any old dickhead who couldn't find my clit with a flashlight and a map in broad daylight but could fuck up putting on a condom. I can fucking take care of myself. And if you're not man enough for the job either, I have a lava lamp that'll do just fine. Better than fine. *Seeing the heavens* fine."

"You...you've fucked a lava lamp?"

"Wouldn't you like to know."

I'd get off his lap, except his dick's straining harder against my pussy, and she's doing that fucking damsel in distress, *woe is me, I need a good penis to help me rub one out* routine that she's never fucking pulled before because I've always given her top-of-the-line toys and paid more attention to what she liked than any man before.

Any man until possibly Zeus.

Who's subtly rocking his dick harder between my thighs while pressure coils deep inside me and blood surges to my clit and my nipples get so hard they're puckering my entire breasts.

"You know what you need?" he growls, low and dirty and bossy.

A spanking? my pussy suggests. "For gender roles to be reversed so I could have a harem of my own?"

"You need the triple Zeusgasm."

Swear to dog, the threat just gave me a mini-gasm right there.

"Where's your favorite spot, Joey Fireball?"

He's hit it twice already today. "You probably couldn't find it with a ten-foot pole and a seeing-eye dog."

"I'm going to find it." In one smooth motion, he lifts me up, goes flat on his back, and sits me on top of his face.

On.

Top.

Of.

His.

Face.

His tongue flicks my clit, my vagina clenches around itself, and my hips buck on their own. "*Ohmydog.*"

"Delicious," he says to my pussy.

His breath tickles the sensitive skin there, and *fuck*, I'm leaking. I'm getting wet and hot and bothered and now he's sucking on my clit while he holds me in place, and it's so intense and hot and *I'm sitting on Zeus Berger's face* and I'm going to come.

I'm. Going. To. Come.

I hunch over and brace my hands against the ground, he nips at my bud with his teeth, that hot spiral deep inside me implodes, my walls clench around empty nothingness, the world goes white and sparkly, and I hear myself crying out his name. Just as I think I'm done, the earth shifts beneath my ass, and then *holy fuck*.

He's got his tongue up inside me. Swirling into my depths. It's long and thick and it's not hard like his cock, but it's clearly strong, because he's stroking me from the inside out with an intensity that's making everything inside me coil impossibly tight and hot and ready again. I'm spun up so fast my ovaries might've just bruised my pelvis.

Something brushes my clit—his nose?—his tongue reaches a mythical spot deep inside me, and I'm exploding again.

Squeezing his tongue with my inner walls while he laps it up and tickles that magic place, coaxing me harder and higher and *more*. Clenching and seizing and spasming with everything I have left, which is borderline nothing, but *dog*, that spot—his tongue—my pussy—my whole fucking life.

It's all there.

The big bang. In my very center.

Coming undone.

Coming together again.

My legs are overcooked okra. My arms turn to silly putty, and I almost face-plant in the grass. Zeus catches me—of course he does—and for the first time in my adult life, I let a man cradle me.

Buck naked.

In a grassy park under the stars.

I stroke a hand down his chest while he peppers my shoulder and hair with kisses. "Jupiter still hanging in there, or is he done?" I whisper. I'm trying to be a badass, but I can barely spell it at the moment.

"He's spent enough time in the penalty box. Learned his lesson."

"Good. Because in about six hours, I'm going to need him."

"Give you six minutes."

"*Fuck.*"

His laughter rumbles in my ear. I can smell myself on him, and it's arousing. I wonder what he tastes like.

If he proves himself worthy, I might see if I can find out later.

When I can move again.

"You're fucking delicious," he murmurs, and would you look at that.

I'm getting another lady boner.

Yeah, he's right.

Six minutes is probably all it'll take.

25

Zeus

I WAS seventeen years old the last time I touched a virgin.

We'd been dating for a month and I was so ga-ga for her I probably would've stuck my dick in boiling oil if she'd asked me to. She said she wanted to fuck, I popped a boner and dropped trou, and *boom*.

She screamed.

My mother came running down the stairs to where we were making out in the basement, Ares on her heels. Ambrosia stopped murdering the piano and started screaming just because another girl was screaming.

It's a monster, the chick had sobbed. *He tried to put his monster in my special lady flower.*

I got a lecture about my responsibility to feed, clothe, and shelter any person whose life I permanently altered, along with my duty to save enough money for a kid to go to college. Also got a reminder that my hockey days

THE PILOT AND THE PUCK-UP

would be over if I made my parents into grandparents before they were fifty, because they'd fucking ground me from everything but work, work, work, diaper duty, crying baby duty, and work.

I thought growing up with Ambrosia had been crying baby duty—and she was actually more terrifyingly devious than she was ever whiny—so that was a scary fucking threat.

Me and Ares compared dicks later, decided we were both fucked in the bad way with the megapacks in our pants, ordered the box-club-size tin of extra-extra-large condoms off a computer at school with the librarian's credit card, and neither one of us did the real deed until we were almost twenty and two older puck bunnies adopted us.

Good times.

Not a good time?

Wondering if my head's gonna even fit in Joey's *special lady flower*.

I haven't been this nervous since that year back home the Baloney Festival almost ran out of deep-fried Twinkies before I got my dozen.

And not just because I think she'd actually find a dickhorn.

She squirms, reaches between us, and strokes Jupiter.

And because my dick's a total dog, he sits up, pants, and asks if he can shake. Soaking up the love while she explores him. She can't get her fingers all the way around his girth, and even with both her fists on him, I'd have to put a hand around him to cover his whole length.

I'm already so fucking ready to blow I'm having to

picture my sister naked when Joey dips her fingers under my dick to fondle my tennis balls.

And yeah, I've compared.

Don't want the tennis balls to feel inferior, so I still say my nuts are the same size.

"Is it going to blow if I lick it?" she asks.

Jupiter strains inside his suit. "No licking." Her hair's that perfect combination of thick and silky and curly, and I'm taking full advantage of the rare opportunity to stroke it.

"Spoilsport." She twists out of my grasp and pushes me onto my back. "You know what I like about you?"

Fuck, like I wasn't terrified enough before. "Can't imagine there's a single fucking thing you don't like about a god like me."

She straddles me again, hands playing on my chest, my demigod trapped between her thighs with his head poking out. He wants to stand tall, but he damn sure doesn't mind being squeezed by her legs.

"Your ego can almost keep up with mine," she declares.

I cup her tits, because they're there, and they're fucking fantastic. "You wish. Stick around a while, and you might learn something about real ego."

She's sliding her pussy along the length of my redwood, and he's threatening to split his bark. Chick has stamina.

But I wouldn't have expected anything different. Not from Joey Fireball.

Fuck, I want inside this woman.

"Your turn," she says, and if she's trying for hard-ass,

she's missing by the length of my dick. "Tell me something you like about me."

"Your pussy's fucking hot." Yeah, I almost came six times while I was licking that tasty treat. But my dick's not in control tonight.

I am.

I'm suited up, in the game, and it's mind over meat tonight.

Because this woman gyrating her hips and worshipping my dick with the goddess between her legs needs to know what she's been missing.

What her fucking *lava lamp* can't give her.

Every time I picture her putting anything up in her pussy, Jupiter threatens to go volcano once more, but he's not doing that to us again.

She pinches my nipples. "Something nice about my personality," she orders.

"You're fucking hot when you give orders."

"Yeah?"

"Yeah."

"Good. Get your dick in my pussy now."

Fuck fuck fuck.

She lifts her hips. Jupiter leaps to his full height. He's standing straight and tall and proud, and she has to lift herself higher to press down on his head.

I grip her by the hips and strain to not buck up into her, because while I don't think she's a normal virgin, I'm not fucking this up.

Joey's not some random chick to blow off some steam with. She's…*Joey*.

I pull myself up to sitting and claim her mouth, because the angle's better and I have to kiss this woman.

I have to taste her. Touch her. Feel every bit of her.

We're both out of here in the morning.

Tonight's gonna fucking count.

My dick glides into her folds. I squeeze her tits and suck on her tongue. She grips my hair, tilts her hips, and *fucking puck on a platter*.

She's sliding over my head, taking it inside her, gasping into my mouth while she rides my head.

Right there.

Just my head.

In and out of her tight pussy, right at her entrance, squeezing the tip of me like that's all she can take. I'm groaning and panting too, because *fuck*, I want more.

I want so fucking much more.

It takes so much control to not push the rest of the way into her that my ass is quaking with the effort. My abs. Fuck, even my boner's vibrating with barely-controlled need.

She inches down my shaft, and even with the condom on, I can feel that slick heat in the tight walls gripping my stick. "Fuck, Joey, that's so good."

"Told you," she pants. "Fucking…fits… *Dog*, so fucking big."

I squeeze her nipples.

She gasps and rakes her short fingernails over my back and takes more of me into her tight channel.

I'm seeing fucking stars.

I'm not even coming, and I'm seeing fucking stars.

"Need more," I gasp.

"Oh, yes, *yes*, right there."

She's thrusting and pumping her hips, taking me inch by inch, higher and deeper and harder, and *fuck*, I want all the way in. I want so far in I'm never coming back in.

I want to be so far inside her that she's squeezing my nuts with her walls too.

She's not cradling my dick. No, she's fucking strangling it with her magic pussy. Strangling and choking it and eating the whole damn thing, and now those stars are black dots in my vision.

"More, baby," I gasp. "Gimme more. You're so fucking good."

"Don't *baby* me. Fucking *fuck* me."

She pinches my nipples, the sun explodes in my chest, and I'm never fucking another woman as long as I live. Swear to pineapple tater tot casserole.

My hips buck into her, driving my dick all the way home. She gasps, and I freeze. "Joey—"

She lifts off me and slams down until she's sitting on my subplanets. "More. Oh fuck, Zeus, more."

That's all I need to hear. I lift us both, twist, pin her to the ground, and I drive home. Her legs clench around my hips, she thrusts into me, my nuts slap her ass, and she's chanting my name.

"*Yes, Zeus, more, yes yes YES.*"

"*Joey.*" Fuck, I'm gonna come. She's squeezing and pumping and riding me and she's so hot and so tight and so slick and so fucking *into* me.

Into *me*.

"*I'm coming*," she gasps.

Those walls squeezing me clench around my dick like

a vise, and that's all it takes. I roar as my own release overcomes me, shooting and firing and exploding harder with every spasm rocking my cock.

She's not just coming.

She's pulling me over this cliff, harder, hotter, faster, stronger, making me come my eyeballs out. There's no fucking room for me to come, there's nothing left for me to give, but her pussy keeps squeezing and I keep coming so hard my dick's probably never going to work again.

This is better than a buzzer-beater. Better than floating weightless. I don't know what's out there at the edges of the universe, but swear on my monster cock, I just saw it.

Joey goes limp beneath me. "Oh my dog," she whispers.

My cock's still twitching inside her.

Her pussy's still trembling around me. Uneven and weak, but still so much fucking stronger than it should be.

That's Joey.

Never weak.

Never quits.

Fuck.

I fucking love this woman.

The realization hits like an enforcer blindsiding me. She walked into my life, said *show me what you got, and don't you dare give me anything less than the best*, and *boom*.

She was *mine*.

And it's not as terrifying as it should be.

I barely know her. She's bested me at every single fucking thing we've done. She doesn't take any shit.

And I'm fucking head over heels in love with her.

Her fingers brush my hair out of my eyes, and this

time, I know exactly what that hot air balloon expanding in my chest is.

"Won't fucking fit," she scoffs as she pants.

Yeah.

I'm gonna love this woman until the day I die.

I lower my head and I kiss her.

Suckle on her lower lip. Swipe my tongue over the inside. Cradle her head and explore her mouth.

She hesitates only a second before she's kissing me back.

I'm not gonna lie and tell you it's because she loves me. Or that I'm letting myself imagine she ever might.

I'm a monster puckhead. She's gonna fly her own ass to the moon without me one day. Probably won't even remember me.

But I'm gonna take every moment I can until it's over. Even if it never comes again, I'm going to fucking have tonight.

She traces my ear with one finger, Jupiter lifts a sleepy head, she giggles and squeezes her pussy around him, and it's game over, lights out.

Because I'm about to make love to this woman.

And this one's just for me.

26

Joey

IF YOU'D TOLD me two nights ago that Zeus could give me a double orgasm before he took his own pants off, and then treat me to a triple courtesy of the same dick that was hair-trigger quick, I would've laughed in your face.

Now, I'm pretending I still remember how to walk while we battle to see who's going to play the gentleman and hold the door while the other goes into the hotel first.

I've never had this much fun in my entire life. My cheeks hurt from smiling. Flying, hockey, sex—I'm *happy*. For this moment, I'm happy.

"Fine," he says. "I'll go first. More cookies for me."

I'd say he already got his cookies, but *damn*. Smells like a fresh batch is sitting in the lobby.

At two AM.

Fuck being a gentleman.

We rush through the door at the same time. He's got

the upper hand for hip checks, so I hit him with a well-placed squeeze to a pressure point in his elbow.

He yelps and freezes in the doorway.

I yelp because the two of us can't fit through at the same time, and I'm stuck between his bicep and the door frame.

Just inside the lobby, several eyeballs swivel our way.

Ambrosia snickers. Ares makes eye contact with Zeus and clearly says something silently, but he's got a mean poker face and I can't tell what.

Chase looks thoughtful. "I've seen this before… Now where was it?"

"Shut up, glitter chin." Zeus dislodges himself by stepping backward, I tumble forward and almost lose my balance, and he scores another point with me by letting me recover on my own.

Nice to know that giving a guy your cherry doesn't mean he forgets who you are.

Not nice?

That gas in my chest that I can't honestly blame on indigestion.

Or the mild panic at knowing my time in Copper Valley ends soon. We're wheels-up, taking Luna back to Huntsville, in mere hours.

I'm busting crew rest big time. Not like me.

But Monkey Butt and Boomer have us covered tomorrow, and my next scheduled flight isn't for three days.

I can have a night of fun.

"Where are those cookies?" I ask.

"If you have to ask…" Ambrosia muses.

Zeus flips her a double bird on his way to the help-yourself coffee bar. He grabs the entire glass tray and makes eye contact with the night clerk. "Bring out all your dough. Man's gotta eat. Pilot chicks do too."

I should get to bed. Even with my crew capable of flying, I have shit I need to be awake for tomorrow.

Instead, I drop into an open seat in the lobby. Unfortunately, it's beside Manning.

He passes me a wine bottle. "Mead?"

I take a swig. It's like wine, but sweet enough to make my eyeballs burn. "Pansy-ass drink."

He grins. "Rather have some tree bark then? Maybe some rubber off a tire?"

I want a hamburger, but I'm honestly too satisfied to be picky.

Or care that the prince drinks girly drinks. He's here. Gracie's back home. She's out of danger. "Does anything ever bother you?" I ask.

"I'm a prince with no responsibilities and all the money in the world. Why would anything ever bother me?"

He's still smiling, but even in my sex-sated state, I can tell I hit a nerve.

Not that I much care.

Unless he's still in contact with Gracie. Then I'm going to fucking care.

Zeus hands me the tray of cookies. "Don't let that royal fucker have any."

"Aren't any royals to fuck in my country," Manning says cheerfully. "We're all male. Which would work out nicely for my cousin, I suppose, if he had the poor taste to be attracted to any of us."

"Was that an insult to you or your cousin?" Ambrosia asks.

He winks. "You know my stepsister. I'm sure you can answer that for yourself."

Ambrosia's still staring at him while I make short work of four chocolate chip cookies. "Were you the one who let the sheep loose in the castle the day her mom married your dad?" she asks.

"I'm quite certain that was a wooly accident."

And as snorts of laughter break out around us, I'm certain I'm glad Gracie went home this morning.

For many reasons.

I take another swig off the bottle, then pass it to Zeus, who's squeezed into a chair meant for a man half his size. He's perched on the edge, his legs spread wide enough that his knee's almost touching mine.

And I wonder if the key card I have for his room will still work.

Motivated by sex?

No.

Willing to jump on another opportunity to ride his rocket around the galaxy?

Only live once. Gotta do what you can while you're here.

Even if it means you hurt tomorrow.

27

Joey

I've been back in Huntsville four days, and I'm getting cranky.

Not because things aren't going well. Meemaw's been moved to a rehabilitation center and has excellent round-the-clock care, so Peach and I are both in the office for the first time in over a week.

I missed her ridiculously perfect face.

Yesterday's flight was just as fucking amazing as it was supposed to be. Couldn't have asked for better weather, no one puked, and one of the passengers was a YouTuber whose video of the flight already has over a hundred thousand views. Our receptionist hasn't taken a full breath since she sat down this morning for all the reservation inquiries we're getting.

She has managed to inhale all four cups of coffee I've brought her between calls though.

Gracie drove the thirty minutes for a visit last night. If she's harboring any lingering irritation with me over my interference with her little whatever-it-was with *Prince Manning*, she's not letting on. Nope, she gave me shit for wearing an orange shirt with purple pants—both gifts from her—and raided my cabinets for my secret stash of jelly beans.

But it's not even the irritation that we don't hang out enough rankling me.

No, that's all Zeus Berger's doing.

He had flowers delivered here yesterday.

Fucking *flowers*.

And not just any flowers. Big-ass pink frilly things with blooms the size of my head. Gargantuan monster flowers. They're the Zeus Berger of flowers.

Do I look like the flower type to you?

I didn't think so.

But now everyone from Peach to my entire crew to Meemaw and Gracie knows that he sent me flowers.

That fucker's probably laughing his ass off at how annoyed I am right now.

Especially since he followed it up this morning with a crate of giant Hershey's Kisses. You know the ones—they're like a half-pound each.

Yeah. The fucking Zeus Bergers of Hershey's Kisses.

Swear to dog, if he sends me lingerie, I'm flying my ass up to Nashville and I'll—I'll—

Dammit.

I can tell myself I'll track down his house, plant spider eggs in his curtains, and leave a lava lamp with a note that it was better, except I wouldn't.

I'd jump the dummy.

And that's what's making me utterly furious.

I let him in. I let him in places I don't let anyone, and I'm not talking about my vagina.

He's in my head.

I grab one of the chocolates and fling it at the basketball hoop hanging inside my office door, and I miss.

It bounces off the rim and plops into the potted plant Gracie insisted I needed and Peach insists on watering, but instead of simply plopping into the dirt, it smashes the edge of the pot, and the plant goes rolling.

I huff out of my chair and around my ancient metal desk to right the damn thing.

And now I need to get a vacuum.

Because I can't work with dirt on my floor.

Correction.

I can't work with *wet* dirt on the floor we *just* had professionally cleaned.

I grab the whole plant—now properly squished by the giant Kiss—stumble through flinging my door open with my hands full, and march it into Peach's office.

She's on the phone, so I slam it into *her* corner.

"That's right, Mr. Jett. You want to get crew-certified, you're going to have to pay our full asking price. And since we all know damn good and well *why* you want you and your girlfriend crew-certified, I'm adding fifty million to the price."

I scowl at the gray carpet while I march back to my office.

Yeah, I can work with dirt on my floor. I can work

with mud, with grass, with sand, and probably even with moldy cheese if I had to.

What I can't work with is being the professional equivalent of a horror film chick.

You know. The recently deflowered virgin who dies at the hands of the psycho because she slept with someone?

That's my brain.

My brain died because I had mind-blowing monster sex with Zeus Berger.

And I don't mean *monster* in a bad way. I mean monster like stupendous, except for the part where *stupendous* and *stupid* share too many letters.

Whatever.

I can get over this.

A run would help. Some weight lifting. Happy private time with my drawer of toys.

I don't need sex.

My pussy gasps, bitch-slaps the three brain cells that led to that thought, and pulls a Carol Kane in *The Princess Bride*: Liar! LIAARRRR!!

A horrible thought strikes me.

What if it wasn't Zeus? What if he didn't send the flowers and the chocolate?

What if someone—like Manning, that cheerful dickhead—is fucking with me?

I bolt out of my chair as someone knocks on my doorframe.

Nyla gives me the constipated goat look. "Uh, you have a—"

She doesn't finish, because she doesn't have to.

Zeus is in the hallway.

He's fresh-shaven. Got a haircut. His jeans fit him like a new paint job, there's a pink sparkly troll dancing on a rainbow on his white T-shirt, and if that's not cologne polluting my office, then he farts cupcakes.

He saunters in. "Hey."

Nyla hesitates a moment. "Go easy on him, boss," she whispers before she pulls the door shut.

That big ol' grin makes my heart do a pitter-patter, which is embarrassing as fuck, and I don't care. "You sent me fucking *flowers*."

The grin gets bigger, and his eyes light up like rocket flares. "Piss you off?"

"What do you think?"

I reach for another one of the humongous Kisses and contemplate chucking it at his head.

"Wanna screw around?" he asks.

My eyes drift to the bulge in his pants, my pussy pumps a fist, and my nipples pop twin lady boners. "I'm at work."

He shrugs and pulls a novel out of his back pocket. I squint. It's pink and girly, with a hockey player and cupcakes on the cover. "No problem. Brought a book."

This is getting weird.

"Is that a romance novel?"

"This? Yeah. My buddy Knox says it's good."

I eyeball the pink troll on his shirt while he props himself against the wall and flips to the first page of the book.

"Are you fucking with me?"

"Not yet, but I can if you want me to."

"Why are you here?"

"Missed you."

More fluttering, but this time *waaaay* north of where I'd prefer to be getting excited.

I'm definitely making a face, and he's definitely noticing.

"What?" he says. "You're hot. I'm hot. Training camp doesn't start for—is that a spider plant? You have a fucking *spider* plant?"

I look over my shoulder at another of the green things Gracie put in my office. "I don't know."

He blows out a slow breath and rolls his shoulders back. "Nashville's just up the road. No biggie to—"

"Nashville's two hours away." By car. And he plays for Nashville's team. So he probably has a house or an apartment or something in Nashville.

It's twenty minutes in the air.

I own a plane.

"Tell you a secret," he says.

The last time he told me a secret, he got me naked.

I wouldn't mind going there again. "What?"

"I hear sex is even better when you're pissed."

Hearing him say the word *sex* practically sparks a mini-gasm. "Who's pissed?"

"I sent you flowers and chocolates."

He wiggles his brows, any brains I ever had in my pants hitch a flight to Tahiti, and I crook a finger at him. "Get naked and fuck my brains out."

"Say *please*."

He's acting like it doesn't bother him that I'm an obnoxious, pushy pain in the ass. Like it amuses him that all I want him for is sex.

But he's not just some big oaf who's good with his dick.

He's funny. He's smarter than he lets on. He's hell on wheels.

And I like that about him more than I like that he knows what to do with that larger-than-life tool under his belt.

"Please," I snap.

He holds my gaze, a silent *thank you* that suggests he's grateful for more than just my manners.

Like he knows about the swelling and palpitating and panicking going on in my chest, and that it's okay.

I suck in the shakiest breath I've ever taken in my life and reach for the hem of my shirt.

He drops his book, strips out of his shirt, and eats the floor between us with one giant step.

And holy fucking dog.

I didn't see him the other night. I felt the stiff hairs on his chest, traced the ridges of his muscles, licked his hard nipples, but I didn't *see* him.

He's a beast.

In the best sense of the word.

Sheer strength ripples out of his every cell. Each one of his pecs is the size of a dinner plate. Veins bulge in his biceps and hands. His shoulders could've been sculpted by a master. His abs are an ode to beauty.

Even his belly button looks like it could chomp a car in half.

Not because it's big, but because it can't possibly exist on this man without being able to stand on its own against every other body part in a battle of strength.

Shut up. Belly buttons can too be strong.

He wraps one big paw behind my head, lowers his lips to crush my mouth, and not a minute too soon.

Because his tongue is an excellent distraction for all the nonsense floating through my head.

And he knows exactly how to use it.

He tastes like hamburger and mint, he smells like a freaking cotton field, and his fingers are making short work of the clasp on my bra.

Who the fuck needs bras anyway?

I unzip his pants and shove my hands into the opening, grip his hard, solid length, and he mutters a curse in my mouth.

"Man up," I tell him.

He chuckles and tweaks my nipples, and *holy sweet dog*, can he do that to my clit?

My pants go flying. He pulls a condom out of his back pocket, rolls it on, and picks me up under my butt. In two steps, I'm flat against the wall, my legs wrapped around his waist while he fills me with his thick length. *Dog*, his swollen head—the veins bulging in his cock too—the sight of him thrusting into me, drawing back, slick and coated with my moisture, and pushing in again, disappearing inside me—has me so spun up, coiled so tight and ready, that all I know is him.

Zeus.

His body.

His strength.

His personality.

His heart.

He pumps into me, holding me under the knees. I'm

spread as wide as I can go, my toes curling backwards, every thrust, every invasion sending me higher and tighter and wetter and—*oh yes there more higher harder FASTER NOW!*

I bite his shoulder to muffle my cry as I shatter from the inside out. He thrusts twice more, groans in the back of his throat, and goes still, neck straining, while we come together. I'm spasming uncontrollably around his thick cock, squeezing and coaxing that rock-hard shaft pulsing inside me.

Dog, I needed this.

Him.

"Fuck, Joey," he whispers while tension leaks out my pores, leaving me a jellyfish tacked to the wall by his massive cock. "You're fucking amazing."

My eyes drift shut and I let my head loll back. "Jupiter and I can be friends."

"Jupiter doesn't let anyone else near his pussy," he growls.

I wave a hand. At least, I think I do. Hard to tell if my bones are working. "Don't tell him I said this," I slur like I'm drunk. Possibly I'm drunk on sex. Is that a thing? If it's not a thing, it is now. My liver needs to process my sexcohol.

"Said what?" he prompts when I go silent.

Fuck, who am I?

"Finding another Jupiter would be too much work," I say.

His chest starts shaking, and my eyes fly open.

If I broke Zeus—

But he's laughing.

Shaking with silent laughter while he pulls out and sets me on unsteady feet.

"Only you, Joey Fireball," he says as he hands me my pants. "Only you."

I don't know what that means, but I hope it means he's coming back for more sex.

Because I know better than to hope for anything else.

Or even *think* about anything else.

Like my daddy always said, doesn't matter how much you love someone. You can't make them stay.

Not that I love Zeus.

He's…a friend.

I can allow that.

But love?

Never.

I'm too smart for that.

28

Zeus

I walk out of Joey's office feeling every bit the god I'm named after.

I rocked her fucking world. We're going out for burgers soon as she's done for the day. And then she says she's gonna whoop my ass in foosball.

She was smiling when she said it too. A full-blown, sparkly-eyed smile that she topped with a smack to my ass.

Best. Day. Ever.

That cloud nine place people talk about? I'm there.

Which is why I don't see the ambush coming.

Something clinks around my wrist, pain shoots through my left elbow, and before I can spin, there's a stick or a broom or something sweeping under my feet.

I don't go down, but suddenly both my wrists are trapped behind my back and I'm shoved sideways. I'm about to fight back when a blonde bombshell dangles something in front of my face.

Fucking spider. A fucking *spider*.

It's not real. It's hairy and thick and horrifying, but it's not real, because it can't—*fuck fuck fuck, it's moving*.

I shriek like a teenage girl meeting Justin Bieber, except terrified, and suddenly I'm trapped in a room that smells like bad whisky with shelves of torture devices lining the walls.

I can fucking break these handcuffs in two, except the spider's still there.

It's moving.

Four fucking inches from my face.

My head's swimming. My pits are raining sweat like a hurricane. I'm having a heart attack.

I'm having a fucking heart attack.

Breathe, big guy. Breathe. You can eat it—fuck. *Fuck*.

I'm not putting something that makes ass yarn in my mouth. It probably wove its fucking coat out of ass yarn. It'd keep spinning its ass yarn around my tongue and suck all the blood out and—*fuck fuck fuck*.

"What are your intentions toward my sister?" a familiar voice demands.

I swallow, and half my tongue gets caught in my windpipe.

That's it. I'm done for. I'm gonna fucking die of archo—araka—arachnafuckingscaryspiderfear.

"Yell all you want, sugar-pie," the blonde adds. "She can't hear you from this side of the building."

"Put the spider away, Peach," Gracie says. "We can't get

answers out of him while he's foaming at the mouth like that."

I can do this.

I can be bigger than the fucking spider.

Air. Lungs. Nose.

Fuck, I'm gonna breathe in spider cooties.

"Fine." The blonde flips the spider over, rubs its belly, and plops it on a shelf. The red glow in its eye sockets fades to black.

Fuck.

It's a fucking fake spider. A hairy-ass battery-operated fake moforantula.

And it's still fucking staring at me.

Be cool, I hear Ares saying. *You could crush its batteries with your ass.*

I picture him taking a sledgehammer to the beast, and my lungs start working again. I snap the handcuffs apart and contemplate grabbing each of the women by the throat, except I don't hurt women, even crazy-ass lady dicks who threaten me with spiders.

I clench my fists and growl.

They share a look, and both scrunch up their mouths like they're trying not to giggle.

Fucking women.

Gracie straightens first. "Peach, meet Zeus. Zeus, meet Peach. If you hurt my sister, that spider's just a hint of what's coming next."

"I'm not going to fucking hurt your sister."

"So what do you want with our Joey?" Peach demands.

I pinch my lips together, because I barely know what I want.

Those feelings that started in Copper Valley? Yeah. They're still there. And they're stronger. I look at her, I hear her voice, I touch her, and *boom*.

She's everything I never thought I could have. Everything I never thought *existed*. Strong enough to put up with my shit. Smart enough to challenge me. And I'd never make the mistake of calling her soft, but she is where it matters.

She's in my head. She's in my blood. She's in my heart.

Gracie takes two menacing steps toward me until she's close enough to threaten my breastbone. She has to crane her neck to glare up at me. "She's not nearly as tough as she acts," she says, and fuck if fear doesn't slink down my spine.

What if I can't handle the delicate stuff?

The world's seen me and Ares as nothing more than two big brutes for too long for me to ever discount another human being having feelings. World sees Joey as a big pilot badass, but she's more.

Yeah, we both have feelings.

Just not a lot of practice with letting them show.

"Nobody's ever as tough as they act," I say to Gracie. I turn a glower to Joey's business partner. "Leave the fucking spiders out of it next time."

Before either of them can get to me any more, I turn and leave.

And I don't slam the door behind me. Or tear it off its hinges.

Turns out, sometimes being quiet makes the biggest point.

I step into the hall and almost run over Joey.

She glances at the closet.

Back to me.

She doesn't say a word, but she grips me by the hair of the troll on my shirt, yanks me down, and kisses me like I'm a fucking god.

Yeah.

Me and Joey?

We're gonna be just fine.

29

Zeus

For the first time in my life, I fucking hate training camp.

Before training camp? Time to see Joey at least three times a week.

During training camp? No Joey.

Fucking training camp.

Drills. Weight training. Scrimmage. Prep for press shit. Team meetings. Bullshitting.

Ares is doing the same in Copper Valley. Last-minute trade between Chicago and the Thrusters. Still not sure he's getting a good enough deal, but he says he likes the change.

After ten years in the NHL, we know most of the guys in the league. Always a few rookies, sometimes fresh blood from overseas, like Manning. Ares will be fine. He makes friends better than I do.

Probably because he doesn't run his trap and he's fucking gold on the ice. One-on-one, he kicks my ass every time.

Still shitty that he's so far from home. Chicago was a short drive back to Minnesota. Virginia, not so much.

If Nashville traded me anywhere, I wouldn't be close enough to drive to see Joey while I'm home.

And the fact that I'm more worried about seeing Joey than I am about my performance during scrimmage today is a problem.

I bang into my condo just after eight.

I don't want to be in my condo. I don't want to be getting shit for letting Giovanni through six times. I don't want to order a pizza and eat it by myself. I want—

"You know security in this building is shit when *I* can use my feminine wiles to get through it."

I want the hot pilot chick sprawled out on my sectional in athletic shorts and a sloppy T-shirt, flipping through my *Sports Illustrated*.

My dick sprouts into a redwood, my cheeks split in a grin, and I drop my bag on the big decorative vase of sticks my mom and sister insisted I needed for *décor* to *detract from the way this place looks like a college frat house.*

Neither me nor Joey pay attention when the weird-ass thing clinks and spills its load.

"You got feminine wiles coming out your ass," I tell her while I stalk the short distance across the scarred wood floor to the sectional.

She cracks a smile, and I high-five my smooth-talking skills. "Must be," she says dryly. She waves the magazine at me. "According to this, you're going to have a shitty year."

"It can eat my dick."

She lifts a brow. A silent *have you ever jacked off with a* Sports Illustrated *wrapped around your dick?*

I grin.

She laughs and throws it at me. "You are such a guy."

I bend down and lick her neck. "Mmm. Bacon."

She grips my hair and holds my head in place so I can lick and suck and nip at her skin.

"I missed you," she whispers in a small voice.

Not my cock swelling now.

No, that's all my heart. Puffing up and sauntering and shaking its dick at my dick, yelling *Suck this, she likes me too*.

Yeah, my heart's such a guy. You got a problem with that?

I know Joey.

And I know those three words cost her more than she'll ever admit. The fact that she confessed them to me?

That's the same as another woman saying *I love you*.

I toss her over my shoulder, because I can already feel her retreating from the emotions, and I'd rather have her here with me than making an excuse to leave.

"Not as much as I missed you," I say while she squirms and protests and takes advantage of the opportunity to hit my secret ticklish spot on the back of my ribs.

By the time I throw her down on my monster-size bed, we're both laughing and squirming like two normal people in movies. Like I'm not some giant freak of nature and she hasn't taught herself to be such a badass so no one ever knows how much it scarred her when her mom left.

So she never hurts like that again.

I might be an ogre, but I pick up on shit. Even when it's two whispered sentences on a blanket under the stars.

I'm also hell with blackmail when I need to be, and I know who Gracie's been texting with, and for some unknown reason, Gracie trusts me.

That, or she's spilling Joey's secrets all over the countryside, in which case I might have to pull out some of my old tricks that I used to use on Ambrosia to get her to leave my shit alone.

"Holy hell, this bed is like a cloud." Joey moves her arms and legs like she's making a snow angel on the moose-emblazoned mega-quilt my granny made when I was in high school.

I take advantage of the situation to settle between her legs with my dick poking her sweet spot. *Fuck*, she feels good.

All of her.

The press of her boobs against my chest. The curve of solid, lean muscle in her arms and shoulders. The strength in her legs.

The softness of her skin. Her silky hair.

There's never been a woman more perfect. And she's pulling me in for a kiss that would make fucking Cupid himself weep.

This kissing shit?

It's making me hard as steel in the cock area, tight as cookies and chocolate chips in the balls, and mushy as cheese curds in the chest.

I reach under her shirt to fondle her boob and do that trick where I tease one nipple with my thumb while my pinky tickles the other. She gasps in my mouth, grips my hips like she's that Bond chick who strangles people with her legs, rocks against my cock, and—

"Fuck." Fuck fuck fuck.

Not again.

I leap off the bed.

Or try.

You ever try leaping when your cock's fucking spurting dick juice up your pants?

I didn't fucking think so.

This woman.

Fuck.

I barrel into my bathroom, fisting my hair in my hands.

I blew it on the ice.

Now I blew it in the bedroom.

I slam the door, lock it, strip, and glare at Jupiter in the mirror.

What the FUCK, dude?

He shrugs as he deflates. *She's the dick whisperer.*

I crank the shower handle so hard it snaps off, and water shoots everywhere.

Out the handle, dribbling out the faucet, all over the walls. I dive to cover it, slip on the tile, and ram my shoulder into the shower tile like Ares fucking checked me against the boards.

Water's shooting into my palms and spraying out between my fingers. If I yank any harder, I'm pulling the whole fucking pipe out of the tile wall.

Water. Off switch. Somewhere.

Something clicks behind me.

"Oh, Zeus," Joey says on a chuckle. She slides a hand

down my soaking wet T-shirt, presses a kiss to the top of my head, and disappears.

A minute later, the water dribbles to a stop.

The good news?

I'm clean as a fucking baby.

The bad news?

I'm a fucking monster dumbass.

I drop my head against the tile wall. Joey comes back in—mental note, locks are impervious to this woman's skills—and her fingers trace down my spine. "We should get you out of this T-shirt."

Jupiter lifts an interested eye.

"Penalty box," I growl.

All he hears is *box*, and he thinks I mean Joey's.

She tugs me to my feet from behind and peels the wet fabric up and over my abs. Her hands slink over my chilled skin and drift down to grab the dick that shall not be named.

"Go easy on him," she says while she strokes him up and down, up and down, up and down. "This is a lot of sexiness for one poor Jupiter to handle."

I growl and turn in her arms, but before I can grab her, she sits her ass on my toilet, double-fists me, leans forward, and licks the tip of my cock. "Mmm," she says.

I brace my arms on the wall over her head, because what Joey wants, Joey gets. "He's been a bad boy," I rasp.

"He's good for at least two more rounds." She blows on my dick, my nerves light up, goose bumps erupt everywhere, even my ass crack, and my ego peeks out from its hiding spot.

"You're a fucking angel," I say.

She doesn't answer.

Instead, she slides my cock into her hot, silky mouth and swirls her tongue around my engorged head. She grips me by the base and fucks my dick with her mouth, in and out, swirling and sucking and licking, deeper and deeper down her throat until my nuts are about to burst and my cock's so fucking hard and thick and long it's gonna bust a vein and die of a dick aneurysm.

"Joey," I gasp.

She sucks harder, squeezes tighter, and swirls her tongue again.

I yank her off me, because fuck if I'm coming again before she's gotten hers. I rip her pants at the seam, set her on my sink, go down on my knees, push her underwear to one side, and bury my face in her pussy.

Sucking her clit. Sliding two fingers up inside her while my dick aches so hard it's bruising from the inside out. She jerks and moans, pulling my hair while I devour her until she's coming all over my fingers and screaming my name.

As soon as she slumps against me, I fumble for the box of condoms under my sink. I roll one on and heft her into my arms. She grabs my face and sticks her tongue down my throat, and *fuck*, I'm gonna come.

I tell Jupiter to hold his shit for *two more seconds*, lay her across the bed, and I slam into her pussy while we're still fucking with our mouths. I pump. She thrusts. I balance over her on my elbows, my arms tight to her sides because I need to touch her. Here. There. Everywhere.

She pinches my earlobes, and *fuck*, nerves explode all over my scalp.

I jerk inside her, she squeezes me so tight I'm never coming back out again, and the earth fucking shakes under us. We're coming together so hot and hard and fast we're making the foundation of the whole fucking world quake and tremble.

Joey's chanting my name.

I'm saying something too, but fuck if I know what it is. I just know this woman—my Joey—she's a miracle.

She's my fucking miracle.

30

Joey

THERE'S an unreal quality to Zeus when he's still. He's a slumbering mountain. Peaceful. Quiet. Almost innocent.

Nothing at all like the man who walked into a fancy golf reception dressed as an overgrown hooker troll.

I'm not sure I'll ever know that kind of peace, but I feel closer to it tonight than I ever have.

My chest is still quaking, but I refuse to give in to the fear.

He said he loved me.

I trace his cheek in the semi-darkness. It's sandpaper-rough over chiseled bone. His lips are full and deceptively soft. And I want to kiss each of the notches in his nose.

Does that mean I love him?

I don't know.

But I know if Dog himself walked into my house tomorrow and said I had to choose between never flying again and never seeing Zeus again, that fucker better be wearing a cup, because I'd be going for the family jewels.

Zeus stirs and tightens his grip on my hip. His hand is so big, his fingers cover my whole butt cheek. "Bed okay?" he murmurs.

"Perfect," I whisper.

A smile twists his lips, though he doesn't open his eyes. "That's the nicest thing you've ever said about my bed."

"Shush and go back to sleep."

"I'm glad you're here."

That's not emotion burning my eyes and stinging my nose. Nope, must be allergies.

Couldn't be feeling wanted, appreciated, *cherished* even, affecting my psyche.

He shifts, pulls me closer, and traps me with a leg across my thighs. His heart thumps in my ear, his skin warms the frost protecting my heart, and I relax into him.

"I know what you did for Bailey," I whisper. *I know what you're doing for me.*

"Hmph."

I press a kiss to his heart. The little spitfire has called a few times since the golf tournament. Once to complain that her mom was too tough. Once to ask if she could trade chores for another ride on Luna. And once yesterday morning, freaking out with excitement because a new girls' hockey league had been announced in her town.

A little digging, and it wasn't hard to figure out who was supplying the gear and making the wheels turn to get the teams going.

"You're a good man, Zeus Berger."

"I love you, Joey Fireball."

Dammit.

I open my mouth, but I can't force the words out.

"Ssh," he says. "Go to sleep."

Like it's okay.

He knows.

And he's giving me all the time I need to figure everything out.

Not helping all those emotions clogging my sinuses.

But if I'm going to cry, he's the only man in the world I'd trust to know. So I fold myself into him, hang on tight, and let go.

31

Joey

Filed under *things I never thought I'd do* is following my boyfriend's family to our seats at Bridgestone Arena to watch him play a pre-season game

There's so much nonsense in that sentence, I don't know where to start.

But I know my heart's in my throat. I know I'm terrified Zeus's parents will hate me. I know I could royally fuck things up with Chase Jett today, when he's about two steps from handing Weightless a quarter of a billion dollars.

Yeah.

More *holy shit* nonsense. I'm a kid from the sticks.

Since when is my business worth a *quarter-billion-dollar* investment? It's worth every penny, but hearing the number—just *fuck*.

I also know Zeus isn't having the best training camp of

his life.

He's off his game.

The only thing different from every other year of his hockey career?

"It's just so amazing to see Zeus so serious about someone," Ambrosia says to me as she offers me some kind of organic nut and fruit mix she pulled out of her purse while we wait for the teams to take the ice. "He sells himself short, you know? Like he lets being a big old ape define him, when we know he's more. I'm not sure he's ever been on a date with the same girl twice before you."

Me.

I'm the one thing different from every other year of his hockey career.

Music rumbles through the arena.

Zeus's family all leap to their feet.

Nashville is playing the Thrusters today, which means Zeus and Ares will both be on the ice. It's literally a family affair. With a side order from me to Zeus to knock some royal ass into the boards every chance he gets, because something's weird with Gracie, and I think I know what it is, but I haven't been able to prove it yet.

Yeah.

I'm dating a hockey player and worrying my sister's sending a prince her own special Pussookies.

My life is so weird right now.

The Thrusters roll out onto the ice. It's not as easy as I'd expect to pick out Ares when all the guys are suited up.

"He's double-zero," Ambrosia tells me. "Crazy-ass. Says it's as high as he can count."

A few fans chant *Force, Force, Force*, and he lifts a gloved hand in acknowledgment.

Zeus gave Ares my phone number right after I surprised him in his apartment a couple weeks back, and I've been getting random text messages from him with nothing but gifs. I've been answering back in emojis, and I think we're beginning to understand each other.

He's actually pretty funny. The gif with faces painted on someone's butt cheeks, so they kiss when the cheeks clenched—I laughed so hard Peach came running. I'm hoping that wasn't a self-made gif.

I'm also hoping his texts mean he likes me. Or at least doesn't disapprove.

Not for my sake.

For Zeus's sake.

He's so much more than the world gives him credit for, and the only people who seem to see it is his family. He needs them.

Me?

I'm optional.

I squelch the shiver in my chest as the introductions for the home team start. When Zeus takes the ice, he circles it while the crowd roars. *The Brute*, they call him.

On the ice?

Yeah.

Off the ice?

He's a teddy bear.

With a big mouth, a brilliant mind for attention-grabbing pranks, and the occasional accident that requires a bathroom remodel, but no one's perfect.

Zeus stops at the Thrusters' bench and shares a fist bump with Ares.

"They'll pretend to beat the shit out of each other at some point before the game's over," Ambrosia tells me.

"No rubber chickens?"

She laughs. "Never know what Ares has down his pants."

"Didn't need that visual," Chase tells her.

Zeus doesn't play in the first period, but he comes flying off the bench as soon as the second period starts. He's a defender, but he's in the thick of things everywhere. I know there's some sense to where everyone is, and I'm watching numbers and checking the program to understand positions and plays and theory. Ares is a power forward—he already scored once in the first period, and when he makes a mad dash up the middle with the puck, my heart almost stops.

Because Zeus is charging him.

And if these two collide, I swear to dog the force will probably make the roof shake.

At the last second, Ares swerves, shoves the puck between Zeus's legs, grabs it on the other side, and slams it past the goalie.

"Holy fuck," Chase says while Ambrosia and their parents scream along with half the rest of the arena.

Zeus scowls at Ares.

Ares grins and takes a fist bump from Manning.

"Zeus'll get him back," Ambrosia says.

Not anytime soon. He's heading back to the bench.

A woman behind us leans forward. "Ohmygod, are you the Brute's girlfriend?"

So fucking weird. "Yes."

"Does he really make weird monkey calls when he... you know..."

Ambrosia chokes on her dried fruit and nuts.

I shift in my seat and look at the woman asking. She's around fifty, draped in a Nashville jersey, with librarian glasses perched on her nose, an oversized locket around her neck, and a wedding ring on her left finger. And she's watching me expectantly like she wants a play-by-play of my sex life.

"Did you see the video we made?" I ask.

And now Ambrosia's possibly dying.

The woman's blue eyes go so round they could double as hockey pucks. She digs her phone out of her pocket like she's going to look it up right now. "No."

"That's because there isn't one. It's none of your fucking business."

She sniffs as I turn back to face forward. "His other puck bunnies say he does."

Mrs. Berger stands now.

Neither Mr. nor Mrs. Berger are anywhere near as tall as their sons, but she's mildly terrifying. "Are you badmouthing my firstborn?" she demands.

"I—"

"Do you want me to ask about *your* children's night-night lives?"

Chase is ducking his head, shoulders shaking while he bangs on Ambrosia's back. She's spewing fruit chunks all over the cowboy hat on the guy in front of her.

"My—" the woman starts.

"If you don't stop being vulgar, I'll have security escort

you out. And by *security*, I mean my son's girlfriend. She's a lean, mean, airplane-flying machine, and none of us need your baloney. Is that understood?"

"I have to go to the bathroom," the woman says.

Mrs. Berger leans over and holds out a fist. "Well-handled, Joey. I like you."

I bump, and I'm pretty sure we just bonded.

Zeus is watching us from the bench, which is just a few rows down. He's got an intense game face on, but when his gaze locks with mine, something warm flickers in his eyes.

Can't take you anywhere, Fireball.

I blow him a kiss.

His eyes widen—*Who the fuck are you, and what did you do with my girlfriend?*—and I smirk.

Go kick some ass, I telegraph.

Five minutes later, he's back in the game. And when I say *back in the game*, I mean he's fucking back in the game.

He's flying over the ice. Stealing the puck. Slamming Ares into the boards. Fighting with Manning.

Earning himself a penalty.

While Zeus takes himself into the penalty box, Manning pulls his helmet off, grins, and salutes me.

I can't decide if I like him or hate him.

It's like he caught a cheerful rash and just can't shake it. Even bleeding from the nose.

Like he's not royalty at all, but just some guy who loves hockey and happiness.

Add that to the list of things that I never thought I'd encounter in my life.

If he has something going on with my sister, I'm going to have to kill him.

Not because that security check I blackmailed an old friend into running didn't check out—it did, and he's clean as a royal whistle. But because he's only here for a year. Then it's back to his home country. To his duties and responsibilities.

And Gracie's not moving overseas.

She can't.

She can't leave me any more than I can leave her.

Which means the only thing she'd get from Manning is heartbreak. And I don't know if I can live through that either.

Gracie isn't allowed to hurt.

Ever.

Nashville keeps the Thrusters from scoring again while Zeus is in time-out. When he breaks out of the box, there's something charged about him.

And I'm not surprised when he steals the puck and takes off on his own down the ice. Charging the goal. The defenders try to stop him, but you can't stop a bull train on skates.

You just can't.

Physics says so.

He's about to crash into the goal when he swerves, swings around the back of it, and taps the puck into the net from the other side.

I'm on my feet cheering. Fists in the air. Feet not even touching the ground.

Dog, he needed that.

He rolls over the wall to climb back onto the bench while a fresh string takes over.

Once again, his gaze locks with mine.

This time, he blows the kiss.

And for the first time in my adult life, I go red.

He notices.

I can tell by his *gotcha back* smirk.

32

Zeus

IF I HAVE TO LOSE, might as well lose to Ares. I can deal with that.

After the game, I get cleaned up, grab my twin, and head back to my place where Joey and the rest of the family are already waiting.

It's family dinner.

A late-ass family dinner, but still a family dinner.

There are ten pizzas on the island between my kitchen and living room. Somebody stacked all my magazines—probably my mom—and somebody else put all the clocks on the right time—probably my dad.

He's the reason we all have months as our middle names. Don't ask.

I squeeze Joey's ass on my way to the pizza. "Good game," I tell her.

"I think you mistook me for your brother," she says.

We both look at Ares, in a purple shirt printed with some red penis rocks and *Second Place Is For Lovers* scrawled over his chest.

"Yeah," I say to Joey. "I can't keep you two straight."

"Explains that kiss on the ice."

"I really like her," Ambrosia declares.

"She's very eloquent," Mom chimes in.

Dad hides behind a paper he must've brought with him. Dude's outmatched and he knows it. But don't challenge him to Cards Against Humanity.

Just don't.

"Did I hear you're remodeling your bathroom?" Ambrosia asks.

"Had a leak."

"Again?"

Before I can tell my sister to fuck off, Joey's phone dings. She glances at it—if it's Gracie, she'll text back. If it's anyone else, she'll put it away.

She doesn't do either.

No, she cracks a grin so big I half expect her cheeks to split to her ears. "You're just screwing with me now, aren't you?" she says to Ares.

He twitches a single eyebrow and digs into the top pizza box.

And leaps back. "*Shit.*"

His phone dings.

He eyes Joey, pulls out the phone, and makes his *that's disgusting* face.

In case you're wondering, yeah, actually, it does take a

fucking pile of disgusting to get any of us to make that face.

Joey takes the top pizza. "Anyone else want jalapenos? No? Just me? Damn. Guess I'll have to eat the whole thing."

This woman was fucking *made* for me.

"What'd she send you?" I ask Ares.

He flips his phone over to show me.

There's a gif from him with—I'm going to fucking kill him. That's me. It's a gif of me falling on my face on the ice during the play-offs last year.

She replied with a spinning jar of—oh, fuck. That *is* disgusting. Who'd put jalapenos in ketchup?

"You're fucking amazing," I tell her reverently.

She shoves half a slice of pizza in her mouth. Pizza with all kinds of green shit mixed in with the meat.

"And there's no fucking way I'm kissing you the rest of the night."

"Your loss," she says around a mouthful of food.

I fucking love this woman.

My mother's practically in tears. "I'm so happy for you, honey," she sniffles to me.

Ambrosia rolls her eyes. "Congrats, asshole. All I got when I fell in love was a warning about getting arrested again."

Dad smothers a snort behind his newspaper.

The rest of the pizzas are sausage or plain cheese, and we clean the shit out of those boxes. Once everyone else is so stuffed they can't move, all sprawled out on my sectional, I pull out my frozen cookie dough balls.

Yeah, *balls*. Heh. And I fucking made them myself. Secret family recipe.

"Six or eight?" I ask Ares.

He flashes two fingers, so I pluck out eight for each of us. He balances a dough ball on his nose. I snap a picture, set two in my eyeballs, and let him take a picture of me.

Season's starting.

World's got expectations.

He smushes six of his balls into a log, presses the two remaining balls to the top, and puts his cookie junk sculpture where it counts.

Yeah, that one's going in Mom's annual Christmas picture book.

So's the one of me that looks like I'm shitting cookie dough across my counter.

"They were…interesting as children," Mom says to Joey.

My mom? Instant pass to heaven.

"They still are," Joey says. She's been checking her phone every forty seconds. "Where's his royal smiley ass?" she asks Ares.

He shrugs.

She pins him with a look that would make one or two of the rookies on my team cry, and they're still fucking hard-ass hockey players.

He grins.

She makes a complicated hand gesture that looks like she's asking for six fish to be delivered to the top of the water tower at midnight if he ever wants to see his chicken again.

Ares goes pale.

What the *fuck*?

Joey tilts her head and crosses her arms.

"Went out for cookies," Ares says.

"*Fuck*," she mutters.

"Break his dick?" Ares offers. He makes a hand gesture we all know that leaves me and Chase wincing, Mom crossing herself even though we're not Catholic, and Ambrosia rolling with laughter.

Pretty sure Dad's asleep behind his newspaper.

Joey sighs. There's defeat darkening her eyes, which is a pretty fucking bad sign. She's not saying anything out loud—not even looking at any of us—but it's not hard to see what's going on in her brain.

She's worried. Knows Gracie's a grown-up. Can't let go.

Because Gracie's *hers*.

Joey takes care of what's hers. I don't know her middle name—fuck, I barely figured out *Joey*'s short for *Josephine* until a week ago—but it's probably something like Loyal or Dependable or Don't Fucking Mess With My People.

"Wanna go find him?" I ask.

Yes, her eyes say. "She's a big girl."

"I'm sorry, did you just say Prince Manning is a girl?" Mom rubs her temples. "Men fornicating with pigs, my daughter in the slammer, and my sons beating up a bisexual hockey player. This year is going to heck in a handbasket…"

"He asked for it," I say. "Said Ares wasn't pretty enough for him."

Ares grunts.

Ambrosia cracks up again, Chase smiles one of those sappy lover smiles at her, and I suddenly want everyone to get the fuck out of my apartment.

Because I hit the road with the team in a week. I'm out of town two days this week for pre-season games already.

Even less time with Joey while Mom and Dad go home together, Chase and my sister go home together, and me and Ares dig into the grind of the show.

He meets my eyes and nods. "Bedtime."

Way more going on upstairs than people give that fucker credit for.

He pats Joey on the head, slugs Chase in the arm, noogies Ambrosia, and points to the door.

I miss that fucker during the season.

"You two disturb me," Ambrosia says as she climbs to her feet.

"You two too," Ares replies.

I snicker.

Joey snorts but tries to stifle it. And fails.

She's so fucking *everything* when she smiles.

Pretty isn't the right word for it, because Joey isn't *pretty*. She's a fucking wonder woman.

Mom hugs her. Don't know if anyone else notices, but Joey's eyes go shiny and she visibly swallows. Dad hugs her too, and now it's time for everyone to get the fuck out, because I think my girl's gonna lose it.

And I'm not having anyone see.

Ares notices though.

He notices everything.

He snags Chase by the collar and lifts him out of the chair, gives Ambrosia the *you're next if you don't hurry your ass up* look, and hustles everyone out the door.

"Getting old, Ares," Chase says affectionately.

"Fucker," Ares replies as I shut the door behind them.

Joey's disappeared.

I find her taking deep, controlled breaths in the middle of my bed. Her knees are pulled up to her chin and she's focusing on something on my wall.

Meatball stain?

Probably.

I climb onto the bed behind her and dig my thumbs into the hard knots in her shoulders. Been a long day. Sucky game. Normal night after a game, I'd be about to crash on my face about now.

But I don't give two shits about me. Or the game. Or anything else.

"We all got your back," I say to Joey.

"Why do you put up with me?" she whispers.

"You see me."

Her shoulders loosen, and she leans back into me. "Everyone leaves."

"Not everyone."

She twists and looks up at me. Not *at* me. *Into* me. *God*, her eyes. There's a whole galaxy in there. Strength and fears, balls and brains. "You won't leave?"

"Will you?"

Her jaw tightens. I hit a nerve.

"I don't fucking walk out on the people I…care about."

I want to tell her the same, but she knows about the ten years Ares and I cut Chase out of our lives for screwing Ambrosia and getting her arrested. She knows it's only been the last six months that I've seen my sister regularly again, even though I missed her ugly face a little more than I missed Chase.

Words don't mean shit.

Action is what talks.

"You know why I fucked around so much every season?"

"Because that dick is a terrible thing to waste?"

Yeah, I get it. Easier to not talk about it. Fuck, I hate talking too. Not like Ares does, but I'm still a dude. *No talk* is in our DNA.

"Because I'm a fucking monster who's too big, too loud, and too much of a freak to find forever outside of a circus or a zoo. Chicks don't want me for this." I tap my head. "Or this." I tap my heart. "But you're in both. To stay. I know what it's like to stare down a lonely forever. *You* know what it's like. I don't want a lonely forever. I don't want *you* to have a lonely forever. Not when we can have each other."

She studies me, those dark eyes taking everything in, weighing me, measuring me, deciding if I'm worthy.

And I'm fucking holding my breath, because if I'm falling short anywhere—and fuck, I've fallen short *everywhere* with Joey—she's gone.

She strokes my cheek. "You're not a monster."

My chest is swelling. Both because my monster heart's getting bigger with every nugget of affection, and because it's all hers.

Every bit of it.

"You might be the only woman in the world who sees through me," I tell her honestly.

A frown creases her dark brow. "Am I the reason you're struggling on the ice?" she whispers.

What? Where the hell did *that* come from? I'm shaking my head before I can find my voice. "No. No way."

Even showing her vulnerable side, she can call bullshit with those eyes. "Are you sure?"

"I'm fucking sure." I squeeze my eyes shut. Not because I'm avoiding the silent inquisition—she's fucking good at asking questions with those hypnotic eyes—but because it's torture to say it out loud. "I blew it in the play-offs last year. Tripped over my own two feet, took out two of my own guys, and we lost."

Ares sent her the fucking gif.

Probably because he knew she needed to know, and he knew I don't talk about it.

She's quiet until I meet her intense gaze again. "That was last year. Let it go."

Just like that.

No bullshit. Let it go.

She could do it.

I should fucking do it too.

I roll us so I'm pinning her to the bed. Her legs go around my waist, her fingertips go to my face, and I dip my head to kiss her.

I love this woman.

And I know she loves me.

I don't care if she never says the words. She doesn't have to. It's in her touch. It's in her kiss.

It's in the way she comes to see me, sends me text messages, and calls to ask how practice went.

Joey doesn't bullshit around. She doesn't stroke egos. She doesn't waste time with shit that isn't important.

She's here because she cares.

It's my job to make sure she knows that's all I need.

33

Joey

"There's something different about you."

I look up from the notes on my flight brief this afternoon—our last day of being just two chicks with a flight adventure company before Zeus's best friend invests a shitload of cash into setting us on a path to the moon—to find Peach leaning in my doorway. "There's nothing different with me. How's Meemaw?"

"Flirting up a storm with the hot manny we hired to keep her in line. And you're smiling."

"No, I'm not."

"Yes, you are."

"No, I'm—"

She holds her cell phone on selfie mode to my face, and I gasp.

Fuck.

I'm smiling.

And I'm—*dammit*. I'm fucking pretty when I smile. Like Gracie. Eyes all sparkly, cheeks flushed, even my lips are rosy.

I try to scowl, and now I look like I'm a sex kitten inviting the entire hockey team to come over to my place for cupcakes.

Yeah, *that* kind of cupcakes.

Because I'm not smiling over a business deal. I'm smiling with fucking *hearts* in my eyes. And now my nipples are popping lady boners.

Fuck.

I push Peach's phone back at her. "Stop it. You're freaking me out."

"Joey, my dear, you're in love."

I'm aware. And it's fucking terrifying. "I said stop freaking me out."

"Why do you think I waited until *after* your flight?" She plops onto the corner of my desk, bending her knee so her whole left leg is crushing my paperwork. Only her foot dangles over the edge. "Deep breaths, sugar-pie. This is gonna be okay."

"I'm not hyperventilating."

"On the outside."

Some days I hate my business partner.

"You tell him yet?" she asks.

"No."

"*Joey.*"

I know. *I know.* He's told me he loves me dozens of times. Over me plowing through a carton of Ben & Jerry's. When I bent over and gave him a view of my ass while we were goofing off in the gym in his building. When we're falling asleep after one of the rarer and rarer nights that one of us sleeps at the other's place, because he's up to his eyeballs in hockey shit and the work keeps piling on here too as we get ready to take Chase on as a mostly silent partner.

But I haven't told Zeus I feel the same. Because once it's there, you can't take it back.

The more you love someone, the more it hurts when they leave.

I press my palms into my eyes. "Regular season starts in a week." I barely recognize my own voice. "We're about to be pulling eighteen-hour days here, and he'll be traveling the country until at least April. Maybe June if the season goes really well."

And I'm terrified.

I fucking hate being terrified. I don't know myself when I'm terrified. I'm a badass. I was the mother my sister didn't have. Served my years in the military. Defy gravity every single week.

And I can't say three little words to a man who's constantly on my mind and has been since the moment he walked into that clubhouse.

Because what if he ever stops loving me back?

"No risk, no reward," Peach says softly. "And, honey, love's the biggest reward there is. Finding your person? That one in a billion who makes it okay for you to be you? If he didn't walk away when me and Gracie kidnapped him with a battery-operated tarantula, you really think him being on the road is gonna change his mind about how he feels?"

I drop my hands and stare at my business partner,

suddenly contemplating murder. "You kidnapped him *with a fake spider?*"

She doesn't scoot her butt off my desk, cower in fear, or show the barest hint of remorse. No, she grins.

She fucking *grins*. "He should really talk to someone about that arachnophobia."

"You have two seconds to get the fuck out of my office before I rack you in the lady balls."

"See? You're still Joey, even when you're in love." She slides off my desk and steps out of arm's reach. Out of leg's reach, and out of my leaping range too. And don't think I can't fucking leap all the way to the door from this desk if I want to. "And you know what happens if he breaks your heart?"

Fuck.

The thought makes my chest squeeze so bad my lungs go inside out.

"You heal, Joey. You remember the good times. You move on." She pauses in the hallway. "And we break his kneecaps after we plant spider eggs in his bedroom."

I stand.

We're signing paperwork with Chase Jett tomorrow. We have forty billion things to do to get ready to take over the world.

And Peach is right.

She's fucking right.

I love Zeus Berger. And if anyone deserves to know he's loved, it's a man with a heart the size of the moon overlooked by the world as a big ol' hockey-playing dumbass.

I can do love.

I can fucking do love like nobody's ever done love before.

I'm going to own the shit out of doing love.

"Going somewhere?" Peach asks.

"Shut up and go get your work done."

She's grinning again. Just like fucking Manning. "You're lucky I—"

I stop in my tracks.

Peach is my sister from another mister. My best friend. One of only two—three—people in the world who know me well enough to understand what a big deal love is.

"I love you, Peach."

She blinks at me, and her eyes go shiny. "Shit, Joey." She tackles me in a hug. "Took you damn long enough, you hard ass. Make sure you're back before the lawyers get here, because you know what I'll do if I have to entertain those boys myself."

"I'll be here." But first, I'm going to go get my man.

34

Zeus

I HANG up my phone and stare at it, like the call I just got from my agent is going to change if I stare long enough.

But it's not.

The world's spinning. I'm hunched on my sectional, knees wobbling, lungs heaving for air.

Two months ago, this would've been fine.

Two months ago, I would've been pissed. Both at the my team and at myself, because I know this is my fault.

I fucked up the play-offs. I'm fucking up training camp —even though I'm getting better this week—but it's still my fault.

Now I'm paying for it.

New York's better than Vancouver, but *fuck*.

I can't drive to Huntsville on an off-day from New York.

A key in my door startles me. I bolt upright, bang my

shins on the coffee table, and I'm cussing a blue streak when Joey pops her head in. "Hey." She's smiling, but the way she shifts on her feet like she's nervous sends a mix of *not good* roiling through my pulse. "Bad time?"

They traded me to the Rangers.

They traded me to the Rangers, and I don't know when the fuck I'm going to get to see Joey enough.

Fuck, I just had my bathroom redone. I don't want to move.

Tomorrow.

Fuck.

"Get your ass in here and kiss my booboos," I tell her.

Get in here and tell me we can work this out.

Her smile fades. "You okay?"

"Didn't know you were coming. Only have a couple pounds of beef thawed."

Shut up. The way we eat, it's a legit problem. Fuck, what am I going to do with all the shit in my fridge? They're expecting me in New York in twelve hours.

"I'll order something," she says.

Because that's Joey.

Solving problems.

I sink back on the couch.

Joey can solve this.

Please, Joey. Please solve this.

She crosses the floor, phone in hand, but she's not looking at it. "Zeus? What's going on?"

I grab her and pull her into my lap. Jupiter leaps to attention. She trails her fingers down the back of my neck, scratching lightly the way she knows I love.

"Bad day?" she asks.

I don't want to say it. Saying it makes it real. I bury my head against her shoulder and breathe. She's got this crazy cool scent—like flowers and hot dogs and a hint of jet fuel—and I need it.

"Got traded to the Rangers," I confess to the cotton of her Weightless T-shirt.

Fuck.

I know it's business. It's the game. But it still stings like being kicked out of your own family. I've been in Nashville for six years. I fucking picked *them* when I was a free agent.

"You…" Joey's fingers stop. Her whole heart stops. I can fucking hear it, and it's not beating. "When?" she whispers.

"Report tomorrow."

Her entire body goes rigid.

Not the good, *I'm having my brains fucked out and I'm going to come so hard the fucking moon feels it* rigid. That was last weekend.

This?

This is *No* stiff. This is *this isn't happening* stiff.

"Joey—"

"Good," she says. "New coaches. A fresh start. The change will be good."

Her voice cracks on the last word. My soul cracks along with it.

"I'm still fucking coming to see you on my days off." I'm not going to cry.

Zeus Berger doesn't fucking *cry*.

She squirms like she wants off my lap. I don't want to let her go. I don't ever want to let her go. "You'll need a new apartment up there, won't you? Can you live near your sister? And Chase? That'll be nice. Being near family."

"Joey—"

She twists out of my arms. "Do you need to pack? Is this normal? Overnight notice?"

My phone rings. Of course it does, because if I know, half the world knows. I'm fucking lucky I heard from my agent and not through *SportsCenter* like some dudes do. I throw it against the wall and stand, hitting my fucking shins on the fucking coffee table again. "Joey."

She turns and looks at me, and I swear to Gretzky I'm staring at a ghost. All the light's gone from her eyes. The fight's gone with it. Her spirit. Her drive.

She's a shell of her normal badass.

"This is life, right?" she says. "I need to get back. We're signing…shit…in the morning."

My phone rings again, a crooked, sad, off-key ring that suggests it's about as dead as the muscle in my chest is threatening to be. "Joey—"

"Good luck, Zeus. You're gonna do great."

Her voice is cracking again. She darts out the door like her pants are on fire. I charge after her, because *fuck*, we're working this out, but she's not waiting at the elevator, and when I yank on the doorknob to the stairwell, the fucking thing breaks off in my palm, because I'm not *normal*.

I drop my head to the door.

Two months ago, she would've been right.

A trade was a good thing. New coaches. New ice. New rhythms.

A fresh start.

Except I found my fresh start in a clubhouse on a golf course in the shadow of the Blue Ridge Mountains a little over a month ago.

And she talks tough. She walks tough. She acts tough.

But Joey?

She's not tough.

She needs to be loved just as much as I do.

And I'm not gonna be here to do it.

35

Joey

WHEN MY DADDY DIED, I refused to cry.

He'd been sick for so long. Hurting. In so much pain. Death was a relief.

I told myself it was for the best.

What would've been *for the best* is if he could've gotten better.

He lived a hard life, and he died a hard death. He knew Gracie and I loved him. He knew I'd take care of her after he was gone.

I told myself he didn't need my tears. That I'd already grieved while I watched him wither away and there was no fucking point to letting my weak side show.

I should've cried.

He was my daddy. He stayed when my mother didn't. He deserved my tears. He deserved to be mourned.

But I refused, because I didn't want to be weak.

Like feelings make you weak.

They don't.

They make you human.

I've spent a lot of years being really bad at being human.

But today? Today, I'm embracing the shit out of being human. I'm angry. I'm sad. I'm *lonely*.

I'm so fucking disappointed in myself.

"Joey, hon, you need to pull your shit together," Peach whispers to me as I trudge beside her on the way to our conference room where a buttload of lawyers are waiting with Chase Jett. Zeus's best friend. The man who probably knows Zeus is moving *today* to be closer to him and Ambrosia, and who will probably get to have dinner with him like a normal fucking friend four times a week, even during the season.

I hate Chase Jett right now. And he's about to invest a metric ass-ton of money in my business baby.

"Either that, or we need you puking your guts out loud enough for the whole building to hear," Peach continues. "I slip you the papers under the door, we'll blow sanitizer on them once you shove them back, and nobody will be the wiser."

"I'm fine," I lie.

And we both know it's a lie.

I'm not fine. I'm puffy-eyed and my throat hurts like a bitch and my nose has been running so bad my snot's making the skin on my upper lip melt.

I have acid snot.

Because I'm in love with a man who's moving hundreds of miles away.

I keep telling myself I didn't actually break up with him. That he didn't say he wants to break up with me. That I'm a strong, kick-ass pilot whose world doesn't revolve around a man.

None of it helps. Because my life doesn't revolve around Zeus, but it's sure as hell been fucking amazing for having been enhanced by him. Am I really going to fall apart?

No.

But I'll miss him. I'll fucking *miss* him.

You have any idea how big of a hole Zeus can leave in someone's heart?

It's about Zeus Berger-sized.

My heart had to stretch to fit him, and now it's deflating on itself because of fucking *fear*.

All the sports channels are talking about how this is a great opportunity for him. Best coaches for his playing style. A chance to really break out. Continue his career for another four, five, eight years.

And he should. He *fits* on the ice. Playing hockey is what he was born to do.

Much like flying is what I was born to do.

Peach pushes me into the bathroom and takes a wet paper towel to my face. "We'll tell them you took some jet fuel to the eyeballs," she says.

"Jett's never going to buy that. He thinks I swallow jet fuel just to fart fire out my ass."

"Honey, don't say that in the meeting. Just keep your mouth shut and sign where the lawyers point."

There's a quarter of a billion dollars on the line this morning.

She's right.

I need to get my shit together.

We walk out of the bathroom, and *shit*.

Gracie's here. Grinning and walking in place with a huge-ass platter of cookies. "I brought..." she trails off as she takes me in, and she immediately looks to Peach.

"She swallowed some jet fuel," Peach lies.

"I'm fine," I tell Gracie. "Love the cookies. They're..."

They're a perfect celebration for what we're about to do. She baked her signature sugar cookies and slapped that printed frosting on top of every one. They're adorned with stars and planets and—*fuck*.

She even has Jupiter and Jupiter's moons. I named Zeus's nuts Europa and Ganymede not four days ago, and he asked if *Ganymede* was some kind of code name for me giving his balls a disease.

Dammit, now I'm acid-snotting again.

"Joey." Gracie shoves the cookies at my partner and smothers me in a hug that smells like sugar and squeezes all squishy and soft and motherly except the part where she's still walking in place to beat Peach with their stupid fitness trackers. "It's not weak to love somebody. It takes fucking *balls*. If anyone can make this work, you can."

"I don't—" I start, but I can't lie and say I don't love him.

Not to Gracie.

"Shh," she says. "Let go and live a little. He's *good* for you."

I don't know how or why, but Gracie knows. She gets it. Maybe Peach is giving her some kind of signal behind my back. Maybe Gracie saw the news.

Or maybe Gracie loves me enough to know me better than anyone, and it's her turn to play Mom.

"I'm scared," I whisper.

"Then pull a Joey and kick the fear's ass," she whispers back. Her shoulder bumps my ear while she continues to walk in place, and if normal wasn't so comforting right now, I'd steal both their fitness trackers and mail them to Ares for him to eat.

I order my emotions to get the fuck out of my way.

I have business to get to, and then I have to...*fuck* again.

I don't know what.

But thirty seconds later, when we walk into that meeting room, my heart swells like it got stung by a monster wasp and my whole chest cracks in two.

Jett's wearing his growly face. The lawyers all look like they've got rotten eggs shoved up their asses.

And the tinny sound of boy band music is coming from the corner behind the conference table, where Zeus is sitting on the floor in blue jeans and a T-shirt with some glitter-sparkle troll on it, back to the wall, earbuds in his ears.

My eyes bulge. My lips part. And I have to bitch-slap some tears to keep myself from falling apart. "What are you doing here?"

Zeus pops one earbud out and meets my eyes.

There's no *hold my beer and watch this shit*.

No smile.

No swagger.

"I'm not leaving," he says.

Jett rubs his temples. One of the older lawyers mutters something that sounds like *worse than raising four girls*.

One of the younger lawyers has black Sharpie scrawled across his forehead.

My chin wobbles. "You have a contract. You have to go."

"Fuck the contract. I'm not leaving."

The oldest dude in the room clears his throat. "Ms. Maloney. Ms. Diamonte. May we proceed, or would you prefer a more private location?"

Peach shoves me in a chair. Gracie's waiting in the lobby, because she hates paperwork as much as I usually hate playing nice.

And she also has an hour or six to get in more steps while Peach is stuck at this table.

"Let's get this show on the road, gentlemen," Peach says. "Or in the air, as the case may be."

"No."

I don't know how many pairs of eyeballs swivel to look at me, and I don't care.

All I care about is that steady intensity radiating out of Zeus. "Do your work," he tells me. "I'll be here."

I don't know anything about his contract, but I know if he got traded and he was supposed to be in New York today, but he's here in Huntsville, at Weightless, he's probably getting himself in trouble.

Possibly jeopardizing his career.

Because that *I'm not leaving* he's spouting?

This is Zeus. He doesn't do anything small. He's *not leaving*. Period.

"You can't do this," I whisper. Not because I don't want him to stay. Not because I don't love him.

Dog, I love him. But he can't give up his career for me. Or anyone.

"You're going to the fucking moon," he says. "Sign your papers."

As though that's the final word on the subject, he slips his earbud back in, shifts to pull a paperback out of his back pocket—another romance novel?—and disappears into his own world before my eyes.

I look at Chase.

"This gonna be a problem?" he asks mildly, as though it's not Zeus making him look like he wants to pull his hair out by the roots.

"Nope," Peach answers for us. "Let's get to work."

"Mr. Berger—" the oldest of the group of suited men starts.

"Shut up before I fire you, Hawkins," Chase says.

He's in blue jeans and a Crunchy grocery polo—his main gig at the moment, though Ambrosia runs a lot of stuff for him—and I think we've identified the source of the teeth-gnashing.

"We doing this?" he asks me.

I look at Zeus.

Sitting there on the floor, silent, out of the way, reading a novel when he's supposed to be meeting his new team and getting ready for hockey season.

"I'm not leaving whether or not you sign those papers," he says without taking his eyes off the book, as though he's some mutantly mature, suave form of Zeus I've never met before, "but I'll be very disappointed in you if you don't. Chase is a good guy. He'll stay out of your shit. And not just because he knows I'll flatten him if he screws you."

Chase smirks like he, too, has a hidden cache of battery-operated spiders and knows how to use them.

I narrow my eyes at him.

I fucking hate spiders.

"This gonna be a problem?" I ask, turning the tables on him and ignoring Peach's heel scraping my shin under the table. I'll begrudgingly admit to liking the guy. And not just because he's known Zeus and Ares long enough to appreciate them the way so few people do.

He's agreed to a lot of stipulations other people wouldn't have. Which means he's either smart enough to realize Peach and I know what the fuck we're doing and can handle expansion, or it means he's doing this for reasons he's still keeping to himself.

I don't like that second option.

He doesn't blink as he taps his copy of the paperwork. "You know what I like about this?"

"That it's going to double your investment in five years?" Peach suggests.

"The training."

Zeus growls.

Apparently he knows about the clause where Chase is entitled to crew training so he can have private flights with Ambrosia.

The part about Ambrosia specifically isn't in there.

The part about Chase getting a flight a month with a guest of his choice is.

I hold his gaze. "That's worth a quarter-billion dollars to you."

He grins.

Like a teenage boy in a zero-gravity sex toy shop.

The weird thing is, I think I get it.

"Mr. Jett—" one of the lawyers starts.

Zeus snorts again. "*Mr. Jett* used to set off cherry bombs in the girls' bathroom," he mutters in full-Zeus mutter, which means the staff in the break room at the other end of the hall probably heard him.

"Pens for everyone," Peach announces. To me, she mumbles quiet enough for only me to hear, "Sign the fucking papers and let's go to the moon."

I look at Jett, who has to know he's taking a huge risk with terms that aren't in his favor if we fuck something up.

Then I glance at Zeus, who's sitting on the floor, *not leaving me* when he's supposed to be in New York.

I'm signing the papers. There's no question. It's a huge step for Weightless. For the next generation of space travel in general, with the added bonus of the local jobs we'll be creating and the research that we'll be taking on in the coming years.

I'd be a fool not to sign, and there's no way I could sabotage Peach by not signing.

But it somehow feels bigger than I ever dreamed it could.

Because I'm not doing this just for me.

I'm doing it for my family.

My hand-picked family. Peach. Our crew. Gracie. My dad's memory.

Zeus.

I pick up the pen, and his expression shifts.

He's not smirking over there over me doing what I'm told.

No, that's his *Proud of you, you sexy badass* smile.

I've always been proud of myself, because there haven't been many others I've let close enough to be proud for me.

It's…nice.

Okay, fine. It's *better* than nice.

It's fucking fantastic.

I'm still going to kick his ass for not being in New York, but I'm going to do something else too.

Just as soon as I sign this fucking encyclopedia-sized stack of papers.

36

Zeus

I ALMOST FELL ASLEEP READING my first NHL contract, and it was maybe twenty pages long.

That stack of shit Joey and Chase and Peach and all the stiff-ass lawyers are going through is like Mount Olympus compared to my little anthill of paperwork. And it's fucking fascinating.

Signature by signature, my girl's teaming up with my best friend to get us all to fucking space. I'm just a puck-head kid from Minnesota who got lucky enough to know the coolest dudes in the whole universe.

And yeah, Joey's one of those dudes.

But she's my dude. You wanna make something of it, punk?

They order in for lunch. Half the lawyers get salads. I get a smile from Joey and two pizzas I didn't ask for—sausage, nothing resembling fucking vegetables or anything spicy—and Joey drips bacon cheeseburger on her contract.

I sit on the floor fighting a woody the size of the sun for the next two hours. My ass is asleep, pretty sure my knees are cramping—had a hard day on the ice yesterday before the news bomb landed—and I haven't read more than six pages in this romance novel my buddy Knox hooked me up with, even though this shit's getting good, because I'm too busy watching Joey.

Finally, everyone's standing up and shaking hands.

"Welcome to Weightless, Mr. Jett," Peach says.

I snicker. Joey snickers. Chase flips me off behind his back and gives Joey a noogie.

She pulls some martial art trick that has him flapping one arm like a broken chicken wing while she noogies him back. "Careful, or we'll get you a call sign next, and it won't be flattering," she says to him.

Yeah, my dick's about to bust out of my pants.

She's so fucking hot.

"Can you teach Bro this trick?" he asks while he's still incapacitated.

"Is this a bedroom joke?" Joey asks while I make a show of getting snarly and overprotective of Ambrosia.

"Yeah," Chase says like it should've been obvious.

"I don't like dickheads touching my sisters," Joey growls.

My lungs freeze and my heart blows up like a fucking balloon. If Ambrosia's one of her sisters—

Fuck.

My eyes aren't wet. Your eyes are wet. Shut the fuck up.

She lets Chase go. Fucker's grinning like he's amused at my expense again. Love that dude. Even Peach, that vicious, spider-wielding, crazy-ass punk face, is beaming.

Joey saunters to me, grabs me by the troll on my shirt, and hauls me to my feet.

Okay, yeah, I help her out a little.

"You. With me. Now."

She turns and marches out, pulling me by a fistful of shirt. I smirk at Chase. Or try to. There's this emotional shit going on in my chest and head and I can't exactly think straight. "Good luck with them, you pansy-ass moneybags."

That shit-eating grin he gives me suggests I'm the one who needs the luck.

But I don't need luck.

Nah. I got the Zeus Berger charm going on.

Somewhere under all these feelings and the fucking fairy princesses twitterpating that muscle in my chest.

Fine, fine.

I've got hope.

And Joey's knuckle punching me in the breastbone every time we fall out of sync. Which is pretty fucking awesome in my world.

Takes a lot to hurt a big brute like me.

Physically. And she's not coming close.

She drags me out the building, across a grassy strip separating the aluminum-sided building from the edges of a runway. We cross the asphalt too, heading to a hangar.

She's not saying anything.

We're walking to an airplane's garage.

Fuck.

She's got a plane. She's gonna fucking take me to New York and dump my ass.

"Joey—"

"Shut up."

I don't know what that voice is. It's thick and heavy and loaded, and it's fucking effective.

She marches me into the hangar through a side door and pulls me toward her massive, gravity-defying plane. The side door's open, staircase rolled down.

I dig in my heels at the base of the staircase. "You're not fucking taking me to New York."

At that, she spins, brows momentarily crinkled in surprise. "You—" She shakes her head, and a devious smile takes over. "No?"

"No. Not just no, *fuck* no. I'm. Not. Leaving. You. I'm staying, Joey. I'm fucking staying *right here, with you*. Because I—"

I don't finish, because she's leaping at me. I catch her, her legs go around my middle, she attacks my lips with her mouth, and *fuck*, she's so strong and determined and delicious and I will fucking love this woman until the day the universe no longer exists.

Her fingers clamp in my hair. Her ankles lock behind my back. And she kisses me like she's trying to reach the stars through my mouth.

"Get on my airplane," she orders.

My legs follow orders and carry her up the steps even though I don't want to. She's not taking me to New York. Can't make me go.

But kissing Joey on her airplane?

Yeah.

Fuck, yeah.

I can get into that.

I turn at the top of the stairs and carry her into the open space where she made me fucking weightless. No windows here—they're all covered by the padding against the walls. The space is dim, the walls curved outward so I can't easily shove her up against one.

Instead, I go to my knees and lay her on her back.

Trapped.

So I can kiss her.

Rub my hard dick into that sweet pussy.

Keep her from getting any more ideas about flying my ass anywhere.

I find the right spot between her legs, and she bucks into me. "God, Zeus, I love you," she gasps.

I lift my head, my heart threatening to beat out of my chest.

Those big dark eyes are shiny and wide open. Committed. Dedicated. Strong.

Not terrified like last night. Not holding back.

She strokes my cheeks, kisses my nose. "I love you," she whispers.

I have to clear my throat twice before I can push words past the damn lump clogging my airways. "I fucking love you so much, Joey."

A smile teases her lips. "Show me?"

Oh, I'm gonna show her.

I'm gonna fucking show her every day for the rest of our lives. I lower my mouth to hers and take a slow, leisurely stroke of her upper lip. She sucks my bottom lip into her mouth and scrapes it with her teeth. Jupiter surges like he's racing around the sun, his moons go hard and tight, and everything else disappears.

Just me and Joey.

Those lush tits. Her strong legs. That mouth. Her eager hands exploring my body and pulling clothing away from skin so she's stroking my chest, my arms, down my pants to—

Yeah.

To where just a stroke of those nimble fingers can put me so close to the edge I lose my fucking mind. "Want you now," I gasp.

She's already snapping the buttons on her fancy work shirt and shimmying out of her pants. I snag a condom from my wallet before she shoves my pants down with her feet—*fuck*, that's hot—and spreads her legs while she rolls it on me.

"Love me, Zeus," she whispers.

I want to thrust in as deep as I can go, but instead, I push just inside her, only my head disappearing into her folds.

Her eyes roll back while she rocks against my tip. "Ohmydog, Zeus, you feel so fucking good."

She's so tight and hot, squeezing my head. Her eyes are glittering with stars, those lush lips parted, her head tipped back in rapture. I reach between us and thumb her clit, and she bucks into my touch, pulling my cock further into her. "*Yes*," she gasps. "Oh, dog, there. *More*."

I jerk into her, press her clit, and her legs go straight and rigid while she cries my name and her walls convulse around the top of me. I grit my teeth and count to potato while she squeezes and pumps, taking me deeper with every spasm while I order Jupiter to wait his turn.

Because Joey's going twice before we go once.

It's the fucking rule.

And she can suck my dick if she doesn't like it.

Fuck, I hope she'll suck my dick even if she does like it.

Her neck arches back and her eyes clench shut as one last wave crashes over us.

She's so fucking hot when she comes.

Her lids drift open, and she smiles. "I love you," she whispers.

Yeah, that's about all I can take. I dip my head to eat the hell out of her mouth while I push the rest of the way inside her, and soon she's gasping and writhing again, scraping her nails over my back, squeezing my ass, pumping up into me while I drive home.

Over and over.

Deeper and harder.

Kissing her mouth and licking her neck and nipping at her shoulder until we're exploding together in a fiery mass of climax, giving and taking and squeezing and thrusting and clenching and shooting fucking fireworks.

I'm coming for fucking *days*. Harder and longer and just fucking *better* than it's ever been, because she's holding me and coaxing me and giving me everything in her pussy, everything in her touch, everything in her whole heart.

After we're both so spent neither of us can move, we lay panting on the floor of her airplane. "You're gonna fucking fly me to the moon for real one day," I tell her.

She laughs, and *god*, I want to hear that laughter every day.

It's better than any boy band song I've ever heard, and I've heard—and loved—all the boy band shit there is to hear and love.

"You think you can boss me around now?" she asks.

"I can ask real pretty."

She rolls to face me, her fingers reaching out to my chest like our bodies are magnets and need to be touching all the time. "You need to go to New York."

"Joey—"

"I know. I know, Zeus. You're not leaving. But we're going to be okay. We can make this work. You'll come back. I'll come to you. Phones. Video chats. Email. Text messages. It's just a few years. You love hockey. You can't give that up for me. I won't let you."

She's wearing that *I'm the boss of you* face. Like that's gonna work. "Too bad."

Her eyes narrow.

I grin.

"You're impossible."

I trap her hand over my heart. "That's why you love me."

There's nothing soft about my Joey Fireball.

Nothing soft except her heart. She keeps that fucker locked up good. Don't think I don't know just how lucky of a bastard I am that she's letting me see it glow in those captivating dark eyes now. "Unfortunately," she sighs with more melodrama than even my sister could pull off in her teenage years, "you're not wrong."

"I know. I'm always right."

She laughs again and pulls me in for another kiss.

Because me and Joey?

We're not normal, but we're perfect for each other.

And I'm gonna spend the rest of my life loving the shit out of her.

EPILOGUE

Zeus Berger (aka the biggest, baddest, most lovesick motherpucker on the ice)

THE ONLY THING I want after an ugly game is to climb into bed with Joey, but that's not happening tonight.

Yeah, yeah, she got her way.

I reported to the Rangers three days late. Meant it when I told her I wasn't leaving, and I parked my ass in her office every minute of the day to prove my point.

When we weren't at her place banging our brains out.

But she finally wised up and threw down a bet. If I won the best sixteen out of thirty games of darts, thumb wars, and boy band trivia, I'd hang up my skates, forfeit the end of my contract, and bake her cookies every day. Sounded pretty fucking awesome to me.

If she won, I'd report to the Rangers.

Fine. It was supposed to be best two out of three, and I refused to concede until game seventeen.

But I was having fun. And who the fuck knew how much she knew about boy bands? That's sexy shit right there.

And considering every time she beat me, I distracted her with sex, she wasn't exactly complaining.

Until that one time Gracie caught us in the fridge.

Don't ask. It's not exactly what it sounds—never mind.

Point is, tonight, we barely pulled off a win against Nashville—yeah, that felt fucking good, even if it was ugly —and since the game was in Tennessee, it was easy for Joey to drive up.

She flew instead, which is good for everyone.

She's a real terror on the roads.

We should be headed back to the hotel so I can bang her brains out. But *no*. She shoved me in a Lyft and dragged me to the airport, and now she's landing the small private jet Weightless owns at a dinky airport in the middle of nowhere while stars sparkle overhead.

Because I promised to be good, I got to sit in the cockpit with her.

Because watching my girlfriend fly a plane is fucking hot, I've got a titanium two-liter in my pants.

"Where are we?"

"The middle of nowhere. I've decided to sex you to death and dump your satisfied body as a warning to all the wolves to not challenge my alphaness."

"I knew that fucking shapeshifter romance was a bad idea." Yeah, I'm in a romance book club. And yeah, Joey is too now. You got a problem with that, you're reading the wrong fucking epilogue.

"Bad idea for you maybe." She howls in the cockpit,

and *fuck*, if I could fit, I'd be crawling into her instrument panel to lick her pussy until she howls again.

Don't ask what happened last time I tried.

"Can we go somewhere we can fuck?" I ask.

She grins. "Soon."

Right.

The problem with dating a pilot? They have to do all this post-flight shit.

Which is really hot.

But not as hot as we make a dinky little hotel room an hour or so later.

Too soon, she's poking me awake. "Come on, sleeping beauty. Time to go."

I'm on a rare day off, and I know she knows I'm probably gonna get my ass chewed six ways to Pluto for not riding back to New York with the team, but I don't mind an ass-chewing if it means I get more time with Joey.

I make her scream my name in the shower before we get dressed, because I'm Zeus Berger, and that's what I fucking do for my woman.

But I don't like the looks of the rental car sitting in the parking lot. Yeah, it's big enough, but— "You driving that?"

"Depends. Can you take orders?"

"Just did, didn't I?"

You know what's different in the three months I've been dating Joey?

She's getting laugh lines around her eyes.

That's what's different.

She surrenders the car keys, and she directs me

through a modest town on a gray, chilly morning to a community center.

The Seven Foxes Community Center.

I know that name.

I grab her wrist before she can climb out. "What are we doing here?"

"In the parking lot? Sitting in a car."

"Joey..." I glower.

She smiles.

Sweetly.

Fuck, I hate when she does that. First of all, sweet's just not *her*. And I don't want it to be. Second of all, it still makes the demigod in my pants surge to attention, because he's fucking helpless.

"An old friend asked me to drop a puck to start her first hockey game," she says on a shrug. "And she asked if you would come along to watch me do what you'd fuck up."

Bailey.

That little turd.

Trash-talking me through my own girlfriend.

"That all?" I ask.

"You think I'm going to put either of us through a parade in your honor?"

Yeah, I do. I know she knows why Bailey has a hockey team. And I don't want to talk about it. Sometimes kids need a hero, and sometimes that hero doesn't want the world to know he's a good guy, because it's way more fucking fun to let everyone think that planting obscene flamingoes in the shape of a Z on a sports reporters' lawn when he calls me washed up is the only legacy I'll leave behind when I'm done at the end of this year.

Which mattered to me a fuck-ton more a year ago than it does today.

Doesn't mean I want a parade though.

"You can sit here if you want," she says, "but I'm going to go see Bailey."

She climbs out like it doesn't matter if I don't go with her.

I let her get almost to the door before I climb out too. "Hey, Fireball," I boom.

A dozen little girls and their families, all tromping through the misty morning to get inside, turn and look at me. A few of the mothers gasp and cover their kids' ears like they're afraid I'm gonna start flinging fucks and turd-wads and all kinds of profane ideas all over the parking lot. A couple of the dads get that look in their eyes that suggests it's a good thing I still keep a Sharpie in my back pocket.

And no, I don't want to talk about how many of those fuckers have gone through the wash and ruined half my wardrobe.

"Get your sass back here," I yell at my girlfriend. "I left my bodyguard at home."

She cocks a hip. "Protect your own sass, Berger. Mine's worth more anyway."

True enough.

I saunter through the parking lot and consider bending over to eat a few rocks out of the asphalt, but that's more Ares's style. If there weren't kids present, I'd drop trou and streak.

"Making me boring," I grumble to Joey when I meet her at the door.

She slaps my ass. "Nah, it's called *getting old*."

I love that she doesn't take my shit and gives it right back. Which is why I'm still grinning when a blondie streaks by me to tackle my girlfriend. "Joey! You came!"

Bailey's mother eyes me with a cross between healthy fear and grudging admiration. Like maybe she knows, too, why her daughter now has more tools in her arsenal of weapons.

To beat the boys off, I mean. Naturally.

Like Fireball used to have to.

Joey squats to Bailey's level while the kid rattles off all the ways Joey's her hero and how many drills she's done this week and how much better she's getting at reading since the foundation hooked her up with a tutor who gets the way her brain works.

"Come on, come on, it's game time." She snags Joey by the hand and pulls her through the crowded hallways to the rink. I contemplate signing Bailey's mother's forehead, but decide against it.

Fuck, maybe I am getting old.

"Holy shiii-take mushrooms, it's the Brute," a girl who can't be more than twelve says as I walk by. "Will you sign my forehead?"

"Mine too?" another kid says.

Soon I'm surrounded by a pack of Zeusleaders all wanting to give me shit about last year's play-offs and me being late reporting to the Rangers, and also whisper in awe about the three hat tricks I've pulled in the last month.

Yeah.

I got my game back. And then some.

But I'm still done when the Rangers win the Stanley Cup this season. Just for the record.

I got cookies to bake for my hot girlfriend every day.

"It's time!" someone hisses. "Come on, Fireball's gonna drop the puck!"

Fuck if I'll miss that. I hustle along with the girls, pulling my phone out. I want video of this shit.

Bailey's mom signals me from down the hall. "Here. The view's better," she says.

I bypass the double doors everyone else is streaming into to follow her, and two seconds later, I'm standing at the edge of the ice.

Fuck.

Joey's not out there yet. No, she's right next to me, with Bailey all suited up and a guy who's probably the coach.

Also there?

Ares.

Ambrosia and Chase.

My parents.

Gracie.

Peach.

"Joey…"

"Shut the fudge up, Berger," Bailey says. "Your stick work stinks this season, and you've got weak ankles. If you hurt Joey, I'll rack you in the pucks."

"Scary short one," Ares says.

"You surround yourself with the best women,"

Ambrosia says while Chase snickers. "Seriously, Zeus. They keep getting better."

"What are you doing here?" I ask her.

"Watching Joey drop the puck. Like family does."

Oh.

Huh.

Even I can't argue with that.

I clap her on the shoulder. Maybe a little too hard. "Nice of you."

"You ready, Joey?" Bailey asks. She's a mini badass in her pads and gloves and helmet, and I can't help grinning.

Kid's going places.

And when I hang up my skates at the end of this season, I know exactly what I'm gonna do.

When I'm not baking Joey cookies.

Because hockey's still my life.

Time to take the Zeus Berger school of ice to some smaller places. I don't need to live large.

Just need to live with my Joey.

PIPPA GRANT BOOK LIST

The Girl Band Series
Mister McHottie
Stud in the Stacks
Rockaway Bride
The Hero and the Hacktivist

The Thrusters Hockey Series
The Pilot and the Puck-Up
Royally Pucked
Beauty and the Beefcake
Charming as Puck
I Pucking Love You

The Bro Code Series
Flirting with the Frenemy
America's Geekheart
Liar, Liar, Hearts on Fire
The Hot Mess and the Heartthrob

Copper Valley Fireballs Series
Jock Blocked
Real Fake Love
The Grumpy Player Next Door

Irresistible Trouble

The Tickled Pink Series

The One Who Loves You

Rich In Your Love

Standalones

The Last Eligible Billionaire

Master Baker *(Bro Code Spin-Off)*

Hot Heir *(Royally Pucked Spin-Off)*

Exes and Ho Ho Hos

The Bluewater Billionaires Series

The Price of Scandal by Lucy Score

The Mogul and the Muscle by Claire Kingsley

Wild Open Hearts by Kathryn Nolan

Crazy for Loving You by Pippa Grant

Co-Written with Lili Valente

Hosed

Hammered

Hitched

Humbugged

Pippa Grant writing as Jamie Farrell:

The Misfit Brides Series

Blissed

Matched

Smittened

Sugared

Merried

Spiced

Unhitched

The Officers' Ex-Wives Club Series

Her Rebel Heart

Southern Fried Blues

ABOUT THE AUTHOR

Pippa Grant is a USA Today and #1 Amazon Bestselling author who writes romantic comedies that will make tears run down your leg. When she's not reading, writing or sleeping, she's being crowned employee of the month as a stay-at-home mom and housewife trying to prepare her adorable demon spawn to be productive members of society, all the while fantasizing about long walks on the beach with hot chocolate chip cookies.

Find Pippa at...
www.pippagrant.com
pippa@pippagrant.com

Made in United States
North Haven, CT
29 December 2025